Bringing You Back to Me

Lelia Long Collins

ISBN 978-1-64559-041-5 (Paperback)
ISBN 978-1-64559-042-2 (Hardcover)
ISBN 978-1-64559-043-9 (Digital)

Covenant Books, Inc.
11661 Hwy 707
Murrells Inlet, SC 29576
www.covenantbooks.com

T he air smelled so fresh and clean. A storm had just passed over with lots of rain as we made our way to a place in the mountains, a place I had planned on visiting for some time now, hoping here I would find what I was looking for—the piece of evidence that would bring you back to me, the answers to this mystery that has kept my life in what you might call "this dreadful unyielding turmoil."

Family who lives in Keokee will be making special arrangements for our arrival. We'll call it a homecoming for now anyway.

As we drove further and further up into the mountains, I could see why my mother kept encouraging me to take this trip, and my grandmother almost demanded that I go.

Now I could see for myself; truly it was such a beautiful place; and, yes, the mountains in and around Keokee were surprisingly beautiful with the narrow winding roads and the valley down below. The trees were naked of their leaves with some new leaf formation as a result of the season leaving winter behind and embarking upon spring. The fir and spruce trees all standing stately, bearing their lush green colors. I was surprised by the houses along the way; they were somewhat smaller than I had envisioned them to be with a charm of their own that seemed so inviting.

David especially loved the winding roads with all the twists and turns, which took us further and further up into the mountain. It made for a good adventure for a young boy.

"K-e-o-k-e e, K-e-o-k-e-e," saying the words slowly, David kept repeating them over and over. "K-e-o-k-e-e!" He repeated them as if reciting a stanza in a love song or a lovely poem.

We arrived a day earlier than expected. This we did on purpose, hoping to settle in a day early before all the guests arrived and family festivities were to begin.

The house was lovely, very charming you might say. Nestled high in the beautiful mountains of Virginia, on the Trail of the Lonesome Pine, was the little town of Keokee.

This was the house my grandmother lived in as a young girl with her mother, father, and her little brother Tim. She had lived here before her father moved the family away. This was the house my grandmother so many years ago had called home.

The caretaker had done a good job getting the house ready for our arrival. The rooms were smaller than I had expected but very cozy, warm, and inviting. The pantry had been stocked for our convenience. Fresh flowers were placed in the bedrooms, and a fruit basket was sitting on the kitchen counter.

I had been told I had lots of friends and family who lived here in Keokee. Here was where I had graduated from high school. Here was where I had started and ran my company.

I myself remembered no one who lived here; however, most of the people will remember me. Hopefully someday I will remember their laughter and voices along with how their lives intertwined with mine, but as of now, I was hoping only for a glimpse into my past.

It was early spring here in Keokee, but it seemed more like late winter on the day we finally arrived. With some snow still lingering on the ground and a heavy wind coming in from the north, we approached the last few miles of our journey.

I had been in Keokee only three days when I received a startling message. The message came from Mr. Carr whom I had hired to take care of some personal business for me. Startled, and, yes, this was totally unexpected; however, I was once again encouraged.

His message to me was, "Carol, don't come home. I'll come there instead. I'll be there as soon as I can get away and make the drive. I am calling from the courthouse, and it will be hours before I can get out of here and on the road. Carol, trust me! Carol, here is Charlotte's message to you: 'Stay where you are. This will be the last chance you will ever get for the truth about what really happened.'

Carol, no time to explain now. Please do what I say and stay where you are. I'll be there as soon as I can." Then the phone went dead.

The truth about what really happened. I didn't know if I should be happy or troubled about this call. I decided I would stay as busy as possible and keep my mind off this message until Mr. Carr arrived.

*****

I had been informed a late lunch or early dinner, whichever one you wish to call it would be served at the pavilion down by Keokee Lake today. The people here were wonderful. They were hosting this event as a welcome back for my mother and grandmother who had been away for some time; however, my mother said it was for me more than them, for my return.

The food, as well as the company, was wonderful. Everyone was so nice. I spent lots of time talking, laughing, and just enjoying myself with my newfound family and friends in Keokee—friends who remembered me but I didn't remember them, which made for odd conversations. However, they were very accepting and welcomed me into their lives and families.

It was so nice down by the lake; it being late winter emerging on early spring. There was just a slight chill in the air. Mr. Carr called once again to let me know he wouldn't be able to make his trip until tomorrow. He apologized for the inconvenience.

"How long must I wait for this nightmare to be over?" I kept asking myself. Always a kink in the road, or so it seemed. When evening finally rolled around, I was ready for bed. George held me in his arms as I cried myself to sleep.

I woke up early the next morning with a start. I realized everyone was still asleep, which seemed to be the case. I heard no one moving about the house. I thought to myself I must be the only one awake. I quickly dressed and went downstairs.

I crossed the living room, headed for the kitchen. Through the window, I could see it had snowed during the night. I quickly found my coat and someone else's boots that were sitting by the door and headed outdoors.

Snow, I wondered. With yesterday's slightly mild temperatures then snow during the night, I was sure the weather here was much different than I was used to, but I loved it all, all of it.

I carefully closed the door behind me, and I walked out into the beautiful mountain snow. It was the most beautiful morning I could remember. The sky was gray, and the fluffy white snow was coming down rather quickly. The green fir trees were white and were bending with the weight of snow that clung to them. Beyond the fir trees were more mountains covered with snow.

I stopped in my tracks; beautiful was all I could say for the sight that lay before me. I lingered there for a while just enjoying the view and in awe at the beauty of these mountains that surrounded me and knowing whatever the news I received tomorrow from Mr. Carr, I would survive.

I was up early the next day in anticipation of Mr. Carr's arrival. By midmorning, Mr. Carr called once more to say he would have to wait until tomorrow.

"Oh no, not another day," I fretted. "I don't understand. What happened?" I asked. "You said you would be here today?" I wanted to know.

"Carol, the holdup is a ten-by-ten inch locked metal box. Charlotte wants me to deliver it to you," Mr. Carr said this after a lengthy pause.

"I don't understand," I said. I was shocked she would want to send me something, anything. This cruel, devious person who had caused me so much trouble and anguish wanted to send me a box.

"Carol, sorry, but I have to go through a little legal process to get this box released to me. However, I won't be able to do that until tomorrow morning. I'll get a quick flight out and be on my way. Carol, one more thing. Do you still have the key that you found?"

"Yes," I told him. "I have the key here with me. I wear it around my neck. I'm afraid I'll misplace or lose it."

"Carol, that is great," came Mr. Carr's voice. "Got to go, busy, and I'll be there tomorrow." The phone went dead.

I kept saying to myself, "I refuse to be afraid. I refuse to give up, and I have to be strong."

*****

"Another day of waiting, and oh how I hate waiting," I kept saying this to myself as I prepared for the day ahead.

I made myself a cup of coffee, wrapped myself in a blanket, and headed for the front porch where I intended to lounge for a while, if the weather permitted. A beautiful sight lay before me. There had been a storm sometime during the night. I had been awakened a few times by the loud clap of thunder. The snow was melting rather fast. I could see a thick mist rising over the lake and the water picking up the rays from the sun. Such a beautiful sight this early morning.

David and George came outdoors and joined me. After lunch, they would be headed for adventures out on the lake, if the weather permitted. Fishing I presume and exploring the lake, and I might just tag along with them for a while.

For me it is better to push away and forget this meeting with Mr. Carr until I come face-to-face with him.

"By the way, Carol, David and I will keep you entertained so you don't have to worry about what's inside that box," George said this as he made his way to my side, took my hand in his, and gave me a kiss.

Then he elaborated on the subject at hand. He said, "Carol, honey, we have no idea what horrors or what happiness lies ahead for us inside that box, but I want you to be prepared. Carol, honey, please don't get your hopes too high. You have seen how things turn out when it comes to dealing with Charlotte."

Sitting there listening to George's words, wrapped in a blanket, looking out over Keokee Lake, I relaxed and laid my head on his shoulder. I rested there for a while just enjoying the view. As the thick fog rose from the lake and more of the surface was revealed, I could see canoes and small boats already on the lake. People were fishing for whatever lurked below the rippling water.

Shortly, we would join them on the lake with our own lures and poles. We would take along our enthusiasm and a big bucket to bring back our catch of the day.

After an afternoon out on the lake with some fish caught by David and his newfound cousins, we headed to the pavilion where what seemed like a feast was being prepared. The menu included some of the fish that was caught out on the lake just today, cleaned and prepared by some of the fishermen and cooked as part of the feast. David and his cousins were eager to donate their fresh catch of fish for this cause. And when it was all fried up, they were ready to eat, standing there holding their plates for this delightful meal.

There was a croquet game going on, and kids were flying kites. There was even live music. Most of the music and entertainment was done by local talent, which was rather impressive. A couple of artists were also present with people gathering around for the artists to capture their best features on paper with pastels and a brush. The weather was holding out—a nice sunny afternoon with a slight chill in the air.

A couple of bonfires were prepared later in the evening, and the kids were excited about this and gathered around in all the excitement. They were roasting marshmallows and hot dogs. There were so many people gathered around. We were all having so much fun.

We were still there when the sun went down, we were still there when the moon was high in the sky. The men and older boys kept the bonfires going as the night went on. Even though the temperature had dropped a lot, the heat from those two bonfires kept the temperature nice enough to endure. People were laughing and talking, just enjoying themselves.

On this lovely night, Keokee Lake seemed to just dazzle. It was such an amazing sight, with the movement of the rippling water, the light from the moon, and a golden glow from the bonfires casting such a glorious sight upon the lake.

We finally made our way back to the house in the wee hours of the morning. I thought to myself I'll sleep in late this morning. That way, I won't have to think about Mr. Carr's arrival. Yes, that is what I will try to do.

However, the sun woke me up early the next morning as it made its way across the bed, warming my skin as I lay sleeping. I tried to fall back asleep, but that didn't work, so pulling myself out of bed, I made my way down the stairs. George was already in the kitchen making a pot of coffee.

Well, it is early spring, I thought, as I made my way outdoors. It was like a ritual with me every morning first thing after I wake up, I walk outside to check out the weather. Rain, snow, or shine—it's like I can't start my day unless I walk out into the morning first. Sometimes I have my coffee first but most likely not.

I could see storm clouds on the horizon. The air was a lot different than yesterday. It was very cool. To me it seemed like an icy mist in the air. I'm not used to the weather here: one day it's warm, and the next day it could be cold with snow.

"Could more snow be on the way?" I asked myself.

George was still in the kitchen when I made my way back into the house. "Too cold for me out there this morning," I said this as I took a sip of George's coffee. "George, I have to say I so dread today. Do you think I will be able to get through this meeting?"

"Carol, you have no choice. I'll be right here with you, and whatever happens, we will just have to deal with it. Sorry."

Mother joined us in the kitchen, made her way to the stove, and started preparing breakfast. The bacon smelled so good, but I knew I wouldn't be able to eat as I was already at the point of being sick from just thinking about Mr. Carr's arrival.

However, the morning seemed to pass so fast; it was like when you want time to go slow, it flies by so fast, and today was no exception.

"Mr. Carr finally called saying his plane had just landed," George informed me.

I thought, *it won't be too long and Mr. Carr will be pulling up into the driveway*. I said this as I made my way into the shower, hoping to wash away the tears that just keep coming and this horrible feeling that I couldn't seem to shake off. I took my time before I made my way back downstairs where the rest of the family was waiting for me.

I had decided to go down and sit in the sunroom, overlooking the lake while waiting on Mr. Carr's arrival.

I was sitting there watching the snow fall when I saw Mr. Carr's vehicle pull up into the driveway. It had been snowing now for almost an hour, big beautiful white snowflakes, which were piling up rather quickly. I had almost hoped the snow would keep him away from my door, away from my living room, away from my mind.

Suddenly the doorbell rang.

George was here with me. He slowly made his way to the door. I wanted to run; I wanted to hide. I didn't want him to be here. I was scared; I had knots in my stomach, but I knew I had to be strong. I had to endure.

The doorbell rang for the second time and I could hear Mr. Carr's voice. I closed my eyes hoping this moment would go away, but I heard footsteps approaching as they came closer and closer to where I sat. My hands were shaking. Mr. Carr didn't say a word to me; he just placed the box on my lap. Panic took hold of me; my throat seemed to be closing. I could barely catch my breath. *I don't know if I can do this.*

I finally took the chain from around my neck that held the key. With shaking hands and an aching heart, I put the key into the lock, opened the lid, and my mind went back to where all this began.

*****

From where I was sitting in my living room, beyond the pane glass, beyond the shadows of the big oak trees that lined our back-yard, I could see a red cap with a little boy underneath. He was emerging from the path that led up from the lake. Swinging over his left shoulder a fishing pole, the one he had been working so hard to purchase from his favorite sports shop with money earned mowing lawns and other odd jobs in our neighborhood. Swinging from his right hand was a gray tackle box, which he had filled just this morning with new fishing hooks and other fishing paraphernalia. There was so much to captivate the imagination of a ten-year-old boy. His mind, his every waking thought, and his dreams were about that

Bass Pro Shop, which gave his young mind the opportunity to dream about all the adventures he could have. The Bass Pro Shop would be an adventure all in itself by just walking down the aisles with all the great merchandise displayed so artfully. In his left hand, he carried a bucket he took along to keep his skillfully caught fish pulled from the lake just this morning. He will clean his catch before bringing them into the house, which I appreciated because cleaning smelly, slippery fish was not my favorite chore to do on such a beautiful Saturday morning. Once he brought them into the house, I will dip the fresh caught fish in buttermilk; then coat them with bread, flour, and a seasoning mixture before frying them up in a very delectable manner. To become a great hunter and fisherman was David's boyish plans for his future. His father and I were so glad to see him taking such an interest in his own little world.

David and his dad were the best of friends. They were constantly planning their next move, their next adventure together. Hunting, fishing, frog gigging, football, you name it—the only thing that separates them is work, school, sleep, and me.

David was in his fifth year of school. He was an exceptional student and had always been focused. History and math were his two strong points. He was energetic, and he took pride in doing odd jobs in our neighborhood. David loved the idea of making his own money. He was a lot of fun and a joy to be around.

Walking through the back door with his cleaned catch of the day, his voice was loud with excitement. "Mom, look what I caught!" This was his first catch in a while.

*****

David's dad, my husband and a doctor by profession, was to be the best man at his sister's wedding in just three days. Julie who thought she would never get married, was very beautiful but overly bossy. She tried to manage everything, to the point of being annoying. Then to top things off, she was also overweight, which she constantly complained about. Being overweight didn't take away from her appearance because she was very beautiful with her long dark hair and flawless skin. She had been engaged for three years. Now that Craig had finished law school, the big day was coming fast.

Flowers were ordered; the wedding cake was made with decorations to perfection; and other decorations were being shipped in daily. The guest list was made; invitations were sent out; and RSVPs were coming back via the mail daily. The catering of the food was written in stone. This subject of food had been gone over and over many times, and finally, all came to an agreement. The main dish to be served was lobster, coming in fresh from a small fishing town on the coast of Maine. Prime rib for those who prefer something other than sea food, and a huge variety of side dishes and salads in abundance: potato salad, shrimp salad, garden salad just to name a few. Then with much planning, there were the desserts with such a wide variety that would please almost any appetite. The best in my judgment will be the strawberry cakes with cream filling piled high with whipped cream and flavored with exotic spices.

The music, let's not forget to mention the music. Craig will be singing to his lovely bride, with his voice robust and powerful. He will be working on keeping a lower tone and a romantic theme, as he sings to his lovely bride-to-be, expressing his love for her.

The garden just outside the entrance of the chalet, which had been rented just for the festive occasion, was lovely. The landscape was being upgraded with flowers and trees being brought in and planted at just the perfect location. This is one of the two main focal points where lots of pictures will be taken before the wedding and as the bride and groom leave for their new life together. The first focal point is the front of the chalet. Beautiful cherry trees lined the entrance that lead up to the chalet. At this time of year, the cherry trees are in full bloom. These old majestic, stately trees have been lining this entrance for some time. These along with the new trees and flowers that were being planted made for a perfect showcase for any wedding. It had taken months and months to get every detail planned and set up.

The second focal point is the main entrance just as you step inside through the beautifully carved wooden door and inside the house. The staircase with its beautiful handcrafted work of dark carved wood wrapped itself ever so slightly to the south of the enormous living area. With gently sloping stairs and with every descending step the stairs and staircase became wider and wider.

Chandeliers hung in a timely manner throughout the house, but the eye-catcher was at the top of the magnificent staircase. Hanging there so elegantly was a beautiful, dazzling four-tier chandelier that cast its light on this enormous open area. The stairs and the chandelier could be viewed from all angles of the room. Roses, along with yellow spider mums, were the bride's choice of flowers to be used in her wedding. With the staircase decorated from top to bottom in satin lace and stunning handcrafted bows just hours before the wedding, yellow spider mums, baby's breath, and an abundance of orange-and-white roses would be put in place.

Two days after the wedding, David, George, and I were to be flying to the Island of Oahu for a three-week vacation, then on to the Big Island for a week. We go every other year, staying at one of the Outriggers. We have some family there and lots of friends. With the wedding and making plans for our vacation, I seemed to be getting a little threadbare on emotions. I was excited about the wedding, but I was so looking forward to Hawaii.

I had spent much time and money and learned a lot while planning for this wedding. For instance, I toured a cake house where cake artists make and decorate wedding cakes twenty-four hours a day to their clientele's specification, with some of these cakes being extravagant, not only in the beauty of the cake but also the nature or theme of the cake. I must say after seeing some of them, I must use the word *risqué*. I also educated myself on the subject of how to select a wedding cake for the amount of people that are expected to attend the wedding and coordinate the color and variety of flowers to match and blend in with the colors and cake decorations. I have enjoyed making the arrangements for out-of-town guests and coordinating the events surrounding the wedding. Such as it is, it has been a very busy and memorable time for me.

*****

Along with having fun planning the wedding and with all the excitement of our upcoming trip to Hawaii, I felt suddenly exhausted, somewhat drained, and fatigued.

The wedding came and went on time and as planned. The planning was precise and well-orchestrated, so the wedding event was fabulous. Julie the beautiful bride, dressed in her overpriced white one-of-a-kind dress designed just for her wedding, surprised her wedding planners with an unplanned song to her husband-to-be. An Italian love song with no music. Although she did not speak Italian and had never taken a course in the beautiful Italian language while in school or college, it was an outstanding performance. To the amazement of everyone present, she pulled it off. But obvious to everyone present, she had worked hard and long learning this song. Craig spoke perfect Italian, but respectfully only spoke English to his bride-to-be and her family, whom had never been introduced to the beautiful Italian language. It was so emotional and beautifully sung that the husband-to-be wept outright. With her performance, it was the making of a very memorable wedding. The reception, perfect; the food, the best. Everyone seemed to enjoy the lobster dishes. Lobster Cantonese with black beans was one of the favorites, and then there was the shrimp with lobster sauce. Also served was beef, pork, and a wide variety of shrimp dishes.

*****

Now that the wedding was over, it was time to make the final preparation for our Hawaiian vacation. Tickets, hotels, and rental cars had been taken care of well in advance. We would make our first stop on the Island of Oahu. We would visit the pineapple plantation, love indulging in the ice cream and shakes, pick out tee shirts to buy and a few other souvenirs, then on to Diamond Head where we would walk all the 173 steps to the top. We always walked these steps every time we go to the island. I think David's favorite part of the trip to the top is the tunnel you go through before the second set of steps. David, being ten years old, has always been fascinated with Diamond Head. I guess the fascination comes with knowing we are climbing the exterior of a volcano that erupted a long time ago. Punch Bowl Crater is very important on his list too but with a different kind of fascination—all the tombstones and the memorial with the names printed of the war dead. From Punch Bowl, you can look down below to the beautiful pristine ocean, just under the water there, you will find coral reefs with lots of sea life. The sunset is fabulous.

One of our all-time-favorite restaurants is Chuck's Cellar, where we will frequent while on the island. We stay in Waikiki, usually Outrigger East. We will tour the shops and buy new swimwear for the three of us. We will go snorkeling, parasailing, and take a couple of trips out on the outriggers, check out Chinamen's Hat then go see the beautiful waterfalls.

Then on to the Big Island, where we go to see lava flow from Kilauea Volcano. When you are around the people who live on the island, you will hear them refer to Kilauea as "the world's only drive-in volcano." You can watch the molten lava pushing forward and slowly change the landscape right before your eyes. To me, this is one of the biggest fascinations I have with the island. David will read and review all his collected information about volcanoes he can find before we take our Hawaiian trip. He is so fascinated with volcanoes.

We will visit Maui last with all of its exotic flowers and the best, sweetest onions on the planet. On our last trip, we visited the bamboo forest and the waterfalls in Haleakala National Park, David has already been asking if we are going back there this time. He let me know he really wants to go back to explore the park again.

Everything was ready for our trip—all the clothes packed, cameras, meds and vitamins. Can't forget the snorkels and flippers. You can rent them, but it is best to have your own, and always buy the best snorkels. It is worth the time and money. After checking everything three times, to make sure I hadn't forgotten anything, my husband said if we have forgotten anything, we can always buy it.

*****

Ruth had served dinner early in the formal dining room. When we were planning a trip or going away for a while she always made our favorite entrees or desserts to be served with dinner. She had made David's favorite dish, chicken divine, plus his favorite vegetable, corn on the cob; George's all-time favorite, which was a mixture of fresh cut vegetables in an authentic Indian sauce complete with Kashmiri peppers, served with a couple loaves of freshly baked nut bread; and my favorite dessert, chocolate cake served with homemade French vanilla ice cream; and at the end of our meal, she served cappuccino with a rich, heavy sweet cream and added just a few sprinkles of cinnamon. It was her special way of saying just how much she would be deprived of our company while we were away. Sometimes Ruth traveled with us, but this year, she was going to go on an African Safari with a couple of friends instead—something she had wanted to do for a long time.

David was so excited; he couldn't think of anything but our Hawaiian trip. I have to say I was pretty excited too. Tomorrow morning, the limo will pick us up at seven o'clock sharp.

*****

I had one more errand to run before bedtime, and I had meant to do it earlier, but here I was at nine o'clock at night, and I was running late. Ruth, our part-time maid, was still here. I'll just leave David with her and be back in no time at all. Martha, my best friend, will be taking care of our cat while we are away on our Hawaiian vacation. Martha was the perfect person to leave Tiff-Tiff with while we were away. She loves cats almost as much as I do. Now I just had to deliver the cat, and I'll be through for the night. I could go to bed, rest, and dream of Hawaii.

It was raining outside, not hard but a steady rain that had been coming down all day. I grabbed a lightweight jacket, put the cat in her cage, and off I went. It was one of those nights when it was hard to see. It was not really the rain that clouded your vision: it was a number of things like the streetlights casting a shimmery shine on the road and on the oncoming cars; lights from nearby shops casting their geometrical shapes on the road in which you are traveling; puddles of water in the low spots of the highway reflecting the light, and then there were the traffic lights casting its own hue of gold, red, or green.

I had just passed the botanical garden entrance. Martha's apartment was only about ten minutes away, and I was making good time. Just before the cut off to her street, I stopped at a traffic light. As I was looking at the light, something happened. I became very emotional. Somewhere in the back of my mind, I had remembered something, something I hadn't known I had forgotten. *My baby, where was he? Oh no, I have lost him. How could I not remember something so important, and yet I could not remember.* It was like an ocean had poured over me. I felt like I was drowning. I couldn't breathe, then I started screaming. "My baby, where is he?" Over and over I screamed the same words. I tried to release myself from the seat belt so I could find my little boy, but I was so scared for him I couldn't move.

I could hear car tires screeching; people yelling off in a distance, soft voices, murmuring, and the sound of windshield wipers streaking back and forth across the windshield; rain, sirens, and a faint sound at first, then closer and closer until the noise was so loud it seemed to swallow me up. I could hear a voice screaming, "Joseph, where is Joseph. I want my baby! I want my baby Joseph. Please help me. Where is my baby?" It was a scream of sheer terror. Then I realized the screams I was hearing were coming from me!

I could hear someone screaming for me to go, horns blowing, tires screeching. I couldn't move; I just kept screaming. I heard sirens and saw even more colors of lights flashing blue and red. Someone was speaking to me. "Ma'am, ma'am, what is your name? Can you give us your name?"

My mind wouldn't wrap around anything they were saying, I just wanted them to find Joseph. Trying to think as hard as I could, what could I have done with him? Did I let someone keep him? Is he dead? Truly, I did not know. *But I have to find him. I have to find him. He needs me. He is so tiny, so helpless.*

I was being gently pulled from the car and laid on a stretcher. The rain was coming down harder now. I could feel each drop of rain as it caressed my face. The colors from all the lights were more vivid now. I was trying to climb from the stretcher, trying to get up, trying to find Joseph. Still screaming, crying, I could feel the sting from the needle of the IV as it entered my arm, then the cool feeling of something going through my veins. *Joseph, Joseph.*

I found myself in a white room somewhere in between consciousness and unconsciousness. I couldn't think. I could barely open my eyes. My head was throbbing, and my hands were shaking; I couldn't seem to keep them still. I heard voices near, then far away, then near again almost as if they were screaming. I tried listening, hoping to hear a familiar voice, but I couldn't make out even one audible voice.

*****

I woke momentarily. I heard voices; they were clearer this time. I heard my husband's voice. What is that he is saying? Something about she doesn't have a son named Joseph. Then it all came back. I tried to speak, but the words wouldn't come. I tried again, but the words still wouldn't come. My throat was dry; my body was motionless. I couldn't move. I felt tears streaming down my face. I saw a nurse come into the room. She was talking to me, but I couldn't make out what she was saying, then my husband was standing beside her. She said something about calming her down. She took my hand, squeezed it, and then added something to my IV.

I woke up many times the next weeks, months, with the same kind of treatment from the hospital staff. They didn't seem to hear the words I was saying. Pills in the morning—they would always wake me up early to give me pills. I didn't mind being woken up. I wanted to stay awake; they talked to me seldom. I needed to keep alert. I had to think things through and try to get out of this place. I would always ask them if they found Joseph. The nurses seemed to hold contempt for me. It was a strange place to find myself. The gloomy halls, the gray gloomy room—I couldn't find any windows here. I like the sun; I wanted to see the sun!

Before lunch, they brought me more pills. The food was fairly good. With what little appetite I had, I would manage to eat a small amount. More pills at dinner—for dinner, they would push me out into what appeared to be a big dining hall. The dinner food was even better than lunch; it might be because they played Beethoven's *Moonlight Sonata*, which gave the sense of a relaxed atmosphere. Then the hours I dreaded most, the night, with more pills. This hospital, for that is what they called it, was so dark and gloomy at night, almost scary and lonely. With all the pills they gave me, I would sleep most of the time. There were questions I kept asking myself and the hospital staff as long as they would give me the time and attention to do so: How would I ever get out of here? And where was my husband? I'll find out tomorrow. I must get out so I can find Joseph; I had to find him. I cried most of the time, and no one seemed to hear or care.

I find this place to be very lonely, a loneliness that seemed to pierce the very soul. A loneliness that seemed to be trapped in every room, every corner, including the hallways, especially the hallways.

The other patients here had their own problems, from extreme to very extreme, or so it seemed. So, therefore, I kept to myself for most of the time anyway.

The cleaning staff seemed very kind and polite as they went about their cleaning duties from day to day. I listened intently to their conversations about their day-to-day life especially the weekends they spent with their family and friends. I asked them questions about the weather or current news that was going on in the world. They were always kind and answered my questions with a respect I rarely saw here. With these conversations, I looked forward to the daily cleaning of my room.

George was here quite often trying to make sense of the situation we found ourselves in. He brought me candy or flowers and news from home. These visits gave me hope. George stayed as long as time would permit. I so enjoyed those visits. He came every other day; he was so loving and kind. I missed our everyday life together.

George and I decided not to bring David here for visits. We both knew it would not be good for him seeing me here. I definitely wanted to spare him from the sadness that seemed to permeate within these walls, which divided us from the rest of the world.

Each time George was here, he talked to the doctor, hoping for word of when I would be released. The lonely, secluded hours I spent alone were almost unbearable but for the thoughts of George, David, and now occupying my mind for the biggest part of each day finding Joseph. I must first get out of this place before I could begin my search.

*****

My best friend Martha came to visit me frequently, which gave me something I could look forward to as I tried to push the gloomy days as far away from my world as life would permit. Her stopovers were very pleasant. Her sweet personality set the stage for delightful visits. She brought me updates on David and his everyday life, now that I was temporarily away from him. Martha always tried to make herself available whenever George needed help in caring for David.

As the days progressed with a slowness, I could hardly bear from day to day. I became more and more restless. I could hear the doctor coming down the hall, even with my door closed. His voice was over-powering, a little muffled by all the noise going on in the hallway—shifting of lunch trays, the sound of footsteps on the under polished tile floors, yet his voice was distinct. It was a voice you could never forget, soothing if not comforting. He had an intriguing and uplifting personality, and he tried to instill in me a sense of importance. He was indeed very kind, and I had to believe he would release me very soon.

*****

Charlotte moved about the room in a manner that showed her flirtatious character, all while helping adjust the lunch tray for Thomas, who two weeks before had had a mild stroke and was regaining his strength. Therapy had done him wonders. Thomas was Charlotte's favorite patient. She had known him even before he had his stroke. Thomas was like a grandfather to Charlotte and Charlotte like a granddaughter to him. The first time she had met Thomas was at the scene of a horrendous car accident. Charlotte had been the first to come upon the accident, which had happened on a lonely country highway about ten miles out of town with not much traffic going or coming, when she happened upon a single car accident the front of the car had smashed into a tree and was resting lopsided at the edge of a cow pasture.

The driver was still in the car when Thomas arrived and offered Charlotte help. His first question to Charlotte was, "Have you called for an ambulance?" to which she answered, "No, I have been trying to wake her up. She is unconscious but breathing, probably has a concussion. She has taken a bad hit to the head, and there is a lot of blood. Her injuries are very severe, I don't think she will make it. Yesterday, my sister borrowed my cell phone, so I don't have a phone."

Thomas quickly replied, "I will make the call."

As Thomas was making the emergency call for help, Charlotte said to Thomas, "I have to check on my baby. She is crying." Charlotte had parked her car just behind the wrecked vehicle. She ran back to her car to put a pacifier in the baby's mouth and was back, checking on the woman. Then Charlotte said she had to go. Thomas thought she seemed a little disorientated, but what did he know, he was just a nice old man trying to help. A policeman arrived about that time. Thomas told him that Charlotte was the first to arrive on the scene of the accident, and right behind was the emergency vehicle. With rescue workers on the scene of the accident taking care of the woman inside the car and conversing with Charlotte, Thomas was free to go. The baby started crying, so as Thomas passed the car, he stuck his head in to try to calm this precious baby. Maybe a few gentle words would help. To his surprise, lying on the front seat of her car was a cell phone. Thomas remembered distinctly the lady working with the victim telling him her sister had borrowed her phone the day before, so she was unable to call for help.

How strange, he thought. *Well, there had to be a good explanation. She obviously was doing all she could to help this poor lady who had been lying in a pool of blood and obviously hurt very bad.* About that time, the lady was being lifted into the emergency transport unit. *Hopefully she would pull through,* Thomas thought.

*****

Dr. Smith checked on me every day. First it was to try to understand where these thoughts were coming from. He had also talked to George, my husband, who assured him we had only one son. His name was David, and he was ten years old and was home with our part-time maid at this very moment—David, whom I missed terribly. I had always been a good mother and put David first, second only to my husband and God. He was such a joy to our lives. He had brought us great happiness. The doctor asked me if I had ever had a child I had put up for adoption. I assured him, "No, I had never put my child up for adoption." But what did I know; I could not remember what had happened to him. I had searched my brain for any memory of what could have happened to my precious baby. The doctor thought this might be the problem, and a feeling of guilt might have caused me to overreact. No, I told him, but in reality I couldn't remember. I just could not remember.

I kept asking him the same question over and over, "When can I go home?"

He kept putting me off with the same statements: "All in good time" or "I'm putting a lot of consideration into this subject." His statement that upset me most of all was, "When you decide you don't have a son named Joseph, then I will start considering your request to leave here and return to your home."

I would suddenly become angry because I knew I had a son. Who was he to tell me I didn't have a son named Joseph; but how did I really know? Was this just a dream, or was my mind playing tricks on me?

Then I met Samantha. That was when my recovery started to come about. She was brilliant. I never could figure out why she was here in this dreary hospital. She always said it was because she wore her clothes inside out. Then she would laugh the most wonderful laugh, not one of those put-on laughs but a real laugh with real feelings. But truly, true to her word, she did always wear her clothes turned inside out. Oh, what a funny young woman she was. She quickly became my best friend. We met together every day for dinner, with the table's cafeteria style and the sound of Beethoven's "Symphony No. 5" playing. We would sit together and enjoy our meal, whether it be pot roast, salmon, or turnip soup, which they served quite often, and to my surprise was quite good. We talked a lot, and our conversations were so interesting. I told her why I wanted to get out of this hospital, about my son David, of course George my husband, and what small glimpse I could remember of Joseph. The first couple of months she talked, but she mostly listened to what I was saying. Then one day she told me I would have to agree with the doctor, that I didn't have a son named Joseph, agree with them that I was schizoid.

At first I was really upset with her. She said, "You will have to do this if you want out of here." I stayed mad at her for about two weeks, which was really hard for me to do because she was just one of those people you just can't stay mad at. After I got over being mad at her, I took some time to think over what she had articulated to me. I decided I had tried everything else, and they wouldn't listen to my plea. So I took her advice because I had to find my Joseph. Three months later, I was packing the few things that belonged to me that hadn't been stolen or mysteriously misplaced. Like a thief in the night, personal belongings just up and vanished. I was now packing my few belongings and heading to the one place I had longed to be—home.

*****

The day George picked me up from the hospital, I will finally allow myself to call it what it really was, a sanatorium, was a day I will always be thankful for. I stepped through the door exiting the hospital and smelled the fresh air. It was almost intoxicating, and the sun shining through the clouds ever so slightly made for a beautiful fall day. This world, which I had just passed into since exiting those heavy doors that had kept me a prisoner for way too long, was filled with fall colors of brilliant yellows, shades upon shades of oranges, and the reds; it was a multitude of colors. The wind was blowing ever so slightly but just enough to send leaves flying through the air. With the sound of the wind blowing through the trees and the sound of rustling leaves upon the pavement, it seemed almost magical. This day would be my day of new beginnings starting with my husband George and my son, David. I had been gone out of their lives for far too long. Getting our lives back together would be one of my priorities. At the top of priorities was finding Joseph, and that I would start immediately.

I would go back to the time I met George, which seemed like a pretty good place to start. I met him at the flower shop where I worked.

I had started working in a small but very busy flower shop just minutes from the hospital where George worked. I loved working for the owner; she was full of life, always bubbly, funny, and cheerful. Just what I needed—someone to keep me laughing and encouraged, someone who was not so inquisitive and always trying to pry into my past. My past was simple: it was just me, my room—which I rented from the owner of the flower shop—and my job. Not much to tell, not much there.

Beth, who was the owner of the shop, and I became good friends. We dined together every evening after work. She had been married, which ended in a bitter divorce. She talked about her marriage and divorce occasionally but didn't linger there, for her bubbly personality always took her back to the fun things of life, like eating chocolate mousse; taking long walks in the park, shopping on her days off; going to the mall; and just for fun, picking out clothes and hats we knew we would never wear out in public and, to our amazement, loving them and buying them. These became our new fashion.

I would come into work every day at six and start making fresh flower arrangements for the day. The flower shop was just down the street from the hospital, so we had plenty clientele. George was one of our customers. He came in often to buy flowers for his mother. He called it "a personal touch for picking a lovely bouquet of flowers."

He never called his orders in, always came by in person. On one of these occasions, he asked me out to dinner, which I politely turned down. I wasn't interested in seeing anyone at this time. I was still trying to make sense of my own life. I need not try to explain myself or my feelings to anyone.

I didn't see him again for at least a month, then one early morning in May, he came back into the shop. He didn't come to order flowers this time. He came just to ask me out to dinner. How did he know me? I knew him. I had seen him many times around the hospital and in town and in restaurants. Everyone knew him; he was a very popular doctor. I didn't want to date, and I told him so. It wasn't that he wasn't wonderful, because he was. If I had wanted to date, he would be the perfect choice, but I didn't want to complicate my life right now. I declined his invitation for dinner the second time.

*****

Samantha had been released from the hospital. She was great, such a dear friend to me. She was still the same wonderful, caring, overdramatic, thoughtful person I remembered from the sanatorium. She came by often and always brought a gift for me or David and, on occasion, a gift for my husband, who had taken a liking to her the first time they met. She knew David loved to fish and camp out, so she would bring him a hat, a new fishing lure, or a new flashlight— something she knew would be of interest to him. David always loved her gifts and looked forward to her visits. She always brought me a new set of earrings as she owned her own jewelry shops. She bought most of her jewelry from Israel. The jewelry was beautiful. The colors and clarity were pristine and very well-made. Samantha had never married. She had been in love once when she was young, but unfortunately, he was in love with someone else. She said he was the only man for her, and she would never marry. Oh such love.

*****

Since I had been out of the sanatorium, things were slowly getting back to normal. It had been a month since I had left that dreary, cold place that was also referred to as a hospital. I was glad things were getting back to the way they were before I had my breakdown. Doctors called it a breakdown; I saw it differently. I call it waking up, my brain waking up and remembering something I truly had forgotten. If only those memories had given me a little more to go on. But that hadn't happened, and this was all I had—a name and a face of my little boy.

As time slowly passed after leaving the sanatorium, I would try so hard to remember back ten years ago to the events before I had my horrific car accident. I stayed in the hospital over two months with injuries to my head, broken ribs, broken foot, and a broken collarbone. Although after time and lots of physical therapy, I had healed fairly well. My memory before the accident was gone, blank—nothing.

I went to the library and searched newspaper articles in the hope of finding information about the wreck, but I found nothing. Well, almost nothing.

I went to the police station, but they wouldn't take the time to talk to me. The sergeant said to me, "Hear all the phones ringing? They are all emergencies, and I have a murder case I have to take care of right now, so please excuse me." I called behind him out loud as he walked through the cloudy, smoke-filled room.

"Well, that got me nowhere." Then I addressed him as "Mr. I don't have time for you." He turned and gave me a dirty look but said no more. I thought to myself as I left the police station, *Mr. Policeman, go ahead and take care of all your triangulating issues. Forget about me.*

Next I tried the hospital where I woke up three weeks after my accident with no memory—no memory of anything in my past. It was strange; I could still read and write, peel potatoes, play music. I could still add and subtract, still tie my shoes, still drive a car, but I was lost to who I was or even where I lived.

My past went back only ten years. The doctors told me there was a medical term for this type of brain trauma or brain injury, "retrograde amnesia." However, this type of amnesia doesn't last for years. The memory loss is usually short-term days or maybe a few weeks; however, in my individual case, something else must have been damaged to cause my memory not to come back. I remember nothing before my accident, except for the fleeting moments when I remembered Joseph, the night as the rain streaked my windshield, and the stoplight turned from red to green; or was that my mind playing tricks on me?

*****

Thomas walked into the kitchen, then placed his worn-out Hokies hat on the table, where he kept all his receipts for the shop stacked in a neat pile. These were old receipts from days gone by where he and his twin brother Fred had run their business for nearly forty years. He picked up his cup of coffee and took a long, slow drink. He then walked over to the window, where he would sit silently watching through the glass plate window waiting on Charlotte to arrive. Her shift at the hospital had been over hours ago. The snow was already pilling up. "Where is Charlotte? She is always on time," Thomas mumbled under his breath as he poured himself another cup of coffee.

Charlotte had moved into Thomas' house over five years ago. It was a large two-story white house with gray shutters on a little over thirty two acres of land. Thomas and his twin brother Fred had been born in that very house to loving and caring parents, who loved this land and farmed it for many years. After their deaths, first father then mother, Thomas and his brother continued to farm the land. Behind the main house stood a large two-room barn where Thomas and his brother Fred designed and put together beautiful stained-glass windows and doors. It was a very lucrative business for two talented men, who had orders coming in from all over the country and a few orders from London and New Zealand. Fred never married, had no children, and had died about two years before. After his brother's death, Thomas hadn't needed all that space, so he allowed Charlotte to rent the top floor. She also had use of the downstairs kitchen. She usually cooked for both of them, which made the arrangement great for an old gentleman who was clumsy around the kitchen, and to beat it all, Charlotte was a great cook.

Two years after Charlotte had met Thomas at the scene of an accident, they met again at the post office. Charlotte was mailing Christmas gifts, and Thomas was buying stamps. Thomas recognized Charlotte immediately. She hadn't noticed him at first, and she was busy standing in line with an armful of Christmas packages waiting to be mailed. Since he was directly behind her in line, they had time and occasion to chat. Thomas asked her how she and her little girl were getting along. Charlotte ignored his question and immediately started talking about Christmas and all the crowds she had been encountering. He asked her if she knew whether the woman in the accident had lived or not; her answer to him was no. She had no knowledge of what happened to her after she left the scene of the accident. A lie she had told herself many times over the last ten years.

Finally Charlotte was next in line. Thomas took that time to ask her to have lunch with him just across the street, telling her they had the best rotisserie chicken and apple fritters on the planet. Charlotte accepted his invitation. Immediately after accepting, she thought, *Oh my, why did I say yes? What if he asks me questions about the day of the accident?* Her thoughts went immediately to the baby boy she had taken from the car, the day the mother lay dying. Charlotte prized herself on being able to manipulate almost any situation, saying to herself, "I'll just have to ask all the questions." Simple as that.

At last, Charlotte pulled into the driveway, which was now covered with about four inches of snow. The snow had been peppering down rather fast the last couple of hours. She was in a mood of preoccupation, you might say, not like herself at all. She didn't explain why she was so late, and Thomas didn't ask; she knew he had been worried. She was a tenant, Thomas the landlord; but best of all, they were friends. They didn't pry into each other's lives—a kind of mutual respect they had for each other.

*****

George's first wife had died of breast cancer about a year before we met. He didn't talk about her much, but when he did, I would give him my full attention. It was usually around Christmas, Thanksgiving, or David's birthday. I wasn't jealous of those memories; I rather enjoyed hearing about all the good times they had shared together. Actually, it showed me what kind of person George was, one who truly cared, and I was blessed to be married to such a person.

Early one morning about two months before George and I started dating, George came into the flower shop and asked me to make him an arrangement of flowers. He asked that I use a variety of different flowers, the nicest ones in the shop. I proceeded to do as he asked and with his instructions on the flowers and the bow to be used. While thinking all the time as I was arranging the flowers, he was very handsome and also wondered if he was here to ask me for a date.

Once the flower arrangement was all finished and had been paid for, and I had been complimented on the beautiful arrangement of the flowers. I asked him for an address where they were to be sent.

George smiled, then he said, "These are for the prettiest girl in the whole city." I was standing there with pen in hand waiting for an address when George said, "These beautiful flowers are for you."

I was so startled by this that all I could say was "thank you," and that seemed to come out all fuzzy and wrong. George smiled that gorgeous smile of his and said, "I must go. I have rounds to make at the hospital." Just before exiting the shop, he said, "Enjoy your flowers," and with another smile, he was out the door.

I must say this brightened up my day! Actually my life. It was about another month before I saw George again.

Once again, he came into the flower shop. It was late evening as I was about to get off work. This time, it wasn't to bring me flowers or candy or even to ask me out to dinner. He came in to the shop to give me tickets to the opera. He said he had bought them months ago in hopes I would attend the opera with him.

However, something had come up, and he wasn't going to be able to go himself, so he said he wanted me to have both tickets for me and a friend of my choice.

I thanked him, and I told him I would be delighted to have the tickets. "I love the opera, and I have friends that would love to have the extra ticket."

After flashing that wonderful smile of his and telling me one day he hoped to convince me to go on a date with him, he made his exit. I thought a lot about him the next few days. How wonderful and kind he was. It seemed as if George was determined to get a date with me. However, I still felt like I needed more time. Not because of George but the holdup was me.

With each visit George made to the flower shop, my decision became a little easier. Would I even be free to date? That is a question I must come to terms with before accepting his invitation.

*****

The kind of amnesia I was diagnosed with is very rare. Mine is an extremely rare case. I was told there was probably damage to my brain, which was the problem more than the amnesia, and I probably would never regain that part of my memory that I had before the accident. I was told my memories before the wreck were probably gone for good.

At the hospital, when I regained consciousness and they were trying to find out my name, they had told me there was no purse, no driver's license, nothing to identify who I was. The car had no identifying marks. The tags and registration were missing. There was a slip of paper that had the word Texas lying under the front seat. That piece of paper was the only thing found inside the car, and my wreck had occurred in Tennessee. None of this made any sense to me; I remembered nothing.

When I left the hospital, I was assigned a social worker and a therapist. In my opinion, the therapist was no help at all, but Mrs. Paul was of great benefit to me. She helped me find a job and a place to live. I owed her so much, and I was so grateful for her hard work and patience in helping me restore a place in society for myself.

*****

Samantha had come to visit for a week. I was so excited. I hadn't seen or talked to her in a while. She had been to Israel for three weeks, then on to Italy where she had been for the better part of a month. Buying different lines of jewelry from different parts of the world was her thing and bringing them back to sell in her upscale jewelry shops. Pleasing her clientele was big on her list. Over the last year, she had even designed her own line of jewelry, but now she is here for a week. When she came to visit, life was so much fun. We loved her visits, and we were so blessed to have her here. Yes, Samantha still wore her clothes inside out, her own fashion statement. Only Samantha could get away with this and look great in doing so.

Samantha had always taken me seriously about finding Joseph. I could talk to her about him, and she would always listen and encourage me, never making me feel like I was imagining it all. So tomorrow, we—she and I—were going to the town two hundred and forty miles away, where my wreck had occurred. She said it was the right thing to do. Seeing the place the accident occurred might help me to remember something about that dreadful day that left me in a world of limbo for years on end.

It was a beautiful spring day. We had gotten an early start, stopped for breakfast, and were making our way to the small town where the accident had happened. The little information I had with me of the accident was from the hospital—which was very limited—and from old newspaper clippings, and a photo of the car. There was also a description of the highway, including the mile post number with the town where the accident occurred, and a picture of me, the young lady with no name. Attached was an article asking the public for help identifying the woman in the photograph. No one ever came forward.

*****

Alice was just going out her front door, looking down at her watch when she realized she was going to be late. She was meeting Noel and Candy, her two grown daughters, for early brunch since all three were off work on Wednesdays. Candy's kids were still at school, and Noel was still single with no kids of her own to rush home to. The middle of the week presented a perfect time for the three to have brunch, catch up on gossip, talk about their plans for the coming week, and still have a little time for shopping.

Noel was the first one to arrive at the restaurant. She was always punctual, and to Noel, always being on time was a necessity if you are an ambitious reporter for a newspaper. Even as a child, Noel was fascinated with events and mysteries of all kinds.

She had always wanted to do detective work. Her sister teased her by calling her a facts collector, which always annoyed Noel, as if collecting important facts on events was equal to that of a stamp or butterfly collector. However, her sister was a detective also and had been for a few years now. They were known in and around town as the two detectives.

Candy and Alice arrived at the restaurant about the same time. Whoever arrived first would always reserve the table by the big bay window, that is, if it wasn't already reserved. Sometimes this table was hard to get because it was a favorite spot in the restaurant, and to add to the scenery was a beautiful flower garden growing just outside the window. Whoever had planned the landscape knew what they were doing. From the bay window, the flowers appeared to grow right out of the lake. Oh so beautiful.

Noel was already seated, sipping on a tall glass of iced tea when Alice and Candy, in heavy conversation, finally entered the restaurant. Noel called to her mother and sister with her singsong voice that personified her bubbly personality and at the same time attracting other customers' attention. She waved to them, and some even gave her a thumbs-up or threw her a kiss. Obviously she was popular here.

She loved having lunch with her mother and sister. Every week was a special time, a special occasion for her. Just being in their presence was the best.

The restaurant was filled to capacity when Thomas and Charlotte arrived for lunch. They were told the wait would be about ten minutes. They had a table seating two that were just leaving. Thomas and Charlotte had been dining here once or twice a week on her days off since they had been reacquainted at the post office.

*****

Samantha and I had decided to start our investigating with the popular town restaurant. We would go in and get acquainted with some of the local people.

Today's special was shrimp salad, barbecue ribs, and the soup of the day was broccoli and cheese in a bread bowl.

My stomach was in knots. I was in the town where my wreck occurred. Could I have lived in this town, and will some of these people remember me or the wreck? As I looked around, I was surrounded by people, busy people, some obviously away from work on lunch breaks, and some here for just a leisurely lunch. One table appeared to be having a birthday luncheon with all sorts of beautifully wrapped gifts sitting on a large table next to them. Over in the corner, a group of four men were talking business, and over by the big bay window were three women flipping through the menus, laughing and talking, while trying to decide what to order. Being seated at the table next to us was an older gentleman and a younger lady. As they took their seats and made themselves comfortable, I was thinking to myself the young lady is probably his granddaughter.

The older gentleman was quite handsome, tall in stature, and with the posture of someone who knows where he is going and where he has been. In other words, a man of importance. He seemed to be popular among the clientele. People were waving to him to say hello, and some approached his table and shook his hand. He seemed like a very likeable gentleman. He had probably lived in this town for a long time, maybe all his life. I thought to myself when things slow down some, I will start a conversation with him. The young lady with him seemed at ease and very confident, sure of herself you might say. Samantha was also scanning the crowd, checking out the people whom she might talk to if the chance arises, all in the effort to gather information about the wreck.

We finally decided on shrimp salad, baked brie served with freshly made potato chips, and a soda. I was too nervous to eat but wanted to keep busy doing something while scanning the crowd. Looking for what, I don't know. Something familiar—perhaps some familiar face, a voice, or perhaps laughter.

My thoughts were on Joseph, and in some strange way, I felt today I would make some progress. I had a feeling of hope. Samantha and I took our time eating and ordered soda refills. The older gentleman and younger lady sitting at the table next to ours were finished eating, so I decided to address him first by asking him a little about the town. I slowly made my way to his table, introduced myself, and then asked him if he had lived in or around this area for a long time. The older gentleman stood and shook my hand, introduced himself, then introduced his female companion. She extended her hand and asked me where I was from.

Something about her seemed familiar—her eyes. I was suddenly shivering; I don't know why, but I couldn't speak. There was something about her voice. Samantha sensed something was wrong, and she took over the conversation. I was trying to keep my mind on what she was saying, trying to stay in the moment, trying to keep from passing out. I felt like I was going to faint. I took a drink of my soda thinking this might help, but instead I swallowed wrong and got choked and started coughing.

I could feel a hand on my shoulder and a woman's soft voice whispering in my ear telling me to just concentrate on breathing, think of nothing but breathing. It worked, and I regained control of myself. The young lady went back to her seat by the bay window. I was still shaking, but I was okay.

The older man knelt down and took my hand in his, and his words were clear. Then he said in a kind voice, "Hope you feel better soon, and God bless you." He slowly slipped through the door along with the young woman who was with him, and they were gone.

The lodge where we were staying was just ten minutes from the restaurant and about ten more minutes to the scene where the accident had occurred. Samantha drove me straight to the lodge. She knew something was wrong from the strange way I was acting after the young woman spoke to me.

Upon arriving at the lodge, Samantha told me to rest and she would make some tea. We needed to talk. She knew something had upset me, but what, she did not know. Yes, indeed, something had upset me; but all I knew was something about this lady, who was introduced as Charlotte, had put me on edge. From the first moment she spoke asking me where I was from, was it her words? Was it her voice? I knew that voice, and I remember those eyes. When I first looked into her eyes, I saw a caring, loving person; then beyond the first look, I realized there was more, maybe the words. *Sinister* or *disturbing* would be a better play on words that would describe her.

It took me about an hour to regain my composure, I mean, really regain my thoughts. Still I kept wondering why this woman had made such a negative impression on me. Something inside me was telling me it had something to do with my past, but what?

*****

As Samantha turned the car off the main highway onto the old narrow country road, which was heavily lined with pine trees, I couldn't help thinking this road looks somewhat strangely familiar, yet there was no real remembrance. Just an eerie feeling, if that makes any sense? As we drove up the winding gravel road, I knew I had been here before. The pine trees grew thick and tall, and every now and then, the sun would filter itself through the vast growth of trees, making dark and light patterns across the nearly deserted country road.

Before turning down this road, I had decided to let all of my five senses work for me. I was here to remember. What would be at the end for me and Joseph? If I do remember. Not knowing really scares me, but remembering might be even scarier. The windows were rolled down. I wanted to hear, to see, to smell anything that would help me in this endeavor.

Samantha's hands clasp the steering wheel as she patiently but slowly drove the Mercedes down the old country road. Occasionally leaning forward over the steering wheel, as if her attention to all the details, which lay in front of us, would somehow make me remember. She would glance down at the map we had purchased just an hour ago. We had marked and retraced, which wasn't hard to do since it was a one lane highway. She kept her thoughts mainly to herself, except for an occasional outburst of, "Carol, do you recognize anything?"

I was in my own little world trying to get my brain to remember something important. Something about the wreck, the road, anything about myself or Joseph that could help me find him. Finally we came upon the mile post where the wreck had occurred. I was hesitant to get out of the car. My legs didn't want to work, but finally, with some vigor, I pulled myself from the car, then I walked around the area several times, hoping upon hope my memory would come back. Off to the right was a thin row of pine trees. Beyond that was a green pasture with a vast number of cows grazing and some with calves alongside.

I said out loud as I walked the vast area, "Joseph couldn't have been in the car with me the day of the accident. They would have found him in or near the car. There was no car seat, no diaper bag, and no bottle—nothing to indicate that a baby or anyone else was in the car with me that dreadful day." I walked and walked this big area looking about, as if in a daze, as if I would find something tangible—yes, something tangible that I could hold or wrap my arms around, but knowing in reality this would not happen, the most I could dream of finding would be a memory.

We continued driving on down the road in the same direction for about thirty minutes. Questioning myself out loud, I said, "What was I doing on this road that day so long ago? I had to have a reason. Had I lived in a house somewhere along this road? Was I visiting a friend or relative? Was I running from someone or to someone?" There was an answer to every question, and this one I must find.

Suddenly the road changed, no longer a gravel road but a very nice paved one-lane road, although it was somewhat wider in width.

No more pine trees lining the road. A beautiful white fence replaced the trees on both sides of the road. Beyond this point stood an attractive two-story white house with gray shutters. The landscape, the trees and shrubs and flowers seemed to be placed in just the perfect spot and left me wondering who might live there.

*****

I woke up early the next day with music coming from the adjoining room. Samantha had been up for hours exercising, which was a very important part of her daily routine. Today was already planned. We had decided to make every minute of our trip as fruitful as possible. Today we would visit all the convenience stores in the area asking questions about the area and the people who lived on the road on White Cherry Drive or if they remember anything about a specific wreck that occurred there ten years ago. With such a long span of time and people moving into and out of the area, we knew the chances of obtaining any new information would be very slim. We also planned to talk to as many storeowners or managers of businesses as possible, hoping against hope for answers.

The two-story white house was on our list. Yesterday, no one seemed to be at home; no one answered. We rang the doorbell, stood around, rang it again, and knocked on the door. We heard no noise from inside except for the chimes the doorbell made. Today we will repeat our visit, hoping to get a good insight of this area and the people who live here.

The first convenience store we stopped at, a little gray-headed lady wearing a very nice straw hat was out front selling peaches. She called and waved to us as soon as we stepped out of the car. Immediately she started talking about her peaches. She was saying you can always tell a good peach from its color. Then she picked one up quickly, sliced it into two pieces, took the seed out, and handed half to me and half to Samantha. "See for yourself" she said. "Now take a bite of this peach." Samantha and I just looked at each other. I could tell Samantha was trying not to giggle.

Then I spoke up, "We are not really looking for peaches."

With a strained little voice, the older lady said, "Then why did you come over here?" Not knowing exactly what to say, being thrown off guard by her comment, I stumbled around trying to find the right words, then I told her we would take a small basket of peaches. Her face lightened up with a smile, and her cheeks turned a pale crimson. I'm not sure if the color was from the hot sun pouring down on us or if she had somewhat embarrassed herself. Handing the lady the money for the peaches and gathering my change and my basket of peaches, I turned to leave. "Miss, miss," she was calling after me, "you didn't answer my question."

"What question?" I asked.

"Why did you come over here?" came her strained little voice.

As I turned back and faced the little lady, I noticed her demeanor had changed somewhat. "Information, I came for information," was my answer to her question.

I stepped under the big umbrella she had attached to her truck in effort to keep the sun at bay. She simply said, "Ask away."

"Ten years ago, there was a bad wreck on White Cherry Drive off the main highway."

"Oh yes, yes, I remember that bad wreck," she said before I could finish my question.

I looked at her with a little more enthusiasm. I was excited now, so I asked her my question. "I was trying to see if anyone in the area could remember any details that might help me."

"Yes, that's the wreck they were asking the public to come forward with information. If anyone knew the young lady in the picture. If so, they needed help in identifying her. The news media had been flashing her picture on television and in the local newspapers. I heard later no one ever came forward to claim her. There were lots of tales going on in this town about that wreck. The woman who helped rescue her turned up with a baby boy. She only had him for about three months. But that was a hoax. Nothing to that story they say."

"Do you know who this woman is, her name, where she lives?" I asked.

"No, honey, I don't know any of the details, but I know the best newspaper reporter, who is more of a real detective than a reporter. If anyone can help you, it would be her. You ask the police, you get very limited information, you ask her, she gets results."

"Her name, please do you know her name?" was my next question.

"Sure," came her voice clear and specific, "her name is Noel Walker. She works at the town newspaper. You can find her easy enough on Main Street West. You can't miss it, right in the middle of town. There is a big sign that hangs over the door: Town Paper the Gazette."

Then she asked me a question, "Are you the young woman that was in the wreck?" I lied to her and told her I was just interested in the story. This lie worried me the rest of the day; it kept nagging at me knowing in my heart there is never a good reason to lie. I thanked her, and we were on our way.

She called after us saying, "Now those peaches are Georgia peaches, the best there are, Georgia peaches..." Then she smiled at us and waved. We waved back to her and departed on our way.

This Noel sounded like someone who can help, and immediately we headed in the direction the lady had given us.

Upon arriving at Main Street West, it only took us a few minutes to locate the building we were looking for. It was an old building, beautiful architecture with huge polished wood doors that were obviously well maintained. We were informed that Noel was out of town and would be back sometime the next day. We left our cell phone numbers and the name of the hotel where we were staying with a brief message.

My thoughts kept going back to the story the nice peach lady told us about the woman who had helped with the rescue. What actually did she mean when she said the woman had turned up with a baby boy and only had him for about three months? I kept asking Samantha just what this could mean. Could this baby have been my baby? Samantha answered by saying, "We will get down to the bottom of all this, but right now, we can't jump to conclusions. The woman also said it turned out to be a fabricated story." My mind didn't stray far from the thought of this baby. Could this baby have been my Joseph?

Gathering information wasn't all that easy. A lot of the people had recently moved here from New Jersey, New York, Connecticut, or a number of other states up north. Their past memories were of some other town back home. They were busy now getting used to living in a small town, away from the hustle and bustle of big-city life. They presented us with no new information.

Our three-day vacation, if that is what you can call it, not really a vacation, was almost over. Tomorrow evening, we would have to head back home. Samantha would stay another day with us, then back to her shop, or should I say shops. I would go back to being mom and wife to my family, but as of now, we were headed back up the gravel road where the accident had occurred, to the white house with the gray shutters. I couldn't wait to see what was waiting for us there.

The road was busier today than it had been the day before. We passed two squirrels without incident. We saw a gray fox and a couple of deer near the pasture where the cows were grazing on the lush green grass. We passed no cars coming or going.

We were coming upon the white house now. "Oh, I am so hoping there is someone there that will talk to us." We repeated our steps as we did the day before, but this time, as we stepped upon the big front porch, we heard a dog bark from inside. *Encouraging*, I thought, then I rang the doorbell impatiently a couple of times.

We heard a man's voice call out, "Hold on, I'll be there in a minute." A man's voice came as he opened that front door, "Well, what a surprise," which was equally a big surprise to us. "We don't get much company here," came his friendly voice. Then his next statement came as a question, "Well, weren't you the two ladies we met at the diner just yesterday?"

Immediately I could see it was the older gentlemen from the restaurant, which had been seated at the table next to ours the previous day.

Just yesterday, he had introduced himself as Thomas and the young lady with him as Charlotte.

Samantha took over the conversation for me knowing that I was probably startled at seeing him here and knowing any minute the young woman who had upset me so yesterday might appear at the door. Samantha told him we were here trying to gather information on a wreck that had happened on this road nearly ten years ago. Telling him since his house was the only one we had passed on this road, we thought we might stop and ask a few questions.

"Sure, come on in. I actually happened upon that accident that day, and it was a bad one," he informed us. Then he took Samantha's hand, shook it, and asked, "Is your friend better today?"

"She sure is," came Samantha's reply. Then he turned to me, took my hand, and said, "Young lady, I am so glad you are feeling better."

Beside him stood a well-behaved, tail-wagging blond lab, and two bays came from the dog. "Don't mind her, that's her way of saying hello," came the older gentleman's voice.

Then the blond lab made her way to my side and just looked up at me, whimpered a little, and nudged my hand.

"Oh I see she likes you. Never mind her, she is a good dog, and she doesn't bite. Not too often anyway," this came from the older gentleman, followed with a laugh.

"What's her name?" I asked as I bent down to pat her head.

"Chocolate!"

"Chocolate?" I repeated as I laughed out loud. Thinking to myself a blond lab named Chocolate, to me that was funny. "How did you come up with that name?" I asked.

"The first time I saw this dog, the word *chocolate* came to my mind. Ever since that day, Chocolate has been her name. She always comes when I call. Young ladies, Charlotte is not here. She works the day shift at the hospital. I'm sure she will be sorry she missed your visit. As I said before, we don't get much company around here," came his kind words.

It was a great relief for me knowing she was not at home now but working. I could ask questions and be at ease with this nice gentleman. I knew if she came through that door right now, I just might grab her and wring her neck; however, I also knew I can't let my emotions get the best of me. I needed facts; I needed information; and I needed to find my little boy.

Thomas described the car and the angle the car settled after the accident. He said Charlotte was already at the accident when he arrived. She was working frantically to save the life of the woman inside the car. He told us about the police arriving, the ambulance arriving and taking the poor lady away. Then he told us he had no idea if the woman had lived or died. He had heard different stories about her fate. When he was finished talking, I asked him questions. The first one was about the baby. "Do you remember if there was a baby in her car?"

"No," was his reply, "there was no baby in the car with the injured woman."

"Was there a baby anywhere near the car?" I asked, trying to control my trembling voice.

"No, there was no baby in the car with the injured woman. Charlotte's daughter was in her car. No other baby that I saw."

I was not ready to divulge to anyone as of yet that I was the lady in the car. I knew I had to be careful. I had to watch my step.

*****

Thomas had lots of interesting pictures hanging on the walls, some of family members and some art he had collected through the years. I asked him if I could go around looking at them. He said, "Sure and there is lots more upstairs in the hallways, if you enjoy looking at pictures."

I thought, *Pictures tell lots of secrets.* However, there were no pictures of babies or children, except for a few downstairs Thomas had told us about when we first entered the house. They were pictures of him and his twin brother when they were youngsters. As he described him and his brother's pictures, I wondered to myself if this was a ritual he does with everyone that comes to visit him. He loved his brother very much; you could tell by the description he gave of each picture. Cute little boys I must say.

As I came back downstairs and entered the living room where Thomas and Samantha were sitting deep in conversation, I noticed a beautiful red vase sitting solo on a side table. It was such a beautiful vase, and looking closer, it was a signed piece. It was as if I knew that piece, as if I had held it, as if I had signed it myself. I made a dead stop, let out a gasp, as if in a trance as I stared at the vase. The signature was signed "Lexi." After the accident, I had taken on the name Carol. I had to be called something and with no memory and no identification. Well, Carol was a good choice. So the last ten years, Carol was the name I answered to. Could this be a memory or some type of wishful thinking? Could it be the mind playing tricks? I was sure it was a memory. Tonight I will do some research starting with the name Lexi, research vases. "The cloud" is a perfect place to start.

I was excited, hopeful for the first time in a long, long time. This trip had been very helpful, and I was so thankful to Samantha for all her help.

Telling Thomas we needed to be on our way was a little hard to do. With not much company coming his way, he would have preferred if we had stayed longer, offering tea or coffee, sandwiches or cookies, which we politely turned down.

I did not want to encounter this Charlotte again anytime soon, not before I had the time to have her properly investigated. Charlotte left me with a sense of danger.

*****

Thomas insisted on showing us his ballroom, and he wouldn't take no for an answer. He walked over to the huge French doors and opened them up to the most beautiful room I had ever seen. It was a huge room. The entire floor was done in white marble, absolutely beautiful. The crystal chandeliers were amazing. Fabulously plush blue velvet curtains hung gracefully, draped precisely over the windows, allowing just the right amount of light to flow in. The light from the chandeliers, along with the sunlight coming through the windows, casting a hint of blue upon the room made for a beautiful scene across the smooth marble floor.

"This room," Thomas said, "was built for a very special person." Then his demeanor changed somewhat. I could see tears rolling down his cheeks. Turning to Samantha and I, he said, "You must promise to come back another day to hear all about the person this room was built for." By now he had our attention. We assured him we would definitely visit him again in the near future. I wouldn't realize for months to come how much this conversation about the person this room was built for would mean to me.

*****

I took my time walking back to the car with Samantha following close behind. She was talking a mile a minute, but I didn't hear a word she said. My mind was working overtime trying to process all that I had learned today. The name Lexi, the signed red vase, finding the lady and the place where she lived, and Thomas. They had both been at the scene of the accident. Oh, what a very productive day. Charlotte, this mysterious person working trying to save my life, or was she trying to save my life? Then the information about the baby, no baby in my car, a baby in hers. No baby pictures in the house, or none we saw, except for the ones of Thomas and his brother, what was his name? Fred. Yes, that's it, Fred!

Thomas had told us there were two more houses on this road. Then a few more miles past the last house, it came to a dead end. No one lived in them. They had been abandoned a few years back. I decided to drive by and check that out too. True to Thomas' word, the houses were abandoned and falling in, then the dead-end road with nothing but forest beyond that.

The next day, upon entering Noel's office, I had been surprised by such a tiny space. I had expected something different. There were no pictures on the wall, no framed awards on her desk. There was only a desk and two chairs in the room, with the exception of a crystal paperweight, a Bic ink pen, and two sheets of paper that lay neatly on the desk. We had arrived about ten minutes early. She had introduced herself, set her laptop on the desk, and said, "I'll be right back. I definitely need a cup of coffee," and disappeared through the open door.

When Noel returned, she was gracefully balancing three cups of coffee. She handed one to me, then one to Samantha, and directed us to make ourselves comfortable.

Noel had an overpowering presence about her—a personality that just commanded attention as she spoke, a seriousness, with an overwhelming drive to get things done. Nothing slothful about her.

As she seated herself behind the desk, her long blond hair hanging over her shoulders, she looked more like Barbie than a news reporter. That thought almost made me laugh outright, but I controlled the urge.

After the formalities of introducing ourselves, we got down to the seriousness of the business at hand. Noel had remembered us two days ago from the restaurant, her being the lady who had touched my back and told me to just concentrate on breathing. When she mentioned the incident, I could feel my face flush. I had never felt comfortable when all attention suddenly came my way. But this quickly passed. What was I, ten? I told her about my memory being flawed for the last ten years, about the wreck, about this Charlotte, who was the first one at the scene of the accident, about Thomas, about Joseph, about the baby in her car. Telling her the reason I was here was for help from anyone that could help me find Joseph. Noel was a native of this area. She knew lots of people and most of the people on the police force. She promised she would find out all she could for me and get back to me in a couple of weeks. I thanked her. We shook hands and said our goodbyes. She followed us to our car just to say, "Remember, I deal only with facts, never hearsay."

*****

Two days later, as we were leaving the zoo in Atlanta, all David could talk about were the lions and elephants, and wow, I didn't realize he knew so many adjectives, and his descriptions were very colorful in describing these big beast. He was so energized by seeing all the animals, his mind working overtime making plans after he graduates from high school—plans that include taking a trip to Africa and going on one of the advertised safari tours he had read about at the travel agency, just last week. Tomorrow is his birthday, and we had spent the day at the zoo with him. George had taken off a week so we as a family could drive down to Atlanta to celebrate with some family and a few friends.

Tomorrow night, David and some of his friends would be having an overnight party at the Atlanta Aquarium. A friend had told George about overnight parties at the Aquarium, and we thought it was a great idea. We had checked on it and decided it would be a perfect birthday sleepover. So George, myself, and seven kids would spend the night with our pillows and sleeping bags in front of the shark tank. I told George this will be a great story to tell to our grandkids one day.

Was David spoiled? Of course, all kids are spoiled nowadays. Since his father was a doctor, he was away a lot, and I was no help other than adoring David. So I guess sometimes, I overindulged when it came to David. How could you help but love him? He was a good kid—never sassed, easygoing, energetic, and fun to be around.

The events for the next few days were filled with fun, friends, and family. We found time to tour the Coca-Cola plant and sampled cola from all around the world. David found three samples he liked best from the countries of Argentina, Germany, and Canada. George liked Tokyo, Kiev, and Colombia. I couldn't get over all the different versions of cola. My preference was Hawaii, although I love just a good cola.

George and his brothers and sisters had grown up in Atlanta. His parents still lived there off and on, spending part of the year in California. On our second date, George and I had driven to Atlanta to meet his parents. The first two times George asked me out, I had turned him down, the third time he had asked me to help him and his son put together a Christmas wreath. Since I knew all about flowers, ribbons, and wreaths, he thought I would be the perfect person to ask. I accepted; he and his son picked me up on a Monday morning the week before Christmas, and we drove to his house. I was expecting a small wreath to put together in half-hour time with a few pine cones, a big bright red ribbon, and lights. Was I in for a surprise? The wreath was huge, I mean h-u-g-e. I was looking at all the pine cones and thinking did he cut the whole tree down and take off all the pine cones? There had to be three hundred at least; what was he thinking? I started laughing so hard and couldn't quit. No matter how hard I tried to quit laughing, I couldn't. It was just so funny to me. I am sure he would have liked to have packed me up and dropped me back off at my house, but I wasn't going anywhere. By now I was just having too much fun. Through outbursts of laughter, I said, "Hand me the floral wire, a glue gun, and of course"—laughing again—a pine-cone." We would joke and laugh about this event for years to come. On our fourth anniversary, he confessed, the Christmas wreath, the bigger the wreath, the longer it would take the three of us to finish.

George said after giving me a kiss on the cheek, "That was my plan, keeping you with us as long as I could. Which of course would give you more time to fall for me and David." Then he said in a very manly tone, "I had already fallen for you."

"Oh how sweet of you to admit this finally," I said after giving him a kiss. We would laugh and talk about that wonderful almost perfect day for years to come.

"Paris!" George had surprised me with a trip to Paris for our honeymoon.

Was I surprised? Yes! Very much so and overly excited as this event began to unfold.

We enjoyed our time together under the charm of this fabulous city. Paris was all I had expected it to be and more. The first four days we spent indoors, our honeymoon suite was all I could have ever asked for. A great place to give our love to each other and start our lives anew together.

George is such a wonderful husband, and I love him dearly. He is so gentle, wonderful, and caring and always a gentleman. I considered myself blessed to be married to this special man.

As our days progressed, we explored Paris and all the wonderful things Paris had to offer. The Île de la Cité and Île Saint-Louis are two natural islands that still remain in the Seine, which is located within the city of Paris. That was where we found the beautiful Sainte-Chapelle with its gothic and French-gothic architecture. George and I found it to be so amazing. The stained-glass windows were magnificent, simply magnificent. The windows were so rich in color and design I could hardly take my eyes away from them, and there were so many windows all beautifully designed.

Neighboring in the same vicinity was where we found Notre-Dame Cathedral. We found this along with Sainte-Chapelle to be two of the best examples of French architecture in Paris. Of course, we could not tour them all for lack of time; however, we did take a bus tour around the city, which took us past most of them and gave us a description in detail of their importance.

Paris is noted for many things; beautiful architecture is just one of them.

Paris, the capital of France, is also noted for its famous French cuisine, which we delighted ourselves in every evening. We would dress in fancy attire for an evening out, and George would take me to dine and delight ourselves in some French cuisine. We found the food in Paris all amazingly good.

George and I slept in late in the mornings, then we would lounge by the pool for maybe an hour, then take a walk, where we would walk—or should I say stroll down—the Rue de L'Abreuvoir. It was springtime when we were in Paris, and the wisteria was in bloom. This walk was so very beautiful. I strolled slowly, and I was amazed at how beautiful it was.

I heard this said while in Paris so many times, and it was true: the best way to see Paris was to walk. I am a believer. There were so many things you would miss otherwise.

The Eiffel Tower was one of my favorite sightseeing adventures. I was amazed at the color of this famous tower, which I consider chocolate—yes, milk chocolate—in color. Some call it bronze; however, I call it milk chocolate.

For George and me, it was a wonderful adventure. Viewing Paris from the height of the Eiffel Tower was amazing, very romantic at night. With the sipping of hot chocolate in the café and the five minutes of the twinkling of the lights, every hour was simply amazing. Seeing Paris from the height of the Eiffel tower is grandeur. I found myself wanting to stay there. Leaving would be hard for me. In just a couple of weeks, I had fallen in love with Paris.

George's parents were great. Both were retired doctors, his mother an anesthesiologist and his father a surgeon. They had retired a couple of years back, young enough to travel and enjoy the fruits of all their hard work. They were great, and David was their only grandson. I had loved them from the first day we had met. They were so loving and accepting and wonderful to be around. They had a way of making you feel like you were the most important person in the room. Never drawing attention to themselves and their accomplishments but rather drawing positive attention to the person they were talking with. Never rude, never judgmental. They both had very unique personalities.

*****

About a week after arriving home from David's birthday party, I started getting unusual phone calls. At first I didn't think much of it when no one answered after I said hello. I would just hang up and think it was probably a wrong number. Then I started writing down the telephone numbers, and to my surprise, it was always a different number. I reported it to the telephone company in the hope that I would find out who was making these calls, but for now, it was just a mystery.

*****

The red vase, the name Lexi, this research had taken me all the way to California—Ojai, California, to be precise and to a little town in the mountains of Virginia, the little town of Keokee, not literally leaving my living room but research on my laptop. Lexi had grown up in this quiet town, studied there and finished high school, and created some very unique masterpieces in the form of vases. She patented them and reproduced them both in California and Virginia. *Now just who is this Lexi, and what does she have to do with me?*

As each day progressed, I found out more about Lexi and about this little town, Keokee, which is set in the beautiful mountains of Virginia.

I had been waiting for Noel to call me and give me any bits of information she might bring to light on this Charlotte character. My days were anxious; my nights were anxious. How could they not be? A small glimpse into the past is all I had to go on. Where will it take me? Where will it lead?

George kept up with all that I was doing. I told him everything—my day-to-day progress and all my findings. He was always the first to know. George had hired a private investigator to find out all he could about Charlotte. Today on his way out the door going to work, he told me I should get the investigator's report in a few days. Then just as he kissed me goodbye, he said, "Then we will know better how to proceed in our search for Joseph. Remember, Carol, it has been ten years since your accident."

I didn't like those words, but I guess they must be said from time to time. Ten years was such a very long time. I had been planning another trip to visit Thomas, but I wanted to wait for the investigator's report. This second trip I would make by myself. Thomas I would trust; Charlotte I would not. I would find out first if she was working before I went to see Thomas. I needed to talk to him alone, to gather as much information about her that he would give me.

One of my questions, what was she doing on that road the day of the accident? Was she following me? Did she run me off the road? I must ask Thomas about the vase. I must ask him if he knows what happened to the baby in her car that day. If he ever saw the baby other than the day of the accident? If he knew what she might have been doing on that road that day. He might not know these answers; he might never have thought about them. However judging by his character, I think he will answer them truthfully. I must get these answers soon. I may not wait on the detective's report. I may go tomorrow. Yes, I need to go tomorrow, and I need these answers now.

Just as we had finished breakfast the next morning, Noel called and said she had some pictures she wanted to show me, and she knew I would want to see them as soon as possible. I told her I would be there in about four and a half hours, which was how long it would take me to drive that distance. I would call Thomas later. I was anticipating a visit with him later in the day. David was spending the day with his Aunt Julie and Uncle Craig, so it would be a perfect day for me to go.

Getting on the road early in the morning was my plan, which worked well. Then halfway there, I noticed a car that seemed to be following me. No, it was probably my imagination—too many horror movies. I told myself, "Settle down and just drive." I did for a while, then I spotted a fast-food drive-in and pulled over to order a coffee. Upon entering the highway, I spotted the car again just a couple of car lengths behind me. I thought, *This is odd.* My first inclination had been to pull off on a side road and see if it goes on. Then fear gripped me. What if I had pulled off back there, oh my, anything could have happened. Then a few scenarios pop through my mind. I could get shot, mugged, beaten, or worse. Again I told myself, *You watch too many horror movies.*

I drove on without any further incident. The car that I thought was following me seemed to just fade away. Noel was there when I arrived. She had friends who worked at the local hospital where Charlotte worked. One such friend, also a registered nurse, had worked the same shift as Charlotte for a couple of years. All Charlotte talked about for six months was her baby boy. She called him Charlie. The way she said his name, you could tell he was very special to her. *Charlie,* Charlotte would say in a slow way of speaking. A friend had mentioned this to Noel.

Noel showed me the pictures taken at Charlie's birthday party. They were clear, good shots of a gorgeous little baby and also clear pictures of what appeared to be a slimmer and frail-looking Charlotte. Noel allowed me to keep these pictures.

I was so amazed by these photographs. I just couldn't take my eyes off this beautiful baby and the thought that he might be my Joseph. My mind became foggy, and tears streamed down my face. Wondering thoughts rushed through my mind, with the question: where could Joseph be at this very minute, this very moment in time? We sat there for some time in silence, then Noel came close and gave me a gentle hug and said, "You have a lot of work ahead of you, which could bring you great happiness or a great deal of sadness in the end, but I promise I will help you all that I can."

Noel informed me shortly after these pictures were taken at Joseph's birthday party, Charlotte just stopped talking about Charlie, just quit talking about him altogether. After a while, people got suspicious and started asking her questions about him. "Where is Charlie? You haven't shown us any pictures of Charlie lately. Can you bring the little guy by for us to see how big he is getting? We miss him." Again and again, people asked her these same questions.

I was given these statements by a few people who knew her or should I say worked with her. Charlotte, with an air of confidence, would use excuses like, "Oh, he is just getting over the flu," or "We are so busy lately," or "We went skiing."

What? Skiing, what kind of explanation is that? Who takes a baby skiing?

Then one day, posted in the nurse's station was a short note from none other than Charlotte herself printed in big, bold letters, which read:

TO ALL CONCERNED

Please refrain from asking me any more questions about Charlie. His father came and took him away from me. I don't want to talk about it at all. Thank you for respecting my privacy.

To all my friends,
Charlotte

Noel told me based on her friend's statement, "None of her friends or coworkers have seen Charlie since."

Fear gripped my heart at that moment. Tears streamed down my face. "What has she done with him?" I said out loud while thinking to myself. "Should this not be a police matter?"

Noel said in a very matter-of-fact manner, "At the time, there was no reason for suspicion. They just took her at her word. Now you are here, this changes everything."

Noel told me to keep in touch with her. She wanted me to call her at least once a day to let me know what is going on, and in turn, she would let me know if she acquired any new information. I told her my next stop, today hopefully, would be to meet with Thomas.

I called to let George know how my trip was going. He told me he had taken work off, and the rest of the day, he would be free. I was to wait for him before I went to visit Thomas. He was already on the road headed my way. He had tried to catch me before I left home but had missed me by about forty-five minutes. I told him to meet me in the parking lot of Clair's Restaurant. His GPS would bring him straight to me.

When George and I arrived, Thomas was sitting on the front porch. I had called ahead to let Thomas know we were coming, so he was expecting us. It was such a beautiful day. The sun was brightly shining. The sky was a beautiful blue color with only few white fluffy clouds scattered across the sky. The cherry trees lining his yard were in full bloom, and the pink blooms were intense.

Thomas was in a jovial mood, quick to welcome George, even gave me a kiss on the cheek. I thought, *Hope he will still be as hospitable after I ask him the questions I have lined up.* After he served us ice-cold lemonade, I told him this was more of a business trip than just a casual visit.

"I have some questions I need to ask you."

His answer to me was, "Anything for a friend. I'll do what I can."

This time I was up front with Thomas, and I told him I was the lady in the car accident ten years ago. I emphasized my suspicions about Charlotte, and I needed some important questions answered. I thought he might know more than he realized. I asked if he noticed anything unusual about Charlotte the day of the accident. He told me, "No, this was the first time I had met her. She was working hard to save your life." After fidgeting with his hat and mumbling under his breath, he told me he had great respect for Charlotte, and his loyalty would probably be to her unless there was reason to think otherwise.

"Thomas, the last time I talked to you, I asked you if there was a baby in my car the day of the accident. You said there was no baby in my car, but there was a baby in Charlotte's car. My question, did you ever see the baby again? Through all these years you have known Charlotte, did you ever see the baby with Charlotte at any other time other than the day of the accident?"

Thomas answered in reply to my question, "The first time I saw her after that accident was about two years later around Christmastime at the post office. That is when we became friends. I asked her a few years past about that baby, and she said it was her friend's baby. I do remember the day of the accident she told me it was her baby girl. I never questioned her on this. Charlotte told me from the first when she became my tenant, she wouldn't pry into my life and I wasn't to pry into hers. I think that is how we have continued to be such good friends all these years. The question of why Charlotte was on that road the day of the wreck had never come up, and I had never had a reason to ask."

"The beautiful red vase, that is signed Lexi, where did you get it? What do you know about it, and who is Lexi?"

Thomas looked puzzled at first. His words were slow when he asked, "What vase? Who? Lexi? Red vase?" He shook his head, repeated again, "Red vase. Oh, you mean the one sitting on the table near the stairs. That vase belongs to Charlotte. She brought it with her when she moved in."

"Lexi, I don't know a Lexi, who is she supposed to be?" Thomas questioned.

"The vase is signed by her, Lexi," was my answer.

"All I know is that vase is Charlotte's, and she said the vase is a collector piece, and it's worth quite a bit of money."

Thomas told us that the only time he had seen a baby with Charlotte was the day of the accident, and she never talked about the baby. "I remembered clearly she said her 'baby girl' she told me the day of the accident." Thomas repeated this to me twice, then looked away as if in deep thought.

Before we left, I changed the subject. I did this on purpose. I wanted our visit to end on a lighter note. We talked about the beautiful flowers and shrubs that bordered his house; they were amazing. Among the many flowers were parrot tulips, which I had never seen before in such beautiful colors. They were outstanding. He told me his brother had planted most of them, and so far year after year, they had grown back to show their beauty.

*****

Charlotte sat on her bed staring at the locked trunk that sat directly in front of her. Her eyes and mind plastered to the trunk thinking of all the things inside this old dark rustic trunk that could put her behind bars for a long, long span of time. Slowly lifting herself from the bed, she bowed down in front of the trunk, unlocked the lock, raised the lid, and slowly began removing one article at a time from the trunk. She sat there holding each item up to the light that flowed through her window, doing so to get a better look at each article. Tears streamed down her face as she removed the little blue and green blankets she had wrapped Charlie in and the clothes he was wearing the day she had taken him from his mother's car—his mother's gray purse with all the contents that were in the purse the day of the wreck lay there among the articles of clothing; a couple of bibs with the name Joseph skillfully embroidered in multiple colors; a stuffed bear and a giraffe; as well as socks, shoes, bottle, pacifier, all the things that were in Charlie's bag. Each article she examined carefully, then laid it gently on the bed. With tears running down her face, she reached for the box where she had stored his pictures for safekeeping. She hadn't opened this box in six years—too heartbreaking, too many good and bad memories; but today, she would look at all the pictures one by one. When she had finished going through all the pictures, she carefully placed them back into the box, tied the box with a white ribbon, and placed it back in the bottom of the trunk beside Charlie's mother's journals.

With trembling lips, she asked herself what was she to do with all of Charlie's pictures and all the things she had taken from the car where Charlie's mother lay dying? She knew she had created problems for herself, for Charlie's mother, and, most of all, for little Charlie. She was not pleased with herself.

When Thomas had first informed Charlotte that a detective had made inquiries about her, she panicked, even to the point of being upset with Thomas, telling him not to answer any of their questions, ignore them totally. This information had motivated Charlotte to open the trunk and take a trip down memory lane.

*****

Thomas was ruffled at the thought that anyone could think Charlotte could do anything underhanded or wrong. She had always been so good to him. He just couldn't understand how anyone could suspect Charlotte of any wrongdoing.

Charlotte had kept up with the whereabouts of Charlie's mother, recently making phone calls to her home and actually following her. Going to this effort only to protect herself, she was home free as long as she, Lexi, couldn't remember anything about the accident.

It was almost time to start dinner, so after the day of sweet and bad memories, Charlotte carefully packed all the baby items from the trunk back into the trunk like they had been before. She shut the lid, then hesitated, opened the lid back up, then taking her time, walked downstairs where the red vase sat on the table. She picked it up, carried it upstairs, wrapped it in a bath towel, and placed it into the trunk before closing the lid.

Two days later, when Charlotte felt a little more resourceful, she hired a private investigator to find out what Charlie's mother might have remembered about the accident. It was expensive, but in the end, it would help her make her decisions. She was convinced they would never find Charlie. Tears streamed down her cheeks as she thought of little Charlie. Oh how she had loved him and wanted things to be the way they were when she had first taken him, but she knew he would never be a part of her life again, and this pain she felt was so intense.

*****

George had hired a private investigator because he thought Carol might be in over her head. From his prospective, it was hard to know what was going on, but Carol was sure she had a baby named Joseph; there might just be something to this. He would help her figure it out. If there was some underhanded kidnapping that had gone on here, he was determined to get to the bottom of the deception.

The reality of it all, Carol had been in a bad car accident ten years ago. She could not remember her life before the accident. If this sudden memory was from her past, and she actually had a son out there somewhere, they had to find him, and he was all for helping her. On the other hand, if this was not a true memory, they would have to try to figure this out too. Either way, he will do all he could to put this right for Carol.

*****

First thing in the morning, George would contact the private investigator he had hired to see what kind of information he had come up with. It had been two weeks now since George had hired him.

He should have some answers, then we have to think about getting the police involved. I thought about going to Charlotte first and asking her for the truth, demanding she tell me what she did with my little baby. But George said no; we have to do this in a lawful manner. I didn't see it the same way he did. Every time I thought about her being devious when it came to other people's lives, I got angry. In my suspicion, she has been playing with mine and Joseph's lives? My patience was getting thin. I wanted answers, and I wanted them now.

The next morning, I drove straight to the police station. I asked to speak to whomever was in charge about a kidnapping. The guy at the desk handed me a form and asked me to fill it out and told me someone would be with me shortly. I took a seat beside two men who had been arguing, and this did not stop upon seating myself. They became louder and louder, then finally a police officer came out and took me to another room. I hadn't written a thing on the paper. The pen the officer handed me seemed to be out of ink. I looked through my purse for a pen or something to write with and found none, so the paper was blank. *This was not good*, I thought.

I handed the officer the paper, and before I could speak, he blurted out, "Can't you write," in a gruff voice. "Never mind," he said, looking at me with an intense stare. "Now what is this about a kidnapping? Name and location please," he asked this in a slightly nicer tone. As I gave him the details, he put the information into the computer. When he got to the part that the kidnapping having been over ten years ago, his attitude changed somewhat. "And you are just now reporting it," was his next statement.

I told him about the small window of memory I had had of Joseph before I spent time at the sanatorium. After this statement, he seemed to lose interest in what I was telling him. Then he said, "Miss, are you sure you are not making all this up?"

"Mrs." I corrected him, "Yes, I am very sure," in a tone I probably shouldn't have used. I urged him to follow up on what I had told him. Then he abruptly stood up and, in the same gruff voice, told me he had all the information he needed. He would get back with me as soon as he checks all this out.

I left feeling like I had not been taken seriously, what an awkward feeling, but at least the authorities knew about my suspicions that a kidnapping had occurred with as many details as he allowed me to give him. Three weeks later, I still hadn't heard a word from the police station. I felt like the report had been pushed to the side or dismissed altogether.

George kept telling me to let the private investigator take care of the crucial work. He would say in a very authoritative voice, "Because, this is what we are paying him to do." After weeks, months, and over a time that seemed way too long, trying to figure out this puzzle, it seemed like the puzzle pieces were coming together too slowly, way too slowly for me.

I decided to do as George wanted me to do for now, let Mr. Carr, that is Mr. Benjamin Carr, do his job. He came highly recommended. He had worked on some high-profiled cases in the past, creating for himself a reputation of being the very best, the private investigator with experience, top dog and highly endorsed by his peers. Tomorrow at 7:00 p.m., we were to meet with Mr. Carr for a full rundown on Charlotte.

*****

David and his two best friends, Artie and Michael, who were both a couple of years older than David, had been swimming most of the morning. This was one of their Saturday morning rituals. First breakfast out on the deck, which usually consisted of eggs, bacon, hash browns, and orange juice. I would always ask them what they wanted for breakfast. Customarily I would get the same answer, which was chips, cookies, soda, candy bars, pancakes with lots of syrup. Whatever foods they ask for was not what they got. I would tell them it will be ready soon. Then I would make them a hardy platter of scrambled eggs, bacon, toast, and hash browns and call for them when it was done. They would carry the trays of food out on the deck, eat, and have a wonderful time laughing, joking, and arm wrestling, just being boys. Later they would bring the trays of dirty dishes into the kitchen. Artie would always say, "Mrs. Wainwright, thanks for the cookies, candy, and pancakes, they were great." Then I would hear them giggle and run out the back door.

Usually they would swim in the pool for a while and then head off to the lake with their fishing poles. It was a great place to play around or fish. The lake was beautiful and had lots of fish, which consisted of bass, catfish, trout, and a few other creatures that I couldn't identify. But before they did any fishing, they would swing out over the lake and let go and fall into the cold lake water. The water ran into the lake from a cold mountain stream. To them, swinging over the lake was the best part of the morning. The swing hung from a big oak tree that George had hung a few years back, making a great swing for the boys to enjoy, and enjoy they did.

Certain times of the year, you could smell sweet jasmine mixed with old-fashion roses, which grew along the river's edge makes for a calming, soothing, delightful aroma. Back further along the mountain ridge grew huge poplar, oak and a variety of fir trees. The cherry trees were a favorite tree the boys like to climb, which grow tall and were full of red cherries in the early part of the summer. Boys, crows, blue jays, and a variety of birds like to cherry pick, so the berries are gone rather quickly. Needless to say, the birds get most of the cherries. It was a great place for a young boy to grow up and roam the lake and surrounding woods with his friends.

When they got to playing, time often slipped away from them, so I would pack them a lunch and walk down to the lake. Usually pack fried chicken, grilled cheese, apples, oranges, and of course, some sweets. I called David on his cell phone and let him know about thirty minutes before in case they were exploring deep in the woods.

If they were not too far out in the woods, they would run, meet me, and carry the basket of food to the pier where they would quickly devour the contents of the basket. If there was any food left, they would tantalize the fish by throwing bits of bread or chicken into the water and watch the fish or whatever may be under there lurking come up and snatch it from the water.

*****

Finally it was Saturday evening, and I was sitting in my living room, waiting for Mr. Carr to arrive. I was a little anxious not knowing what to expect. I was also hopeful that he would have more information to go on. George was out back smoking a cigar, something he seldom did. So I guess he must have been a little nervous too. We were not used to private investigators or police being involved in our lives. The telephone rang. As I walked over to answer it, George hurried back into the house through the side door. He told me he was expecting a call from an adoption agency. "I don't understand," I said to him, "an adoption agency?" Then I repeated my statement again. "I don't understand."

"Have they found Joseph?" I asked, following George to the telephone.

George shrugged his shoulders and whispered in my ear, "Honey, I don't know. I'll let you know as soon as I talk to them."

About that time, my cell phone rang. At the other end of the line, I heard Noel's voice, "Carol, is this you?"

"Yes," I answered in a strained voice, my mind still wondering why George was waiting for a call from an adoption agency. "Yes, yes, this is she," I managed to say.

Noel's voice came clear and precise, "Well, Carol, it seems as if Charlotte is trying to make friends with a few of the men on the police force. She doesn't understand these are men who will not be manipulated. She has been making accusations about you, terrible accusations. She wants you investigated."

"What?" was all I could get out of my mouth before she came back with, "and she has been telling them you might have lost your son on purpose. This is not hearsay, I am telling you. She told me this herself. She came into my office yesterday making the statement I was helping a criminal. Just wanted you to be aware of what was going on."

I told Noel, "Thanks for the information. I will get back with you later. Mr. Carr, the detective we've hired just pulled into the driveway. Thank you so much." We hang up.

George had finished his conversation and had just hung up the phone and was on his way to answer the door.

It was just a few minutes before he entered the room. "Mr. Carr I presume." I walked forward and extended my hand.

He took my hand and answered, "Yes, and you must be Carol." Since George had hired Mr. Carr, this had been my first opportunity to make his acquaintance.

He was a big guy—muscular—and sported a black-and-gray mustache and heavy dark eyebrows, which seemed to fit him well. Mr. Carr had an air about him that gave the impression of being a go-getter. He seemed very sure of himself and very comfortable in his own skin. I guess that goes with the line of work he does for a living. After our introductions and a couple of comments about the heavy traffic and a few remarks about the mild sunny weather we had had the last couple of days, we finally got down to the business at hand.

Mr. Carr informed me that without a doubt, Charlotte had a baby that she claimed was hers. "After about six months, the baby was gone. None of her friends that I talked to had seen him after that. She called him Charlie." I thought to myself this was the same story I had already heard but from a different source altogether. In my mind of reasoning, with what I was being told for the second time, this information must indeed be true.

Then came Mr. Carr's controlled voice, he chimed in by saying, "The odd thing about all this is none of her friends or acquaintances I spoke with remember her ever being pregnant. Her explanation to them once she had the baby, was 'I concealed it well, lots of exercise, and the right kind of food.' Before Charlotte lived here, she had lived in Ojai, California, where she worked for a thriving business at the time. She had worked there for about three years. Previous to this job, she worked as an RN in one of their local hospitals."

"Excuse me," I said, "did you get the name of the company?"

"Yes, indeed, I did, Carol," was his reply. "Lexi is the name of the company. The company was started by a young lady, and her name is Lexi McGruder. The artist, Lexi, who started the company just up and disappeared. Hasn't been heard of in about ten years." This statement startled me a little, "What? Ten years?" My grasping at his explanation was coming slowly as I was somewhat stumbling this thought through my mind.

So let me get this straight: Charlotte worked for this Lexi and some-how ended up as the first person present at my accident. What was he telling me? Just what did this mean?

This was very alarming to me. Could this Lexi be me? Then my mind went back to the beautiful red vase signed by Lexi that sat in Thomas' house on the table near the stairs. I remembered when I first saw that red vase, it was like I knew it, like I had touched it, like I had signed it myself. Could I possibly be Lexi? True, I couldn't remember anything past the day of my accident except the small glimpse of Joseph and the red vase.

I was thinking I was so glad George was here with me because my mind could deal with only one thing at a time. Right now my mind was back to Joseph. Where was he? What has this unethical creature done with him? What has she done to us? Is he safe? Does he have someone taking care and loving him? If she took him from my car the day of the accident, he would be maybe around eleven years old, maybe eleven and a half by now. That would depend on the age he was the day of the accident. I wanted to remember so badly, but all I could see in my mind's eye was a glimpse of a little baby, my baby. He would be close to David's age. I dream one day when we find him, he can run, play, fish, arm-wrestle—do all these things with David. I know David would love to have a brother close to his own age. Please let him still be alive. Deep inside this was my ever haunting fear.

I was suddenly brought back to reality when I heard George's voice, "Carol! Carol! Are you okay? Are you hearing what Mr. Carr is saying?"

"No, I am sorry, I am trying to take all this in," I managed to say.

Mr. Carr was saying, "Charlotte has no criminal history here or in California where she worked before going to college and earning her nursing degree. She is a hardworking registered nurse and a very good one at that. She has been married but separated. We know his name. We are trying to find him to see if her story's accurate. We need to know if he came and took Charlie away from Charlotte, and also we need to know Charlie's whereabouts. We should be getting that information about anytime now. Then we need to get the district attorney involved and bring her in and question her on kidnapping charges. We know she had a baby in her possession for about six months. Then the baby just disappeared from her life, gone."

Mr. Carr was removing something from his briefcase. "Carol," he said, "I brought these along with me. I thought you would like to look at them and tell me what you think." He handed me a gray envelope. "Go ahead and take it," he said. "You might be surprised by what you find inside."

Sitting down and almost tripping in the process, I managed to rip open the gray envelope. The envelope smelled malodourous, like it had been packed away among smelly rotten vegetables, but the envelope itself had only a few small stains. The sending address had faded somewhat, but it was still legible. It was addressed to a Lexi McGruder. The address looked strangely familiar, on taking a second look, I suddenly realized it was Thomas' address.

My mind was flooded with questions, and I hadn't even seen what was inside the envelope. Opening and sliding the contents of the envelope onto the highly polished mahogany table that sat directly in front of me, falling to the very bottom of the pile of envelopes and papers was a chain anchored to a locket.

Turning myself halfway around in the chair to where George and Mr. Carr stood watching me, I simply said, "What does all this mean?"

I paused for a few moments, looked back at the envelope, and then repeated my question slower this time. "What does all this mean?" startling Mr. Carr by the emphasis I put on my question.

Mr. Carr put his hand to his face, then shook his head a little and said, "Keep going. It will all make sense soon enough." I turned to George, and he just shrugged his shoulders and pointed to the envelope, then nodded his head as to say for me to continue. I returned to my task at hand. One by one, I opened and read all the contents of the envelope.

George and Mr. Carr circled the room and stood directly in front of me, watching my expressions I was sure, looking to see how I would react to all the information inside this envelope.

The letters were signed by a Mary Sinclair, who was writing about her granddaughter Lexi. If I am Lexi, then the woman writing these letters must be my grandmother. I turned over the envelope to make sure I had read the address right, then I looked to see if there was a postmark. The postmark was clear, almost eleven years to the day. Eleven years ago. I grabbed for the letters to check the dates on them. Some letters were written weeks and months apart. Then they had all been mailed in this old, smelly gray envelope.

George had taken a seat beside me. I looked at him and said more to myself than to him, "Is this my grandmother? Where have these letters been all these years?" I wanted to know.

I looked at the envelope again; it was addressed to Thomas. "Why Thomas, and what does Thomas have to do with me or my grandmother?"

George kept looking at his watch. He seemed a little nervous, but I didn't think much about it. My emotions were up and down like the waves of the ocean. Before I could say anything else, the doorbell rang. A few minutes later, Ruth came into the room. "Carol, you have a visitor," she said.

"A Mrs. Shirley Lucy McGruder is here to see you."

George lunged to his feet, and his voice was high-pitched as he turned to me saying, "I am so sorry, Carol, your moth...," his voice trailed off as he rethought what he was saying, "Mrs. McGruder was supposed to arrive sometime tomorrow, after I had a little time to talk to you, giving you time to process all this information that Mr. Carr has gathered." His next words came quick, "She has arrived a day early," and then he disappeared through the French doors.

I stood dumbfounded, unaware of my surroundings, thoughts swirling in my head, my heart pounding with a strange rhythm. I felt lightheaded as if I would pass out, then suddenly everything went black.

I woke up lying on the couch with an excruciating headache. "Lexi, Lexi are you okay?" came a woman's voice. Looking up slightly to my left, I saw George with a strange look on his face standing beside the lady who had called me Lexi. When she spoke, I remembered the voice, soft and soothing. It was a strange sort of feelings. You know the voice yet you don't know the voice.

I could see her clearly from where I lay awkwardly sprawled on the couch. She was dressed in a long straight-cut dress. It was very pretty. I thought it was of a designer Indian print. I especially liked the designs of the print and the bright, vibrant colors. The dress and the woman were strikingly beautiful. It is strange the things you think of in a moment like this. However, this was the way my mind addressed the subject at hand.

Her hair was cut just below her shoulders and stunningly almost the same color blond as mine, except for a little hint of gray here and there. Her face reminded me of a porcelain doll. She was very pretty.

As she talked, I listened, still trying to grasp all her words. With a splitting headache and a flood of emotions, I tried to manage to pull myself to a sitting position. First try, I landed right back where I was. I felt embarrassed and very uncomfortable lying there.

She was sitting on the antique couch, just inches from where I was lying. What a strange situation to find myself in. I finally pulled myself to an upright position, feeling very much embarrassed and a little overwhelmed to say the least.

I wondered to myself, *If this is my mother, she is very beautiful. Her eyes were a striking blue in color, beautiful you could say.*

Then her voice came. "Can you fancy my thoughts?" She said, "When I got a call telling me my daughter could be alive, I came immediately. I had to see you to see for myself if this could be true."

She seemed amazing. Her personality brought a high level of energy into the house, with an amazing ability to make you laugh. She seemed to never second-guess herself, which is a quality I truly admired. I liked her immediately, but what was she doing here? Was she my mother?

Awkwardly lifting myself from the couch and facing her, in a shaky voice that didn't sound like me at all, I asked her, "Well, what is the verdict? Am I your daughter or not?"

I was embarrassed immediately as soon as my question awkwardly rolled from my tongue. Then came her sweet answer, "From the minute I saw you, I knew it was you, Lexi."

Nervously, I said to her, "You will have to forgive me if I don't know what to say."

I watched her as she gracefully stood and walked to the door. I saw tears in her eyes as she turned to face me.

As she reached for the door handle and turned again to face me, she said, "Lexi, honey, I'll be back tomorrow. You need time to rest and think all this over." As she walked from the room, I suddenly realized my comments must have seemed very rude to her, which I had not intended; the wording had just came out wrong.

But one thing I realized, I didn't want her to go. With an overpowering urgency, I ran after her, "No, please don't go, and please stay."

David walked into the room about that time. I said to David, "Meet your grandmother. She is staying the night."

David, and should I say my mom, and I walked up the stairs together. After showing her the room she would be staying in, we left her to rest a little while, and as for me, time to gather my thoughts. The next few days were very pleasant. Lucy was my mother's name, and she was a bombshell, full of life. She brought with her wonderful laugh, a beautiful smile, and a road map back to my life. Yet she was serious, very intelligent, and well accomplished.

*****

The next day, we talked a lot—her telling me things about my past life. She talked to me about Keokee, the place in Virginia where I had grown up. About Keokee Lake, where we had spent lots of our time years before I disappeared from their lives. About my family there, about my working with pottery, and going off to college, starting my own company, creating some famous vases and selling them all around the world. About commissioned pieces I had done for some famous clientele. Keokee was where it all started, my business, that is.

It was hard not being able to remember your own life. It was surreal having your mother, of whom I had no memory fill in all the blank holes of my life, anyway the ones she was familiar with. But who else better to fill you in but your mother, even though you can't remember her. Only a faint sound of her voice, nothing more, but I count that a blessing, a wonderful blessing. As the days and weeks passed, we will have many talks together.

I quickly realized how wonderful my mother was. She was so much fun and an encouragement to me. She was so charming in her ways, very dainty, graceful, and such a pleasure to be around; and to top that off, she had such sweet laughter, which added to her personality.

I was up early the next morning giving consideration to my plans for the day. I wanted to visit Thomas today, and this time, I had someone I wanted to introduce him to. I would take the gray envelope the detective had given me along with the locket. After I had met with Thomas, I would make a surprise visit. I would wait for Charlotte to get off work. I had waited long enough. I wanted answers today. I had made arrangements with Thomas, and he delightfully agreed to meet me. We would meet at Clair's Restaurant. My preference would have been to meet at Thomas' house, but Charlotte had taken off a few days of work, and he wasn't sure if she was working today. The next time I met with her, I wanted it to be on my terms. Hopefully today would be that day.

As we drove toward our destination that morning, the clouds were dark and moving fast across the sky. They looked as if they would spill over at any moment. It was a warm day, and there was a heavy mist in the air. I considered waiting until the next day, but the weather report said the sky would be clearing up by midmorning. By that time, we would have arrived at Clair's Restaurant.

My mother Lucy and I talked most of the way there. I have to admit it was so nice having her along with me on this trip. I knew almost nothing about her, so everything she talked about was new to me. Her stories were mesmerizing. Even though I had lived through most of it with her, I remembered nothing. She talked a lot about Keokee and how beautiful the mountains were. She said there was no other place like it on earth. She told me no matter where she lived, Keokee would always be home to her. It was where my mother had grown up. Her mother, my grandmother, had moved back to Keokee when she was only four years old, she informed me.

"Lexi, Keokee was where you were born, and you lived there till you graduated from high school. Your two best friends Samuel and Norma Jean took up lots of your time when you were home in Keokee. You three were almost inseparable. They were either at our house or you were at one of their homes."

She talked about how wonderful and creative the people were who lived there. She was very possessive and protective of the people in Keokee. She informed me Keokee was a mining town and had been a mining town for as long as she could remember. Lots of coal had been taken from those mountains, and there was lots more to be mined.

Our conversation took many turns as we continued our morning travel.

She avoided the subject of Joseph. When I would mention him, she would start crying, so I decided to keep my thoughts about him to myself for our morning drive anyway.

Thomas was at Clair's Restaurant when we arrived. He was talking to a few of his old buddies. He told us later they were friends he had grown up with. They greeted us with a handshake and a few comments about their childhood days way back when. He had arrived early and reserved the table by the big bay window. I could see the lake from the window. The wind was producing ripples upon the water, and the small waves were drumming against the bank. I could see some cattails growing along the south side of the lake in a wet swamp area over by the water's edge. Yellow butterflies fluttered among the assorted flowers and hummingbirds that seemed to never get their fill of the nectar were keeping themselves busy down by the lake.

The roses just below the windowsill were in bloom, and I loved roses. My favorite of all roses were the yellow rose, and they were budded out and gorgeous. Among them were also red, white, and pink. They all looked like they were just waiting to be picked. I could just imagine myself as a child running out and picking a handful, and I would fill that bouquet with all those colors with only one exception: there would be more yellow roses than all the rest. How peaceful it was looking out over the water and thinking what I might have done as a child—wishful thinking for someone that couldn't remember their own childhood. Then my attention was pulled back to reality when the waitress came by to take our drink order.

I introduced my mother to Thomas. As I sat there watching them converse with each other, I realized for the first time they looked like they could be from the same family—the same eyes, the same dimples, even some of the same idiosyncrasies. Wow, this was even a shocking experience for me. Thomas' hair had long ago passed the blond stage and was mostly gray, yet there were patches of blond here and there still. He was very handsome. I just couldn't get over the thought of how much they looked alike, and if Lucy realized it, she kept silent.

Shortly the waitress came around to take our order. Since Thomas had been dining here for many years, he knew all the waitresses. He introduced us. We conversed with our waitress for a few minutes and then we ordered brunch. Just coffee for me. I didn't think I would be able to eat and comprehend all that was going on. Mother ordered a small platter of eggs and toast, and Thomas ordered a huge breakfast, said he had been up all night thinking all this through, and now he was hungry and was ready for a big breakfast. They ate in silence as I slowly sipped my coffee.

Thomas finally broke the silence by asking my mom, Lucy, if she had grown up in Keokee, and her answer was yes. Then she started talking about her life as a child and all the fun she had while growing up there. "Keokee, what a beautiful name for a town," Thomas said this more than a couple of times during brunch. Mother was pleased with him taking an interest in the area of the world where she had lived most of her life.

Then there was a long period of silence as the two sat in front of me eating their breakfast. The coffee was very good this morning; you might say a perfect cup of coffee. Sitting there, I looked around at the people and wondered about their lives. Were their lives as complicated as mine? I wondered if anyone else here had lost their son and had no true idea where he was. Looking around, I saw families laughing and talking while enjoying their food. Across from us was a gray-haired man and his son talking about things that happened in their lives many years ago. As the words pass from one to the other, I pick up part of their conversation. They seemed to be enjoying each other's company.

A young lady seated at the far end of the room kept glancing at her watch, and every now and then she would wipe her eyes, as if trying to hold back tears. Who knows the heartbreaks that others go through? The sadness that live within their hearts or the joys that make their lives worth living or worth proceeding on to the next day. Would anyone here sitting in this restaurant looking at me think I had forgotten about my son and for all those years did not remember him, not even once? Even if it was no fault of my own, it seemed so, so very terrible.

Then my thoughts were abruptly broken up by the sound of a cell phone. It happened to be Thomas' cell phone, and it was Charlotte on the other end of the conversation. She was at work and had called to let him know she wouldn't be home for dinner. She would be working a double shift. After the conversation was over, Thomas said, "Charlotte has been working a lot of double shifts. Told me she had hired a private investigator to take care of some of her personal business."

Interesting, I thought. *Yes very interesting.*

It was good that Charlotte was working a double shift, I thought to myself. When brunch was over, we could now go to Thomas' house where we would be able to talk in a more private setting. Thomas went on ahead of us. We would meet him a little later in the day. I had promised Noel I would meet her at her office and, since I had driven this far, I needed to meet with her and see the information she had for me.

With every new piece of evidence, whether it be large or small, I received it with gratitude, so thankful that all the missing pieces were finally coming together.

*****

Noel was working on her computer when Mom and I entered her office. She greeted us with her contagious smile. Noel's smile came with beautiful white teeth and bright, shiny blue eyes. You couldn't help but smile when you were around her. Seriously she had a very contagious smile. I introduced my mom to Noel. With that smile still on her face, she gracefully stood, circled the desk, and gave us both a big hug; then with a wave of her hand, she offered us a seat.

Noel started the conversation with the details we had come to hear. She said years ago, her mother was a volunteer for an adoption agency, and she had kept in close contact with one of the workers. "She had had lunch with her recently and was telling her about your story and your plight to find Joseph. They also discussed Charlotte."

Her mother's friend, I think she said her mother's friend's name was Danielle, knew Charlotte, and she remembered years ago her coming to their agency and asking questions about placing a baby with them. The reason she remembered Charlotte was she kept coming back week after week but never brought the little boy she called Charlie. She made plans to bring the baby boy in on different occasions but never did bring him in. She had no idea what happened to her son as Charlotte had referred to him. Noel's mother's friend thought she may have placed him with another agency.

Noel handed me a folded piece of paper with the woman's name and address on it. She said, "You are welcome to call her anytime, but she doesn't know any more than the information I just gave you." We said our goodbyes and were on our way.

Our next stop was to visit Thomas, and he was sitting on the front porch waiting for our arrival. He greeted us with a smile but looked somewhat tired. I asked him if he was okay, and he said he would be when we got all this figured out. He invited us inside so we would be out of the heat. Then he turned to me and said, "Before we talk or do anything else, I have to tell you about the room with the marble floor and why and whom it was built for."

Thomas led the way into the room, and it was as beautiful and magnificent as the first time I had been there. The marble floors were lovely, the crystal chandeliers stunning. The draperies, sky blue in color, with their deep velvety texture was opened just enough to let the right amount of light into the room. The light coming through the window flooded the marble floor with just enough light to add to the mystery of the room. The room had been well planned. The walls were covered with a wall covering made of cloth but a lighter shade of blue than the draperies. The cloth covering the wall was interweaved with strands of gold, green, and silver. The rods the draperies hung on looked to be made of high-quality material, I would think brass, and on both ends of all seven rods was carved a ballerina in flight or different poses might be better words to describe them. At the end of the room set a beveled glass table with a side bar, and hanging from this bar were four pairs of ballerina shoes, all in different colors. The floor reverberated with all the colors of the room. Wow! Is the best description I could give for this magnificent room? By far, it was the most beautiful room I had ever seen.

Thomas, with his mannerism of a perfect gentleman, ushered us off to the far side of the room to a sitting area. The Victorian-style chairs were upholstered in the same high-quality fabric as the walls. The pillows that adorned the chairs were a deep black in color and were embellished with small patches of green, gold, and silver. A perfect dissimilarity for the room that seemed to make this range of this lovely room so inviting.

After walking around the room and standing gazing out the window, Thomas made his way back to our side of the room. Seating himself in the chair directly in front of us, Thomas began his story.

"At the age of eighteen, I fell deeply in love." He voiced the words the second time, "I mean deeply in love. My brother Fred and I had been working felling trees. We were clearing the land for a neighbor who had just moved there and lived about half a mile down the road from us. Mr. Sinclair, the gentleman we worked for, invited us to have lunch with his family on the days we worked for him. By the time twelve o'clock rolled around, we were ready to eat, and we were always there on time. They had a son about seven years old. His name was Tim and a daughter which we had not met until the third day. Their son was always full of energy and asked a million questions and even made more comments. He was always making comments about his ugly sister. His mother continuously called him down and threatened to send him to Siberia if he didn't quit making remarks about his sister being so ugly.

"I thought to myself, this sister, she must be really ugly. So, therefore, I was looking forward to seeing her for myself. 'How ugly could she be?' I asked Fred on our second day of work. He just shrugged his shoulders and laughed. Then he said, 'I can't imagine a young girl being that ugly.' He paused for a few minutes, then added, 'I think Tim is just a mischievous younger brother.' The third day of working for the Sinclairs is one I shall never forget. I remember Mrs. Sinclair served fried chicken that day with corn on the cob, rolls, and a bean casserole, and she always had two pitchers of ice-cold lemonade sitting on the table. Some days she would serve the meal on a large table under the shade trees on the front lawn, and on other days, we would eat inside in the big dining room. This particular day, we ate inside. It was always a joyous event at their table whether we ate inside or outside. My brother and I were joking around just having fun while trying to eat. My mouth was half full of food, and I had just taken a big bite of chicken when she entered the room. I swallowed wrong, got choked, and nearly died. I could feel my face turning red, partly from embarrassment, but mainly from the lack of oxygen. Couldn't breathe, couldn't suck the air in, couldn't push air out. I was gasping for life or air, you might say. My brother hit me square in the back of my shoulders, and out plopped a big bite of food right onto my plate. Then I started gurgling and making all kinds of weird sounds trying to breathe. I finally caught my breath, almost wish I hadn't when I looked up and saw everyone staring at me. Then I heard Tim say, 'See I told you she was ugly!'

"His statement caught me off guard, and I started laughing. Couldn't quit laughing. I quickly excused myself and went back to work. At this point, I was so overwhelmed with embarrassment. When my brother finally joined me, I asked him, 'Fred, what is wrong with Tim? Are his eyes bad? His sister is the most beautiful thing I've ever seen. What good will that do me now? She probably hates me.' Fred wasn't any comfort to me. First thing he said, 'You know, she probably thinks you're a funny guy with a red, red face. You eat too fast and you can't hold your food, and I am sure she had noticed you laugh like a hyena.' We finally got back to work after I chased Fred around for about an hour, hoping to hurt him bad for all those crude and unwelcome remarks. It took me about three days to get the courage to join them for lunch again.

"However, after the third day, I was up early every day, couldn't wait to go to work, couldn't wait for lunch, and I could hardly wait for the next day to come. It seemed that Mary occupied my every thought. We bought a little house, this Mary and me, she seemed to like me as much as I liked her. Mary was her name, and this room was built just for her. We were married for five wonderful years, may I say, happily married. We had the best of times, wonderful times. There are no words to express how happy I was, and I was sure she felt the same about me. Then one day, I came home, and she had left me a letter propped up by the coffee pot saying she was sorry but she had to leave. That was the last time I saw her. 'Had to?' The words in her letter have always bothered me. What did she mean? I even contacted the police trying to see if they could help me find her. The only thing the police department said was she must not want to be found. Even her parents couldn't give me any information on her and where she had disappeared to. They also were very distraught about her decision to just up and leave. She had likewise left them a note or might I say a letter with a message for each member of the family, which consisted of her mom, dad, and Tim. The messages were telling each one how much she loved them with a personal note of love, letting them know this was her decision and her decision only. There was also a footnote that said this decision has nothing to do with Thomas. Then in parenthesis it stated, 'I will always love Thomas,' and a signature, then nothing more.

"So I built this beautiful room just for her. I know the years have slipped by, and she is much older now, but I know wherever she is, she is still dancing, and I'm hoping one day she will return!"

My mother interrupted Thomas. My mother could not contain her thoughts any longer upon hearing this information. In a voice unfamiliar to me, my mother said, "My mother's last name was Sinclair before she married."

Thomas continued his story. "Ballet was Mary's life back then. She was a great athlete, had a lovely singing voice, and played the piano in a very professional manner. Seems like everything she put her mind to turned out a success. I am sure there was a good reason for her leaving. I just don't know the answer. So I have to trust that she knew what she was doing. I always hoped there was no outside foul play involved. This has always bothered me. I would have always been there for her if she had allowed me that.

"I thought she might have gone back to her beloved Keokee home in the mountains. I drove to Keokee many times the first three and a half years after she left, looking for her. She wasn't there. Heartbroken I discontinued my search. I have to say the first few years after she left were very hard on me." Thomas became very emotional, and I noticed tears running down his cheeks. He then stood up and said, "Excuse me, ladies," and left the room.

I could tell the conversation about Mary's leaving was a sad topic for Thomas; however, when he talked about Mary, you could see his face light up.

My mom and I made our way out to the front porch swing where we sat talking and getting to know each other better while we waited for Thomas to make a reappearance. When he finally did join us, he was carrying a tray with three cups and a pot of coffee. Along with the coffee were three slices of apple pie. He made his apologies for leaving so abruptly.

I looked at my mother and noticed she was very quiet; something was bothering her. She began to speak, "Thomas, you said her name was Mary, Mary Sinclair. Is this correct?"

"Yes, that's what I said, Mary Sinclair."

Then Thomas repeated her name again very slowly, and for a moment, he seemed to fade into another time. Perhaps the time many years ago when they shared wonderful times together—glimpse of her face or a touch of her hand.

"Thomas, Mary Sinclair. That is my mother's name!" came my mother's soft voice.

"What are you saying? I don't understand?"

I excused myself just long enough to retrieve the envelope I had brought along with me. Upon returning, I handed Thomas the gray envelope and told him, "Mr. Carr, our private investigator, had given this envelope to me. I informed him I had read all the letters inside the envelope. Thomas, Mr. Carr told me you had provided him with this envelope. Can you explain? Please! Remember my mother has not read the letters, she has not had the privilege of reading these letters as of yet. She is sitting here because I ask her to be present when I talk to you because in the end, this will probably be more important to her than to me."

"Ladies, regretfully I only found this envelope a few days ago," said Thomas in a strange voice I hadn't heard before.

"I don't understand," I said.

"I didn't either at first," came Thomas' voice, "especially after I looked at the postmark."

"The envelope was dated a little over ten years ago, so where has this envelope and letters been all this time? Letters written to me," I said looking straight at Thomas.

Thomas said, "As you can see on the envelope, it is sent from Mary Sinclair Dunlap, which is why I wanted to tell you and your mother a little about her before we had this conversation. The address on the envelope is addressed to me. However, the letters inside the envelope are addressed to Lexi.

"When Carol started asking serious questions about Charlotte and about her missing child, I became curious about what was going on, and I couldn't get over the thought of that precious child in Charlotte's car at the scene of the accident all those many years ago. Then her telling me later it was her sister's baby. And according to Carol, Charlotte told the people at the hospital her ex-husband came and took the baby away from her. There is something really wrong here, a bizarre mystery, and I want to help find the answer if I can.

"As I have said before, I have always had great respect for Charlotte, but now things have changed. A little child is missing. When Charlotte moved in, she stored some of her things in the basement, so I went downstairs to have a look. I hadn't been down there in years. Boxes pilled on furniture, boxes on top of boxes, furniture stored away in a haphazard fashion. While I was looking around to see if I could find anything that might help among her belongings, I came across this envelope. It was in a box of what appeared to be trash, and there was other unopened mail in the box also. Lying on top of the box was an old jacket of mine I hadn't seen or worn in years, and if I hadn't moved that jacket, I would have never found this envelope.

"I was shocked when I saw that gray envelope with Mary as the sender and unopened at that. Then I saw the date, and I was immediately sick. It was a little over ten years old. You can only imagine how I felt. I had waited most of my life to hear from Mary, and all this time, the envelope has been downstairs among clothes, socks, furniture, and whatever is in those boxes.

"You can only imagine how upset and distraught I became upon finding this envelope. I found it just two days ago. Seeing it was from Mary, I became distraught and was overwhelmed in a way I cannot explain. All I had dreamed of all these years was hearing from her. Whether it be in the form of a telephone call or a letter. My twin brother, Fred, died about the time that letter was sent out. We had grown up together. We were almost inseparable, ran a business together, very close. His heart was always weaker than mine. Ever since he was a little boy, he had some problems with his health, but for the most part, he was in pretty good shape. So when he died unexpectedly, it was a great shock to me. For months I didn't want to get out of bed. My thoughts were, what's the use? I would wake up to the same nightmare I had went to sleep with. My brother was dead, and I would never see him again on this earth.

"It took me a couple of years to come to terms with it, but then I realized my brother wouldn't want me to be unhappy, and he would have told me to 'straighten up' and 'get on with your life,' and 'be happy. So that is what I decided I was going to do, and I did it for him as well as for me. Friends came in to help me after my brother's death. Things were moved about, and that pile of mail must have gotten misplaced and ended up downstairs. Now that I know where Mary lives in Seattle, I'll be leaving in two days. I have already made my traveling arrangements."

My mother was quick on her feet. She faced Thomas. "Let me get this straight, Thomas, are we talking about the same Mary Sinclair? My mother lives in Seattle and her name also is Mary Sinclair."

Thomas' voice came with a hint of relief, "So she is still alive." He took his wallet from his pocket and removed a picture and handed it to my mother. Thomas looked straight at my mother and said, "This is my beloved Mary, and now my question to you, is this your Mary?"

Lucy, my mother, after looking the picture over for some time, handed the picture to me. As I took the picture from Mom and looked at it for the first time, I kept thinking to myself, *Wow, she is so young and beautiful.* Then Thomas asked about Mary's health. Mother told him she was in good shape and very active doing benefits for charities and so on. As I handed Mom back the picture, I realized I had been looking at my grandmother. She was as lovely as Thomas had said her to be, yet I had no memory of her. What could all this mean? Is Thomas my grandfather?

*****

Standing looking through the window, I could see the sun had just went down below the tops of the sycamore trees when I heard George come through the front door. David was beside him as they cross the threshold of the kitchen, they both wrapped their arms around me giving me hugs and kisses. I was so glad they were back. George had been on a three-day camping trip with David. Gatlinburg had been their destination, with camping and fishing as just part of their activities.

Mother had been upstairs resting. She was a little exhausted after our visit with Thomas and then our long drive back home. She was also overwhelmed with the fact that Mary was the love of Thomas' life, and all this was news to her, as well as me. Dinner was running late and would be ready soon, and I was looking forward to hearing all about the camping trip.

Ruth had finished part of the dinner before she left, and I would finish it off. The salad was all I had left to do. George and David had excused themselves while they cleaned off the smell of fish before joining us for dinner. Mother, after resting for a short time, came downstairs and joined me in the kitchen where she was sampling the chicken cordon bleu, then she asked me what we were having for dessert. I told her that was a surprise; she would have to wait till after dinner. I had overheard Mom telling David the week before that she loved blackberry cobbler, so with that knowledge, I had prepared blackberry cobbler as today's dessert. Alice had made homemade vanilla ice cream to go along with the surprise dessert. "Yum!"

After a late dinner, we would share with George all that we had learned from our visit with Thomas. My one regret from this visit was that Charlotte was working a double shift, so I would have to confront her at a later time.

*****

Our dinner turned out to be in line with dinner and entertainment, with David elaborating on setting up the tent, a bear encounter, getting soaking wet from an unexpected storm and a lot of unwelcome lightning. He was chattering about all the rain and catching the biggest fish he had ever caught, weighing in at 4 lbs. and 2 oz. As I watched him eat and talk about all the excitement of his camping trip, my mind kept thinking of Joseph. If only he could have been with David and George on this trip, what a wonderful time the three of them could have had together. I have to find him so he can join in on all the love and excitement we share.

As this thought passed, as thoughts suddenly do and was quickly replaced by another thought, I was overtaken by a very sad feeling, or may I say something I had not considered before.

Joseph may have a wonderful family, with brothers and sisters, a mother and father who love and adore him. Yes, he could have been adopted by a wonderful family. I tried to convince myself this could have happened; he may be content, happy, and well taken care of. I then asked myself, could Charlotte have done this one good thing for him?

Even when I find him, could I just pull him away from what would be his family now, that is, if he has a wonderful family? He may have brothers and sisters and ideal parents. How wrong would that be of me to just tear him away from all he has known? Could I do that? Could I? He probably would be going on eleven years old by now. I had to concentrate hard to push this thought from my mind, an extra added worry I didn't want to have to struggle with at this moment.

Early the next morning, Mr. Carr called me on my cell phone, and unfortunately for me, I missed the call. I spent most of my morning trying to get him to answer his telephone. When I finally got back in contact with him, he told me he had tracked down

Charlotte's ex-husband. Her ex-husband had assured me that they had no children.

Charlotte's ex-husband also said he never came and took a child away from her either and therefore had no idea why she would say such a thing. Besides, he hadn't seen her in years.

"Carol, he was cordial and gave me all the information I needed to further investigate him, if the need arises. Assuring me he had nothing to hide. So far, all that he has told me has checked out as being the truth."

Mr. Carr informed me that today, he would be going to talk to the district attorney about bringing kidnapping charges against Charlotte. I was pleased at first, and as the day dragged on, I got to thinking what if she just picked up and disappeared? If that happened, we might never find Joseph.

I told George again I was going to go myself and ask her what she had done with Joseph. I told him I was going today. He made me promise I would not go and I would leave it to the authorities.

"It will all work out," he kept saying. "Just please let the authorities take care of dealing with her." He made it clear to me by saying, "Don't go!" He was firm on that.

I couldn't sleep the next few nights. I was afraid she would skip out and we wouldn't be able to get the information we needed to find my son. The detective told me at some point I would have to go and file a formal complaint with the office of the district attorney. He also told me the State would also file kidnapping charges as soon as they pulled all their evidence together. They had to have enough evidence against her before any charges could be made. This made me angry; what more do they need? They need to be looking for my son now.

Not only had George hired a detective but also a lawyer. He said before all this was over, we would probably need legal advice, and more and more I caught myself wondering about dealing with different aspects of this dilemma.

Two days later, Mr. Carr called again. This time he told me a police officer had been dispatched to the home where Charlotte lived, for questioning. I immediately called Thomas to let him know so he wouldn't be alarmed by the officer's arrival.

My first question to Mr. Carr, "Will they search Charlotte's room?" He assured me the district attorney will decide on the action he will take after questioning her.

My description of Charlotte would have to be a disingenuous, misleading, and deceptive person along with being cruel, heartless, devious, and manipulative. She was a kidnapper and an outright horrible person. When I thought of what my son must have gone through living all these years without his mother, I became angry, very angry, and I thought to myself when will this all end? Surely she will tell the authorities where my son is, and I can bring him home to me.

*****

Mother and David were up early. I had overslept for a change, woke up a couple of times, but it was one of those mornings. I just wanted to stay in bed. As I was pouring myself a cup of coffee, I could see them outside through the kitchen window. They appeared to be pulling weeds from my flower garden. It had been unattended for months now. The weeds were growing strong amid the pink Texas star hibiscus and dinner-plate dahlias, which I had planted in assorted colors. I had decided to let them go this year to compete with the weeds the best they could. I didn't have the time or energy for the task. I had more pressing issues that needed my full attention. They were strong plants, probably stronger than me at this point. Each year I had taken all the necessary precautions to keep them through the long, cold winters. This year would be different; it would be a contest between the weeds and the flowers. Survival of the fittest was my theme here. I'm pulling for the flowers. I just hadn't had time to worry with the grooming of the garden, so it made me very pleased to see that Mom and David had taken the time to do this for me. Before I could get breakfast ready and served, most of the weeds had been extracted from the rich, fertile, dark soil they clung to.

It was such a beautiful Saturday morning. I served a late breakfast outdoors under the gazebo. Lots of white bilious fluffy clouds were scattered across the blue sky as the sun made its way up above the treetops. The jasmine with its vines clinging to the arbor and producing the sweet smell of jasmine mixed with the fragrance of assorted scented geraniums filled the air with such a pleasant aroma.

Mother and David were both pleased with themselves, surprising me with this monumental drudgery of removing weeds. I laughed and thanked them at the same time for being so pleased and prideful about the work they had done. They worked well together. David was so pleased to have a second grandmother to worry over him.

David's two best friends, Artie and Michael, would be stopping by any moment to eat, swim, go fishing, and play in the woods. Saturdays were almost always a day of food, fun, and adventure.

Thomas was leaving to fly to Seattle, Washington, tomorrow to see Mary, my grandmother. I talked to him just yesterday, and he was so excited, almost like a schoolboy. So many years had passed since the last time he had seen Mary. Now he knew where she lived, and nothing could keep him away. He had to see her and find out the reason she had left him and if she would come back to him.

I was finding out more and more about myself and my family every day. I had a mother and grandmother now, and I am sure there is a lot more family I will have the privilege to meet when all this is finally over. Mom said most of them live in the beautiful mountains of Virginia—the small, quiet town of Keokee and the surrounding small municipalities. The people are friendly and known in this part of the country for their Southern hospitality, their artistic ability, good looks, and hard work.

I was sure most of my extended family will know me, except for the generation that was born after my disappearance, you might say. Yes, I hadn't thought of it that way before now. That was what it would have been to them, a disappearance. How could I have just disappeared and no one find me? Did no family member know where I was going the day of the wreck? Why were the letters sent to Thomas from Mary? How does Thomas play into all this? So many pieces to my life still missing.

Sometimes I wish my mind would be still and quit trying to figure all this out. Deep down inside, I knew this was an unrealistic way of wanting to deal with this whole situation. More than I could put into words, I wanted to find Joseph, my little son, whose face flashed through my mind on that gloomy, rainy late evening while I was on my way to deliver my cat to my best friend. "Joseph, where are you? If only you could answer me."

Mother came out of the house waving my cell phone. "It is for you, Lexi," she said. "Samantha, the caller's name is Samantha." I took the telephone and walked out into the front yard. Her voice came clear even with the barking of a dog in the distance and birds overhead chirping. I could hear her clear voice.

"Hello, Carol, can you pick me up at the airport? My flight has been bumped, and I won't get another flight out till tomorrow, but, Carol dear, this I ask only if it is convenient for you."

"Sure, I would be delighted to pick you up from the airport. I've been hoping you would come our way. We miss you. Oh, I am so excited," I said.

Within thirty minutes, I was on my way to the airport. After calling David and telling him fishing was fine but no swimming in the lake while I was gone. The pool was fine. Ruth was always here on Saturday, cleaning and keeping everything tidy. And Mom's plans for the day were to be outside sunbathing by the pool. I let David and his friends know Mom and Ruth were there in case they needed anything.

Samantha was waiting for my arrival inside the airport lobby, sipping on a cup of Norma Jean's Coffee. She called quickly for a porter and directed him to take her luggage to my car, directing him out to the car and told him it is parked in the "hurry and get out of here" lane. A funny young lady she is.

Hanging from her left hand was a designer purse. In her right hand that was dazzling with rings and on her wrist three or four bracelets that she had probably bought on her last trip abroad was the latest book *Executive Power* by Vince Flynn. She wore her clothes well. Draped across her shoulders was a cashmere scarf, and with her designer skinny jeans, she looked as if she had just stepped out of a glamor magazine.

After the luggage had been arranged in the car trunk and we were out on the main highway, she asked first about David then

Joseph. I told her David was loving life, happy, healthy and would be extremely, so extremely, delighted to see her.

"Joseph, we still have no idea where he is. As soon as the district attorney has enough evidence, they will bring her in and charge her with kidnapping. That could be as early as today. They are working on getting a search warrant as we speak. It is terrible. I have no idea if Joseph is loving life, if he is happy or healthy, or even if he is…" then my voice trailed off, and I was silent for the remainder of the trip.

Samantha changed her flight arrangements and stayed a couple additional days, so we decided to visit Thomas. We set out on the four-and-half hour drive to our destination. I was determined this would be the day I would confront Charlotte. Face-to-face I would put her on the spot. She would have to tell me where my son was, where she was hiding him.

Samantha called Thomas' house and asked to speak to Charlotte. He said she would be out most of the morning, but she would be home about eleven o'clock. We decided we were going to be there waiting to speak with her when she arrived. I was and was not looking forward to this meeting. Unforeseen and unexpected by Charlotte, by surprising her, maybe I could get some much-needed answers. I remember in phycology class studying about how surprising a guilty person, by throwing them off guard, they let slip out more information than they would otherwise divulge. We thought this over for a while and decided this was the course we would follow. I'd rather use brute force, and I would, but I guess I had better use common sense and stay within the law. Whether I maintain control or completely lose it will, to some extent, depend on Charlotte.

I will come right to the point. *What have you done with my son, Joseph? The son you called Charlie.* Running this through in my head now seemed easy. I knew it would be much harder in person, but I planned to control how the conversation would go. I only hope the answers will be forthcoming and truthful.

I had promised George I would let Mr. Carr take care of this matter, and in all good conscience, I had planned to do just that; but today, I felt like I really needed to see her and talk to her face to face. I wanted her to weave her words in a truthful answer to me. Hopefully the weaving of her words would bring this kidnapping and what seems to be a never-ending nightmare to an end.

Our trip was half over when we stopped to grab a cup of coffee. My telephone rang, and it was Mr. Carr who informed me that the police had just taken Charlotte in for questioning. *Finally, it's about time*, were my thoughts. I had to pull off the road. Tears were streaming down my face. I was suddenly overcome with emotion. I cried for about half an hour, which was very unusual for me. Every time I thought I had the tears under control, I started crying all over again.

Samantha took over the driving, and as she drove back onto the bumper-to-bumper traffic-filled highway in an attempt to make our way back home, I felt a sigh of relief. I was not sure what spurred my sense of relief. Was it from the knowledge finally the authorities were getting involved, or was it the relief of not having to confront Charlotte today for fear of what she might tell me of my son's demise? I must not feel like this; I must be strong. I kept telling myself, "Yes I must be strong."

Before we were back home, Mr. Carr telephoned me a second time. This time to say the authorities had issued a search warrant to go through Charlotte's belongings. "Have they found out the whereabouts of Joseph?" Was all I wanted to know.

"No," came the answer from Mr. Carr, "but, Carol, we are hoping for the best outcome."

"Joseph, we are getting closer," I whispered out loud.

The next few days seemed like a waiting game—waiting to see if the authorities had received any information as to the whereabouts of Joseph, waiting to see if they had searched Charlotte's personal effects or if she had told the authorities of his location, waiting to see if they had found any items belonging to Joseph. Waiting! Waiting to hear any helpful information that could help bring this all to an end. I thought, *Why can't they just make her tell where he is?*

Not realizing I had made the statement out loud, Samantha answered, "It doesn't usually work that way, my dear."

The next two days were full of activities: tennis, soccer, movies, and, of course, cookouts. Nevertheless the time passed rather quickly, with lots of entertaining, merriment, and making memories. Mother and Samantha were lost in their own conversations about self and adventures and travels in their past. With both having a business mind and both running very successful businesses, each having traveled extensively through the years, they had a lot in common and a lot they could talk about. They had both visited Paris several times and studied abroad in Switzerland, which was also the place they had each learned how to ski. They had taken a mesmerizing yet exhilarating African safari, complete with sweat, bugs, and lions. Mom's overseas studies were in the '80s while she was in her early twenties, whereas Samantha, the early 2000s and in her late twenties—a different generation, a different time, which made the inquisitive want to eavesdrop on their comparative conversations about their journeys through life.

Mother had been on the telephone for hours talking with her mother. The conversation was mainly about Thomas. He wanted to surprise Mary, but Mother had a different take on this. She thought it would be better to prepare her mother for his visit. My grandmother, Mother's mother, had been very secretive about most of her life. My mother had never met her father. The only thing Mary told Mother about her father was that she loved him very much, and she would never marry or love anyone else, but that was all the information she had given her about her father.

I had many questions I would love to have the answers to. Questions like, what would have kept her from the man she loved all these years? Perhaps she had lied to my mother, or perhaps she is hiding something. Why would someone just walk away from a wonderful life, a wonderful marriage as Thomas had referred to their five years together? I was sure we would find out soon enough. Thomas' plane was to touchdown in Seattle in just thirty minutes. Will she be there to meet him? This would be a big surprise to Thomas now that Mom had informed Mary of his arrival. I was excited about this because I knew Thomas was so thrilled about this trip and seeing and talking to Mary again. He was so curious to find out just why she had left him and their happy, idyllic life together. He gave the impression of being still in love with her. You could see it in his eyes when he spoke her name or when the conversation turned to Mary.

I would love to be a fly on the wall when they finally met. Thomas had promised to call in the next couple of days and tell Mom and me all about his trip. I thought to myself, he had better call since he was probably Mom's father and my grandfather. Did I actually say that? Wow, what a thought. If Mother had thought about this, she hadn't expressed it to me nor did I think she would until she had talked more about it with her mother.

Samantha was just putting the last of the luggage into the car. She was flying back to California on an early-morning flight. David had told her goodbye earlier in the morning just before his bus arrived to take him to school. He always hated to see her leave. He missed her pleasant, playful personality and her jubilant spirit.

Mother would be riding with me to the airport to see Samantha off. Whereas Samantha would be back on her way to California, she promised David she would return in the fall, and we would all go horseback riding. This will be the topic of conversation for some time to come, especially around the dinner table.

We had been horseback riding a few years back that was on our last trip to Hawaii. It was such a fun time for all of us. Ruth had come along with us on that trip and had enjoyed horseback riding also. She had planned to make this trip with us several times but always backed out at the last moment. She said compared to housework, she preferred riding a horse in the foothills of the north shore of Hawaii any day. David got a chuckle out of that. I guess he remembered when she slid off the back of her horse and went a little ways down the hillside. He still laughs when he thinks about it. I try not to laugh, but it was so very funny. Fortunately she lived to tell her funny version of the story. We loved that lady; she kept us all in line.

The afternoon was dragging by slowly. I found myself walking back and forth through the kitchen to the sunroom, something I usually did if I got anxious. He was late, and he should have been here thirty minutes ago. I couldn't get him on his cell phone, and I was getting worried.

Mr. Carr had called earlier in the day, hoping to meet with me early in the evening at my convenience. We had set the time at ten minutes after one. Early afternoon was perfect by me. Now where was he? At this time it was one forty, and his secretary said, "He is seldom late." She was sure he would be along any minute. Another forty minutes passed, and he finally pulled into the driveway. He made his apologies by saying he had been held up in court longer than he expected. "Finally." He seemed a little disconcerted at my agitated tone. I found his reaction a little amusing. He mumbled a few excuses under his breath. Then he let go a hardy laugh, which I thought was arrogant after leaving me waiting for such a long time. "You will see things differently when you see all the interesting things going on with your case," said Mr. Carr. "However, I am very sorry that I was so late in meeting with you. I am very sorry, Carol. Please accept my apologies."

Mother stepped into the room as well as into the conversation about that time. My mother met him with a polite smile and addressed him in a gleeful tone. "Well, Mr. Carr, may I ask, have you brought us any advantageous information? Anything we can use to achieve our goal in finding my grandson?"

"Now, Lucy," Mr. Carr said, "beneficial information is how I make my living. When I set out to do a job, I always do it to the best of my ability. I always do it in a professional way, a way that will be pleasing to my clientele."

Turning to me, Mr. Carr said, "Can we sit down? We have a lot we need to discuss."

Mother, in her sweet tone and pampering attitude said, "Sure, have a seat, and I will pour us some coffee. Would you like a sandwich or a slice of apple pie, Mr. Carr?"

With a tilt of the head and a gruff voice, he said, "Only coffee for me, no cream or sugar, please and thank you!"

After settling down, Mr. Carr gave me some good news, the best I had heard in a while. First he said, "A search warrant had been issued, and the police have searched the property, and a lot of incriminating evidence had been taken to the police station. There were articles that belong to you and Joseph in Charlotte's possession. Yes, they were found in an old locked trunk stored in one of the rooms she rents from Thomas."

"Articles such as what? Personal belongings?" I demanded to know.

"Articles of a personal nature, your wallet for one. I am not privy to all the information and details. That is under the police jurisdiction now, and you will be informed shortly to come by the holding station to identify the articles in question."

"Was there any information as to the whereabouts of Joseph?" I kept saying out loud and thinking to myself.

"No, I am sorry, Carol," was his reply. "Carol, we don't know that information, but we are getting closer to finding out where he is." He looked at me as if he was trying to read my thoughts as he spoke these words. "I am sure the district attorney has enough evidence now to bring charges against Charlotte for kidnapping. She will be arrested and booked for the kidnapping of a child. That piece of police work is probably being done as we speak."

I felt such a bit of relief. "Now we are making some progress, finally!"

Mr. Carr told me he had been talking to people who ran some of the "in-state orphanages and adoption agencies," but there he said is where you run into problems.

"Most adoptions are closed adoptions. Sometimes they will work with the courts if they think there was any foul play involved, but the process has to go through proper legal procedures. We have several leads as to where she could have placed the child, but right now, they are just leads, and we shall see where that will take us, but you have to remember, he could be anywhere. Hopefully she will volunteer that much-needed information."

He had me read a few memos and sign a few papers before he took his leave. I walked to the door with him, and he said, "It shouldn't be too much longer, and we will have all the answers to this puzzle."

Just before he exited the door, he said, "By the way, there were lots of pictures, lots of baby pictures in that old dark trunk I was told by a good source."

As I closed the heavy door behind him, I almost lost consciousness. I could feel myself gasping for air as if my lungs wouldn't take any more air in. The thought of Joseph's pictures stored away in an old dark trunk brought an uneasy feeling to my mind. As I made my way to the sofa in the den, I could feel hot tears streaming down my face. I sat there for who knows how long. I lost track of time. I just kept thinking of his pictures being stored away in that old dark trunk. Just knowing about these pictures made him even more real, and I couldn't wait to feast my eyes upon them.

Little more than this thought had gone through my head when the doorbell rang. Standing there as I opened the front door was the chief of police, whom I recognized immediately. This was the same officer that I had talked to once before who seemed, at the time, to ignore me.

"Mrs. Wainright, I am Chief Gent, and this is Officer Crane. May we come in?" he said this to me in a respectful manner, not like before when I tried to report to him my story of Joseph's kidnapping.

"Sure come on in," was my reply to him.

The meeting was nothing like I expected. His first question to me once we had made ourselves comfortable was indeed surprising. "Mrs. Wainright, do you know where your son is at this very moment?"

The question gave me the impression they had found him. "Oh my, you have found him. Can I see him? Where is he? Is he Okay? Please!"

"Mrs. Wainwright, you have the wrong idea, and we are asking you because we think you might have had something to do with your son's disappearance."

I couldn't believe what I was hearing. How could this be? Why would they ask me such a preposterous question? I could feel myself getting very livid, which I infrequently did.

Speaking of bad days, this one was about to get much worse. Mr. Gent stood up, and in a voice full of authority, he told me he would like to ask me more questions.

"Just what do you want to know?" was my question to him.

"We would like you to come down to the station for more questioning," came a voice I hadn't heard as of yet.

The second officer made his presence known. He was verbose and just kept the questions coming my way with his rather demanding type of personality. I thought to myself this officer likes the sound of his own voice. I asked "Why? Why are you questioning me? Shouldn't you be talking with Charlotte?"

Suddenly the front door flew open, and David rushed through the door and down the foyer. He was just getting home from school. "Mom, Mom, why's a police car out front?" Then he stopped in his tracks as he almost bumped into one of the officers. Looking from the officer to me, he came and stood by my side. David didn't say a word; he just looked up at me with a puzzled look on his face.

I introduced David to the police officers, then I directed David to go upstairs and ask my mother to come downstairs. He took off running up the stairs two steps at a time. Nothing slow about him when he was excited.

When Mother arrived downstairs, I instructed her to call my lawyer and have him come to the police station right away. "Call George and tell him where I am headed." David had tears in his eyes. I reached down and wiped them away and assured him everything would be okay. Mother was obviously upset too. I reach over and squeezed her hand and walked out the front door.

*****

I was glad when my alarm clock went off the next morning, my sleep through the night had been sporadic. I kept waking up with a frightened feeling, a feeling that my world was turned every way but the way I envisioned it would go.

The evening before had been long and drawn out, so many questions. My lawyer was there, which made questioning bearable for me. George was there too but wasn't present while I was being questioned.

Before I left the station, my lawyer and I were taken to a room two stories down, to a dusty old basement, where a large sturdy white box with big black bold numbers was brought in. I was informed that the items inside this box were taken from Charlotte's living quarters.

I was asked not to touch them, but I was to see if I could identify any items in this box. I stepped forward and pulled the box closer to me. Inside the box were lots of pictures of a child, two stuffed animals, a ladies' purse, a baby bottle, pacifier, and baby clothes. I reached my hand into the box and took out a little baby blanket, then pressed it to my face, at the same time my other hand reached for a picture. I was told again not to touch anything inside the box. I gazed at the pictures, beautiful picture of a little boy, and the blanket. It was so soft against my cheek. I could almost smell Joseph, or was I imagining the smell of a little boy who wore the scent of baby powders and a hint of baby oil. Again I was told not to touch the items in the box. The lid was placed back on the box. Then the box was taken away along with the pictures and the blanket. I was mad; I wanted that box. The things inside belong to me and Joseph, and I wanted them, but I was told they were to be used as evidence. At that point, I had to gain control of my feelings. I wanted to make my thoughts known as to how I felt about this officer for being so cold and unfeeling. With much restraint, I managed to keep my feelings to myself. Deep down inside, I knew they were just doing their job, and in the end I was sure I would appreciate all that they were doing for me.

To George and my surprise, the next evening, the officers came back to the house. This time they wanted George to go down to the station to answer some questions. This made no sense to me at all. Mr. Crane insisted George go down to the station with him for questioning.

The next day, while describing the unwanted visit to the police station, George was obviously a little upset. Of course, his lawyer had been called or he would have been detained for a longer period of time. He had been cleared of any wrongdoing and was clearly upset with the whole situation.

He asked me several times over the next three days, "How could they think I had anything to do with a kidnapping when I know absolutely zero about any of it, except what I have heard from you?" *Upset* was not the word I would use for what he was feeling after the interrogation. His words would have been a little more heated and a lot less kind.

Thomas had called me two times since he left for his trip to try and reconnect with Mary. They were pleasant conversations with not too much detail about how their first meeting had gone, except he said Mary had surprised him at the airport. He had no idea my mother had told Mary of his soon arrival at the airport, along with the flight number and the arrival time.

Thomas said, "Carol, this was the second happiest day of my life, seeing Mary standing there waiting for me at the airport. Carol, after all these years of her being absent from my life, you can only imagine how I felt. My love for her was as strong as the first day we had met, and, yes, I had fallen in love with her the first time I saw her. The happiest day of my life was the day I stood waiting for Mary to walk down the aisle to become my bride. Love is a mysterious thing. True love is eternal."

After my conversation with Thomas was over, I kept thinking how extremely happy I was for him. The mysteries of life and how our lives can be so unexpectedly intertwined with one another are amazing. I started this search for my son Joseph, and in doing so, I had found my mother, grandfather, and my grandmother. In this process, I had also learned so much about myself. My search for Joseph must continue till I come full circle, starting from the day I realized I had lost him, till the day I embrace the knowledge of knowing he is okay and happy.

After talking with Thomas, I expressed to Mother my thoughts of my conversation with Thomas. He was so happy I could tell it by the tone in his voice and the way he talked of Mary. Thomas had told me, "Carol, finding Mary again has completed my life, and I am in love with her as much today as the first time I met her. Mary is my life, and she has always been. She was all that mattered to me even during all those years we were apart. My heart only beats for her."

In a spirited conversation, Mother told me, "Lexi, when I told my mother that Thomas had flown out to Seattle to find her, she became so excited and so happy. At first I thought I was talking to a different person. I kept saying to myself this can't be my mother. I have never seen her so happy or so excited in my entire life. She was crying and laughing while trying to talk all at the same time."

So you can imagine how surprised Thomas was when he was asked to meet his party at a specific destination inside the airport, especially when he had made no arrangements for anyone to meet him. Even more surprised when he saw that it was Mary. I wanted details, I really wanted details of this meeting, but I didn't push. I knew it was a private matter, one I had best leave alone. He had told me all I needed to know.

His second call to me was to tell me he had decided to stay another two weeks, which gave me the impression that all would turn out well.

Mom, on the other hand, wanted to know every detail. She wanted to know all the whys and why-nots and everything in between, and she didn't want to wait for the answers; she wanted to know them right now! So my mom and grandmother were on the phone a good part of the day. Even though Mom had some of the answers, I was not privy to the details. I didn't press the issue, for I was sure they would be forthcoming in their own sweet time. I was happy for Thomas. I had witnessed his strong feelings for Mary through his speech and mannerisms when talking about his beloved, and on the other hand, all I knew about Mary's feelings for him was she had left him with only a letter saying goodbye. I was like Thomas; I had to know the reasons for her departure from her wonderful idyllic life. I also wanted her explanation, not from hearsay or through someone else but from her own mouth. For this, I would have to wait.

*****

It was early morning, and I decided to take a walk, a good way to clear my mind; and besides, I needed the fresh air. I invited David to come along with me, which he happily accepted. It had rained a little during the night, and there was a slight mist in the air. The sun was just coming over the distant trees, and the lake was already picking up the reflections from the sun, which cast an almost glasslike shimmer upon the water.

David kept asking me, "Mom, when are you going to find Joseph and bring him home?" He always got so excited when talking about Joseph, and he couldn't wait to meet him, saying, "I will finally have a brother."

"Hey, Mom, I just thought of something. He will still be here when all my friends have gone home." Then he skipped a few more rocks on the shimmering water and jumped all around and made all kinds of happy sounds. I laughed at him. We laughed together. We fed the geese and ducks, talked and laughed, and just soaked up the sun.

I sat down on the edge of the pier and watched David the biggest part of the morning. He kept himself busy collecting rocks to throw into the water. He liked throwing the rocks at a slight angle to see how many times he could make them skip the surface of the water. Every time he threw the rock and it skipped more than three or four times, he would let out a loud y-hoop of a sound, as if victoriously winning at some great competition.

Summer was almost over. The leaves were still green and clinging to the branches, but soon with the chilly nights, summer would become only a fading memory. Fall would bring on a substantial amount of color, with the turning of the leaves, our world would change from many shades of green to a pallet filled with oranges, yellows, and reds as if by a magical hand, dotting the landscape with much beauty. As I sat there pondering the changing of the seasons, I was so thankful that I had David here with me to enjoy the seasons and our special life together.

David always took interest in bugs, frogs, turtles, even snakes that made their sanctuary in and around the lake hiding themselves among the trees, rocks, and shrubs. Other than bugs and slow-moving turtles, we found a couple of tree frogs that were almost white in color, with the exception of a few black designs here and there on their small bodies. They both were facing the sun, perched on a small branch in a tree, with their back side up against the trunk. They seemed so content and carefree. Our presence didn't seem to bother them even the slightest. David even got a few close-up pictures of them from different angles, with a small camera hanging from his neck, which he brought along just for these great finds. After lingering there for a while near the water's edge watching the frogs, we slowly made our way back to the house.

Mother was at the window watching for us as we ascended up the path from the lake. She had hot chocolate ready for us and served it outdoors. David was excited; he always got excited when served hot chocolate. It was one of his favorite drinks. He played around with Bounce, the neighbor dog, a blond lab with an extreme playful personality while Mother and I relaxed and just enjoyed the moment.

As it seemed the items in the box at the police station did belong to me, not that I remembered any of them of course. But eventually, Charlotte confessed she had taken them from my car. However, she would give no information about Joseph. She said she didn't know anything about him and kept saying she had never seen him. When asked about Charlie, that was a different story. She would talk on and on about him, giving all kinds of details about his looks and his sweet personality. When asked where he was, she would give no more information. I was informed that asking her information about Joseph was like hitting a stop sign with her shutting down and giving no more information—nothing.

*****

Charlotte was now behind bars on suspicion of kidnapping charges and possible murder. The second charge I had to ignore totally; this thought I must push far, far away from my mind. I cannot let my mind be troubled with such a thought.

Her lawyer was trying to get her out on bail. My lawyer said that will never happen. I hoped he was right. The story was being talked about in the paper daily. I was hoping some new information would come forward. Someone out there had to know something.

Mr. Carr had gone to California at my request to find out how my company was being run and if it was still my company. I wanted to know what position, or positions, Charlotte had held in the company and as much information as he can find out about her from the people who had worked with her—why she had left her job there, and if she now, present day, had any strong ties to the company. I was at such a disadvantage not being able to remember these important facts about my own company, but such as it is, I must rely on others, and hopefully, I get the right information.

*****

It was Monday morning, and I had been up for hours, drank a cup of coffee, skipped breakfast, and was planning my day. David was already at school, and George was out of town at a medical convention, which had been on his schedule for some time—destination, Atlanta. He had invited me to go along with him, but I had declined. I wanted to be home in case Charlotte divulged any new information of the whereabouts of Joseph. David was into soccer now, and I didn't want to miss any of his games. As the day slowly passed, I decided tomorrow I would drive the four and a half hours to the police station and once again to ask if I could have a meeting with Charlotte. My lawyer had already told me this was out of the question, but I was determined; I would call every day. I would go back every other week until they decided to let me talk to her. Just maybe she would tell me the answer to the question I wanted answered so badly.

After David's game was over, I took him and some of his friends to the nearest pizza parlor—wow, can they put away the pizza and soda. Celebrating—they called it after winning the game, although I am sure they would have celebrated just as hard if they had lost the game. Enjoy it while you are still young and still carefree is what I always say. Enjoy life; it is a gift from God, and this thought I regularly impressed on the mind of David and his friends, encouraging them to be happy, and with this happiness comes along responsibility.

We got home late, and Mom was up waiting for me. I could sense there was something she wanted to say to me, but she held back from starting a conversation. After helping David with a small amount of homework he had not finished earlier and after he had gone to his room for the night, I knocked on Mother's door to see if she was still up; no answer, so I decided to have a cup of tea and go out on the front porch and sit for a while and enjoy the nice, cool air. Fall was slowly making its way into our world, and with the fall came cooler nights. I loved going out at night and just relaxing in the swing on the front porch, which I would label as pleasure, peace, and serenity. Sometimes you could hear an owl in the distance or a dog baying, but what I enjoyed most was just the silence that brings a certain peace to the soul.

Mother was up early the next morning, sitting at the kitchen table with the newspaper spread out in front of her. She was already dressed and ready for the day when I entered the kitchen. I was still half asleep as I made my way to the coffee pot looking for that rich, robust caffeine, which would give me that morning lift I so needed. I took my coffee into the solarium, one of my favorite spots in the house. I enjoyed the early morning sun as it filtered through the big bay window and on into the room. The room was overgrown with vines and potted plants of all assortments. Mother came in and sat down beside me, then I heard her whisper, "You know I never met him!"

Looking at her, I said, "Never met who?"

Her soft reply, "Joseph. You were so busy with your life in California, and I was so busy with my life in Keokee. When you left, you stayed away for years. We hardly knew you. I am not saying it was intentional, but you were so busy running your company, and you were so very far away. What were you doing in that part of the country when you had your accident? Why were you there?" I could only look at her, I didn't know the answers. "None of the family knew where you were!" She informed me, "None of us." The second time she repeated the statement was somewhat a little more agitated than the first time. "No one knew about that town but your grandmother, and she had never talked to me about the place she had once lived." Continuing her conversation, she whispered in a low voice," I knew nothing about that place or Thomas."

Our conversation ended almost as abruptly as it had started with my silence on the end of all her questions. Questions I didn't know the answer to. Why would I answer without some knowledge of my past?

I could see she was a little agitated maybe not with me but with my not knowing the answer or just the whole state of affairs. She walked back into the kitchen where she took her time making a second cup of coffee. I sat in silence pondering these questions and just wondering.

She seemed to avoid me for the biggest part of the morning. Then just before noon, she came into the living room where I was sitting. She took a seat beside me, then she said to me, "You know, your grandmother had her reasons for leaving. One day she will tell us."

Turning to her, I asked, "What do you mean her reasons?"

Mother slowly walked across the room, pulled back the curtains, then turned to me and said, "She is coming back with Thomas, so she will talk more about this with you upon her arrival."

"She is coming back with Thomas!" I asked, suddenly overcome with emotions.

I couldn't help but laugh and cry at the same time. For some reason, it made me so very happy. I can't remember my grandmother, and Thomas I had only known for a very short period of time, but when he talked of Mary, you know the words are said with love. If Mary feels the same way about Thomas, oh how wonderful.

Mother interrupted my thoughts by saying, "Lexi, remember, Mother is the one that left their happy marriage, and this one she has to explain to me. Just yesterday, Mother told me she had never stopped loving Thomas. *Never* was her words."

That is when I said, "Mom, you know you look so much like Thomas. The eyes, the same blond color of hair minus a little gray here and there. Even some of the same mannerisms." Not saying a word, she turned and smiled at me, opened the door, and walked out into the beautiful sunlit morning.

Shortly after my conversation with Mother ended, I started out on my four-and-a-half-hour drive to the police station back to the little town in Tennessee. Intentionally, I lingered awhile, pretending to be busy with the last details of my trip. I thought Mother may try insisting on some kind of answer to those darn questions. Then I realized, she was out by the pool lounging and reading a book, even though it was midfall. She took every opportunity to soak up the sun before the real cold weather arrived, and it appeared to me she had fallen asleep.

*****

Words, words are so important especially when addressing important issues that deal with everyday life. If I am given the opportunity today to talk to Charlotte, I am hoping to use words that will appeal to her good side, if she has a good side, therefore allowing me to have the information I have been longing for.

However, after my arrival at the police station and a lot of arguing back and forth, I was told once again I would not be allowed to talk to Charlotte. Nevertheless, with the help and urging from my attorney, I was finally allowed to take copies of the photos of Joseph from the police station. I was elated and so happy to have them in my possession.

As the day dragged on, with the sun spreading its rays of light and warmth into my little world, I carefully placed the pictures in the passenger seat and headed for home. After arriving back home from my trip, I carried the pictures of Joseph straight to my formal dining room where I spread all the pictures out on the large dining room table. There was plenty of light and lots of room to display them. I was glad they were out of that old dark stuffy trunk, where they had been hidden away far too long. Now these pictures were out in the open where everyone could see them as they entered the house. I spent most of my waking time for the next couple of days looking at these pictures marveling, hoping, thinking, wondering about this precious little boy.

Just yesterday, David and I were looking at those pictures when Mother walked into the room. The first one Mother picked up, she said, "Well, David, these are pictures of your brother." Oh David loved that; it made his day. He turned to me with a big grin on his lips, a grin that quickly spread to his entire face. He let out a big "Yes!" A voice of sheer excitement flowed from him, "Yes! Wow, we're brothers. Can't wait till we find him."

David had always wanted a brother, but his mother had died of cancer about four years into his young life. And with my marriage to George, he was still an only child. This comment from Mother was very pleasing to him.

*****

Hours dragged into days, then days into weeks, and weeks into months, then we got our first real break, or so we thought it was our first break until seven days later when we realized we were only being toyed with.

Charlotte had given Mr. Carr a name and an address where supposedly that would be the place we would find Joseph. After a plane trip eight hundred plus miles away, three taxis, a rental car, and a week of investigating, it all came to a dead end. She had sent us away knowing we were about to embark upon an adventure that would lead us right back to where we started. *Oh, what a mean and devious woman she was*, I kept thinking to myself as I exited the airplane. George would be here to pick me up and take me home, which would make a great ending to a terribly wasted trip.

*****

Frustrated and very tired, I returned home. I spent the next two days in bed feeling sorry for myself. On the third day, I decided to go to Ojai, California. Three days later, I was boarding a plane headed west. David and George would fly out and join me at the end of the week. Then we, as a family, would explore what was at one time my life my home and my workplace.

Fortunately for me, all those years long ago when I started my company, I had made good choices in whom I hired to help in running the company. I was told the vice president of the company who also had the power to write checks and make important decisions in my absence had indeed done a great job in keeping the company afloat, both here in Ojai and in Keokee. The company was still listed as a top-rated company, still produced top-rated vases, and beautiful decorative glass. Usually no more than three pieces of each design, which kept them very pricy, highly sought-after, and made them collectors' pieces. With their rich colors, unique designs, and with my being unavailable to keep designing the pieces to be produced, a couple of famous artist had been hired. Their work was very good, and the demand for their pieces was high.

When I arrived, I was impressed at the size and efficiency of this company. Lexi in huge letters was displayed across the upper face of the building. Was I impressed? Yes! Awestruck when I entered the building, and I gazed upon the beautiful unique vases surrounded by glass, displayed on pedestals in the lobby and on the first and second floor. Some of the vases on the first floor sitting on pedestals surrounded by glass were signed by LEXI. Impressive, they were beautiful; and as I looked at them, I had the same feeling, the same inner impression that I had when I first saw the red vase sitting on the mahogany table in Thomas' house. Now as I looked upon these vases with their brilliant colors and design, it was as if I knew these pieces, as if I had signed them myself.

I was told later these pieces signed by Lexi had been produced by Lexi just months before her disappearance.

The president, in her absence, had decided to keep her last masterpieces as a tribute to her. These were some of the ones on display this present day. Collectors were very desirous to get their hands on these highly sought-after pieces; however, he chose not to sell.

With the unique designs of the other two artists who were hired in her place, the company ran smoothly, and there was no need to sell the last vases Lexi had designed.

My arrival was expected, but only hours before I stepped through the door, arriving with just a small amount of warning. This I had planned, why I don't know. I just thought this would be the best way to make my way back after my being absent for so long. Mr. Carr was already in Ojai, arriving here days ahead of me. He had come earlier to do further investigating, and just this morning, I had him inform the vice president of my imminent arrival.

As I stood looking almost mesmerized by the vases in front of me, I heard shuffling and footsteps behind me. Turning to face whomever the footsteps belong to and finding there standing in front of me, a middle-aged woman and two men all well-dressed, all three with a brief case in hand, smiling with outstretched hands as they introduced themselves. To my surprise, I recognized one of the faces. The woman did look somewhat familiar but nothing more. I was not sure who they were or what role they played in the company or maybe even my past life. I was here to listen and learn.

Standing just behind them was Mr. Carr. He was staying in Ojai a few more days in case I needed moral support and/or help with any problems that might arise that he might assist me with.

"Lexi," came a booming voice from one of the gentleman that stood in front of me. "Lexi, what happened? Where have you been all these years?" I just stood very quiet and let him talk, trying to take in all that he was saying to me.

These top three people running the company had already been informed of my lack of memory or amnesia. I stepped forward and asked each one to tell me their names again and what position they held with the company and how long they had worked the position they held now. I paid attention to their answers very closely, hoping to recognize a voice or a name. The one with the big booming voice informed me he was the vice president and had held this position since the company was in its first stages. He was distraught at the thought that I could not remember him. After introducing the head project coordinator and the company financial coordinator, he invited me to his office where we could talk in a more private setting.

As we were making our way to his office, which was located on the first floor. He introduced me to all the workers that we passed by. They were all congenial and extended their hand, giving me a good hardy handshake, except for one, who ran toward me screaming, "Lexi, is it really you?" Looking me straight in the face, she screamed, "Yes, Lexi, it is really you." With much excitement, she threw her arms around my neck and gave me a big hug. When she finally let go and looked up at me, I could see there were tears in her eyes, and in a timid voice, she said, "Lexi, I thought I would never see you again. I know you don't remember me, but we were best friends, the best of friends. My name is Norma Jean."

For me there was no memory, no connection whatsoever, which was sad because she was a very interesting person, and I could imagine being her best friend. She made me promise we would meet for lunch before my two-week stay was over. I took her telephone number and promised to make the call.

*****

Samuel, with his medium build and slightly dark complexion, had very wavy dark hair. He had a salt-and-pepper pencil mustache and, to add to all that, a very pleasing personality. Samuel informed me that he was hired by me at the beginning of my business career, which I do not recall and is still vice president of my company.

The entrance to his office was very charming. With vases and glass designs methodically placed with great thought here and there, some sculpture glass designs were very cleverly hanging from the ceiling, some very tall pieces setting on beautiful pedestals. The pedestals were also works of art, which worked well together. All were signed pieces.

Samuel's office was very plush with lots of photographs hanging or mounted on the wall. Upon my inquiring about the photographs, he informed me these pictures were people who had a big impact on the company—people who had been promoted to a higher position, top awards, great achievers, etc., etc. Their names were under each picture mounted on a bronze plate.

I stepped forward to get a better look. The biggest picture was of Lexi, hanging somewhat higher than all the other pictures. I guess with the title of president of a company merited that position. I was very surprised to see a representation of myself hanging here on this wall of marble. I had to look at it two or three times to make sure it was really me. I had to say I almost didn't recognize myself, and yes, it was a much younger version of myself. This was the first image I had seen of me taken before the accident. This was a little uncanny to me looking at a picture I did not remember and a life I cannot comprehend. After scrutinizing my picture for some time, I kept wondering, contemplating about that time long ago when I worked here day after day as president of this company. Sadly, the memories I had hoped for were still unavailable to me.

I stepped forward to take a little time to study the other faces and carefully read their names, trying to link some type of connection between them and me. As I moved forward to picture after picture, I recognized a face. Yes, it was Charlotte. Her hair was different. Before the color was a dull blond instead of the dark brown that she wears now. In a voice I almost didn't recognize, I turned to the vice president, "Samuel," I spoke with authority in my voice, "I want this picture taken down immediately. I also want a board meeting scheduled for early tomorrow morning, first thing."

Samuel immediately made a phone call, and within ten minutes, someone with a stepladder was there to take the picture of Charlotte down. I thanked Samuel for his prompt removal of the picture. We continued our tour of his office, then we took a seat at his oversized desk.

Samuel told me how he had been running the company without me being involved both here in Ojai and in Keokee. He was so eager to tell me everything. In his eagerness, he forgot I had amnesia or this complex memory loss that was such a big flaw in my life. However, I tried to cling to all his words and learn all I could from this man who had taken such good care of the business in my absence.

He was an amazing person, very smart, a gentleman, and obviously an honest man. He had kept my company running, kept it making money and a top-rated company at that. He brought to my attention that Mr. Carr had informed him of a few of the details of my life since I had just up and disappeared. "I was so sorry to hear about your accident and the loss of your son. I remember your son well." Okay, with this statement, the company talk was over. For now, I wanted to hear all he knew and could remember about Joseph.

"Joseph, you knew him?" I asked in a voice that stumbled from my mouth in a most awkward way. Feeling a little embarrassed, along with being a little uncomfortable, I repeated my question for the second time, this time with a little more control of my emotions.

He hesitated before answering, "After your son was born and after your husband's death, you brought him here quite often."

"What? My husband's death? What? What are you talking about?" This statement I did not expect. I had considered this question many times. Yes, I had thought about this. I had a child, I must have a husband somewhere. Again no memory.

Thoughts were racing through my head at high speed. Mr. Carr hadn't mentioned anything about my husband. He had come here to prepare me for this meeting, why hadn't he said anything about this prior to my arrival?

"A husband dead? What?" I repeated this statement more than once, trying to come to terms with what I was hearing from Mr. Cook, Mr. Samuel Cook.

"Lexi, there was an accident here at the company. It happened about a year before your disappearance, and it was a fatal accident that took your husband's life. The situation is still a mystery. The police said they suspected foul play was involved. Lexi, do you remember any of this?" was his next question. All I could do was shake my head.

"No," finally escaped from my mouth, which seemed to come from somewhere deep inside me. I could barely hear the answer. "No! No!" I repeated no for the second and third time in a more controlled response.

Why hadn't Mr. Carr prepared me for this conversation? I kept thinking to myself.

"Mr. Carr knew nothing about your husband's death," Samuel said as he walked over to where I was sitting.

Then I realized I must have asked the question out loud. Did I? Had I asked that question out loud, or had he read my mind?

"It was his job to find out," I said, gravely annoyed.

"He would have found out soon enough, but I instructed my staff to keep quiet about that bit of information. For a few days anyway."

"Why? Why would you do that?"

"I thought it was best for the company, and I knew if it was really you, then you would be showing up soon enough. I was convinced of that."

"Samuel, how were you so sure that I would actually come? I myself only decided a couple of days ago to come back to Ojai and try to reacquaint myself with my previous life."

"I just knew you would come. I just knew!"

After Samuel filled me in on what he remembered of Joseph, which consisted of stories of get-togethers for the staff or dinners I held in celebration for the jobs well done by my staff and workers, he said he and his wife were almost always present at these dinner parties. Joseph was usually the center of attention. He informed me that these occasions were almost always at my house.

"Lexi, you threw the most amazing dinner parties, as an extra thank you for your employees."

"Matthew would come to work early in the morning, and after about ten o'clock, you would come into work with Joseph in tow. You actually had a crib brought in for him so he could have nap time. I remember you were very happy, the perfect family you called it.

"Joseph was a great kid, healthy, alert, we all thought he was such a cool little man. I think he was about eight months old when you and he disappeared. It was very hard on you after your husband's death. You didn't come to the office quite as much. You were in disbelief, in denial. Just one day you weren't here anymore, gone! Those were very trying days for me as well as the staff. It was very hard on us not knowing what happened to you or Joseph. Then there were many questions from the police. We were at a loss to tell them anything. We knew nothing of what happened to you.

"Whereas dealing with your personal belongings, I made the decision, so we left your office almost as you had left it. Plenty of photographs still line your desk, most of those photographs are of the three of you." His next question, he addressed to me, "Lexi, would you care to see your office?" I was thinking photographs of the three of us.

"Yes, I would love to see my office." What an odd statement to come from my mouth. *My office,* I can't believe I said those words. "My office!"

*****

As we entered my office, I was awestruck once again. My eyes feasted upon a plush, beautiful office with a huge window overlooking a terrace covered with beautiful flowers. This I noticed as I proceeded straight to the desk Samuel led me to.

Here sitting in front of me, on the highly polished dark mahogany desk was my past life, a picture of three. Joseph, I remember only a small glimpse of him, myself, and I do not know my "husb—" the rest of the word seemed to stop somewhere within me. I couldn't get the rest of the word past my lips. Him, I did not remember and yet how could I not remember.

They together appear to be a happy family. All I could do was stare at the pictures. They looked so happy, so beautiful, with a smile glowing on each face. Joseph was so beautiful. Oh, I thought what a lovely family, one I should know well, but I did not. Then I felt tears streaming down my face. I don't know how long I sat there looking at that beautiful family. When I finally looked up, it was dark outside, and Samuel was nowhere to be seen.

I finally picked myself up from the chair, walked to the window still thinking, wondering, crying; and as I turned away from the window, there to my left was a baby crib. I just stood there for a while looking. Suddenly I had an urge to run away. Why? I don't know. I can't explain that feeling. Instead I slowly walked over to the crib, picked up a blue baby blanket that lay resting, neatly folded at the head of the crib. I gently took the blanket in my hands from the crib and held it close to my face. Feeling like I was in a daze or in another life, I crossed the room to the desk, hesitated for a moment then picked up one of the photos. With both blanket and photo hugged tight to my chest, I took a seat on a sofa near the window.

*****

I woke up the next morning to the sound of Mozart's *Moonlight Sonata* playing softly, so softly. First I thought I was dreaming, and upon opening my eyes, I realized it was no dream, and I was still in the office. Looking at my watch to check the time, I realized it was late, and I had a board meeting to attend, one I had ordered myself.

Still clutched in my left hand was the baby blanket and the family photo. I put the baby blanket around my shoulders and the photo in my purse. I proceeded to Samuel's office where I was met by his secretary. After a good morning greeting, I told her to inform Samuel I would be back in an hour, and we could start the board meeting.

I barely made it back to my office in time for the board meeting I had ordered. I would have preferred to have been there ahead of them. However, after thinking about this move, maybe this is the right approach after all. After the meeting was over and just before I made my exit, Samuel asked to speak to me just a few minutes alone before I left.

"Lexi, the board members and I could have sold you out a long time ago because your long years of being absent from the company. Instead I hired consultants and using the lawyer we retain here to take care of any legal matters that might arise. I informed them both I wanted to keep things running like they were, as if you were still here, always hoping for your return. Both the consultants and the lawyer through a long process of time and paperwork got this matter legally and ethically taken care of. Lexi, I hope you will find all this to your satisfaction once you have had time to go over all the paperwork with our legal department. You are welcome to have this checked out with any lawyer of your choice."

"Thank you, Samuel," I finally managed to say.

My emotions were overtaken by his kindness, with him remembering me and caring about my interest in the company with the thought that someday I would return.

With me not being able to remember, this wonderful man was sad for me and for him; but from this day forward, I am sure we will become the best of friends once again.

*****

Hours after the meeting, I met with Norma Jean. I had used the telephone number she had given me, and we were meeting in a local diner, one not far from my office. She was on time, arriving a few minutes after me. She greeted me with a smile and a gentle hug.

As she took her seat, she asked, "What did you learn from the board meeting, and did you get to see your office?"

I assured her I learned all the important issues I needed to know, and yes, to her second question. I wasted no time. We greeted each other, and I started with questions. I suddenly realized this was somewhat rude. I rethought what I was doing. We looked over the menu, we ordered, and just talked for a little while. Our food came, and we enjoyed our meal. I ordered coffee, and only then did I start with my questions.

"Now that we are talking about important issues, here is one for you, Norma Jean. Since you were my best friend, I guess you would be the best one to ask some very important questions." I addressed her by saying, "Norma Jean, convey to me a little about yourself since you remembered all about me and I don't remember anything about you. Sorry for my loss of memory, but that is the way the situation stands as of present day." As I spoke to her, I realized I was very tired, and this get-together should have been scheduled at a later date. But here I was; I needed to make the best of this occasion.

She started out by saying, "You and your husband with your ability to gather and make new friends and the laughter and happiness that radiated from you two was amazing. You were so easy to love. Joseph and Matthew, they were the best. Then when Matthew died of an untimely and very unfortunate accident, you became very distraught. I loved them dearly. Then when you and your son disappeared, it was bad. You were such a big part of my life, and then you were gone."

"Lexi, you and Joseph were just gone, I mean gone, just disappeared from our lives. I had such a hard time with your disappearance. I never really got over it. I knew if you were still alive, you would contact me or Samuel, but as the years went by with no word from you, I knew something dreadful must have happened. I kept in touch with your mother and your grandmother hoping you would turn up there, and this nightmare would finally be over. But as you know, this did not happen. Time just kept passing.

"When you disappeared we checked with the airlines, the bus stations, and even the train stations with no results. If you took a plane, it was not from the state of California. All the records of passengers were searched. Your car and both sets of keys were still at your apartment. All your friends and coworkers were at a loss as to what happened to you and your precious son.

"As the years went by, Lexi, I tried to push all this from my mind, but it didn't work. I caught myself time after time looking for you everywhere I went—a crowded street, the airport, wherever I found myself I scanned the crowd hoping to find you and Joseph."

I believed Norma Jean was genuinely sincere. She had such a dramatic personality and such a sweetness about her. She filled me in on some of the people who had left the company since I had been gone and some who had been hired. This conversation I listened to intensely; however, it was almost meaningless to me because I didn't remember any of them.

I asked her many questions about her life, questions about her education and if she had children or if she was even married. She was very polite in answering and very forthcoming with her answers. I asked her what brought her to work for my company and did she like the position she held now.

"Lexi, I think you have the wrong idea. I don't work for your company. I guess you got the wrong idea the other day when we met in the lobby. I didn't intentionally mislead you. I overheard a friend telling a coworker you were returning to your job after years of being absent, and I had to see for myself if this was true."

"How did you get passed the security?" I asked her.

In a very innocent, charming way, she answered, "Samuel. Oh that was easy, Samuel."

"So, Norma, did you ever work for this company and if so how long?"

"I was with the company from the very start, ground level. We were friends even before you planned your company. Growing up, it was almost always the three of us you, me, and Samuel. We were best friends. We went through school together. You hired me and Samuel when you started your work in Keokee. We both have been with you from day one, you might say from the ground floor.

"Lexi, you were the one with the business mind and very determined at that. You were always coming up with all these great ideas." Then she elaborated further, "You producing beautiful vases and with your advertisement adventures, 'trial run as you called them,' you made it happen. Lexi, you were a genius the way you got this company running. You did so good with the sales, and the way the company was growing, you decided to expand, and here we are. Starting your second headquarters was a great idea, and Ojai, California, was the perfect place."

"Norma, how well did you know Charlotte, and were you good friends with her?"

"Friends? Lexi, are you asking me if I was friends with Charlotte? Oh! Honey, you really don't remember! DO YOU? Oh no, Lexi! I kept telling you there was something about her I didn't like. She was a professional manipulator, oh, and was she good at it. She was very charming and quite attractive, and she used both of these qualities to get what she wanted. People just fell for it, and they were drawn in by her charisma. It was as if she cast a web and caught her victims."

"Norma, did you see me as a victim in her web?"

"Yes, and I told you so many times."

"Now, Norma, you being my best friend at the time of my disappearance, did you know why I left? Did you know where I was?"

"Lexi, in all honesty, I had no idea where you were. I was devastated when you were no longer here and you were gone, just disappeared! I had left the company about six months before. However, we talked every day. We had lunch at least once a week."

"Why did you leave the company?" I asked in a tone coming from me I almost didn't recognize.

She just skipped passed my question and kept talking. "You know you always kept a journal with you wherever you went, and you made an entry at least once a day. Where is your journal? Or Journals? Lexi! If you can find your journals, you will probably find all your answers or most of them anyway."

"Norma Jean, why did you leave the company?" I ask for the second time.

"Charlotte!" she answered, "it's as simple as that."

"Norma Jean, nothing is simple when Charlotte is involved," I managed to say. "Norma Jean, can you please explain?"

"Sure, Lexi, I will try. However, it is a little complicated. She and I, we didn't get along at all. We were always at each other. Our personalities just clashed. I don't know what she had against me. She tried to make problems between you and me. I was determined not to let that happen. Lexi, I had plenty of reasons why I didn't like her. When you weren't around, she was always trying to get Matthew to notice her. It wasn't good, and Matthew detested her. He avoided her at every opportunity, at every turn. I told you many times my thoughts. She was an opportunist, and she was trouble. I told you one day I was resigning from my job. I refused to work with her any longer. You begged me to stay. I made my feelings known to you and the company the only way I would ever come back was if she was no longer working for the company. You were about to terminate her position when she just up and gave her two-week notice. Said she had found a job in Seattle, Washington."

"Where did I live when I was here in Ojai?"

She smiled at me, then answered, "About three miles from where we are now. I believe all your belongings were put in storage, but I am not sure, however, Samuel can provide you with a key and the information you need. Maybe your journals are there, and you can find some answers."

"Norma Jean how was it that you saw this taking place and others did not?"

She took a moment to think about her answer then she said, "Lexi, it was like I was watching a rat chewing its way through a wall to get to the jewels. It was just obvious to me."

It wasn't easy asking questions about my personal life to someone who was a perfect stranger to me; however, it was the curvy one-way road back to my past, which I chose to take. In her enthusiasm to rekindle our long-lost friendship, she listened silently as I asked her questions about my family. "How well did you know my husband and Joseph? Anything you could tell me about them would be more than I probably already know. Was Joseph a healthy child? Was he happy? What color eyes did he have? What color was his hair?

Were Matthew and I as happy as we looked in the photos laying on the desk in my office?"

Some of these questions I already knew the answer to, but I wanted her to bring their personalities to life. I wanted a clearer picture of the two people I had loved so. All I knew about my husband was his name. Matthew had died in an accident while doing some work at our company, and all this was before my disappearance.

"Well, Lexi, as I remember, you met Matthew at a Christmas party. It was a party given on behalf of local artists and designers, which benefitted local charities. It was a rather big event with lots of talent and most had money to throw around donating to charities. With Matthew's impressive work in the field as an architect/designer, he was on the guest list. It was a wonderful party with many in attendance. Lexi, there we were the three of us—you, Bonnie, and me. As I remember, you saw him from across the room, and you were almost spellbound. I remember you saying that guy is gorgeous, and wouldn't you guess Bonnie was the one that had the pleasure of introducing you to Matthew."

"Now who is this Bonnie you are talking about?" I interrupted wanting to get a clear picture in my head of this event that should be everlasting in my mind but was not.

"Bonnie is a nickname for Bonita. Bonnie was another one of your best friends. She is a friend that could compliment any stage or should I say someone that attracts a crowd. Oh, and by the way, Lexi, you always called her Bonita. She has been out of town on vacation but will be back in a couple of days. Bonnie will be so excited to know you are back in Ojai."

I thought to myself, *Two best friends one I don't remember, the other one I'm looking forward to meeting.*

As Norma Jean continued with the tale of events as they unfolded about my previous life, I tried to visualize myself there among the guest as she spoke the words so eloquently. I visualized in my mind the manner of events as they progressed into what became a very passionate romance, marriage, and a beautiful child. Norma Jean paused just long enough to catch her breath, then she continued to describe the party as where the romance between Matthew and I had begun.

She asked me in what seemed to be a caring manner if I remembered any of this. I would shake my head no, and her voice would continue with the presentation of my life. "Yes, the party went great, and as far as you and Matthew, you were attracted to each other from the first time you met. After that first meeting, you two were almost inseparable. You were very sensible and dated for about a year. However, you couldn't wait for him to ask for your hand in marriage. Then the big day finally arrived June 1, with a small wedding with just a few friends."

"Was any of my family there? At the wedding," I asked, blurting the words out before I thought about what I was saying.

"Only your grandmother, the two of you always kept in close contact. She would come quite often to Ojai to visit with you. She would stay a week or sometimes a month."

"My mother wasn't present at the wedding?" I inquired.

"No," came her answer with no further explanation except to say, "she called to wish you well."

My mind drifted somewhat as Norma filled me in on my family's lack of attendance and my lack of invitations on such an important day in my life.

"Lexi, you had decided to have a very small wedding. You knew if you started writing a guest list, it would morph into a lengthy complicated mess. Therefore, you made a few calls, and all that extra stress was over, the wedding was on. One year and three days later, you were wrapping Joseph in a blanket, leaving the hospital, going home where the three of you would live happily ever after, or so we thought." Norma Jean bowed her head, then looking back up and meeting my eyes, she said, "Well, that was how it was supposed to be, and it was for a while.

Matthew was an architect by profession. His office, which was located nearby, had grown into a good-sized firm. He had started his business about four years before he met you. Now, Lexi, Matthew was one of the kindest people I have ever known. He was good-looking, talented, kindhearted, and wonderful. He adored you and Joseph. Lexi, you loved him so."

The waitress refilled our coffee cups. I took time to add sugar and fresh cream as I was processing what she had just said. After a few sips of coffee, our conversation continued.

"Norma Jean, you say we were best friends that we talked often, had lunch together at least once a week. Tell me how it is that my son and I traveled from California all the way across the country and you knew nothing about my plans. You have no idea why I made that trip, is this correct? How no one at this company knew I was leaving? It just doesn't make sense. Was I different or indifferent before I left? Was there anything that would have led you to believe there was trouble ahead for me? Anything?"

"No, Lexi, the only thing out of the ordinary that I remember happened about a month before you just disappeared, you had a very heated argument with one of the secretaries that worked for your company. However, I never understood what that was all about. I remembered it bothered you tremendously. You seemed to be tight-lipped about that argument, and you told me it wasn't a subject for discussion. I wouldn't have known anything about that argument if it hadn't been for Bonnie. Bonnie was the one that told me about it. When I ask you about that argument, you told me to drop it. It wasn't open for discussion. I never mentioned it again, but from that day forward, you were somewhat different. That was just before I left the company."

"What was her name, the secretary, what was her name?" I asked her this question as I waved to the waitress.

Norma Jean answered by saying, "I never knew her name. Bonnie will know, you will have to ask her."

"Coffee please and more cream." I elevated my coffee cup as the waitress passed by. I sat there talking to Norma Jean through two more cups of coffee, listening to every word she could tell me about my past and the time I had lived in Ojai.

Before Norma Jean and I parted and went our separate ways, she made me promise to keep in contact with her. She also empha-sized the importance of finding my journals. "Lexi, your journals will probably have the answers you need, so please, Lexi, find your journals," was her last words to me as she waved goodbye and pulled away in her car.

*****

I slept in late the next day tired from all the excitement of the last week. I also needed a little time to think about what I needed to do next. As midafternoon approached, I made my mind up on something I had been struggling with since the day I had arrived in Ojai. I would talk with the detective who had investigated Matthew's death. Even though I couldn't remember Matthew, the evidence was lying on my desk in the form of photos which told a story of love and happiness. Deep inside me, I knew I owed Matthew this much.

I had Mr. Carr make arrangements for me to meet with Mr. Swede, the detective who had been in charge of Matthew's case, and today our meeting had been confirmed.

I arrived at the address where we were to meet and immediately thought this was a very unorthodox place to be holding this meeting. I entered the church/school through the side doors as I had been instructed. It was a weekday, and no church services were going on at the time. The door to the office was just a few feet from the side entrance.

As I entered the office door, a well-dressed, well-mannered young lady met me just inside. After introducing herself and inquiring if I was indeed Mrs. Carol Wainwright, or did I go by Lexi, I informed her yes, that indeed I am Mrs. Carol Wainwright. I am used to the name Carol, so that is usually what I answer to but telling her I was getting a little more acquainted with the name Lexi. Everyone here in Ojai who knew me before my disappearance called me Lexi. The name Lexi was a little hard to get used to after going by the name Carol for so many years.

Then she instructed me to have a seat and Mr. Swede would be with me shortly.

"He was directing a play here at the school, and it was a big event for the children. Unfortunately, he is running a little late today. However, he should be here with you momentarily." Then she excused herself and disappeared through the door.

After I waited for what seemed like a long time, I began to wonder if I was in the wrong place. *What did she say?* I asked myself, *directing a school play?*

Momentarily turned into about thirty-five minutes, and just as I was about to leave, he walked through the door. After introducing himself and apologizing for being late for our meeting, he stumbled over some explanation as to why he kept me waiting so long.

"I volunteer every year to direct the holiday plays the kids put on at the church. It is a big event for the children as well as the parents. So please forgive me for being late."

"Lexi, if you would follow me please, there is an office down the hall where we can talk in a private setting without being interrupted. In just a few minutes, the kids will be dismissed, and things will get pretty loud till they are dispersed and on their way home."

He stood to leave, and I followed close behind. It did get very noisy down the hall, with children just being children. Mr. Swede seemed to be very popular with them. As the children passed by us, you could hear their words, "Bye, Mr. Swede," or "See you tomorrow, Mr. Swede."

"Finally, here we are, Lexi," he said as he closed the door behind him leaving the noise behind in the hallway for ears more acceptable. "Have a seat, Lexi, make yourself comfortable, and we shall talk. I was deep into the investigation of your husband's death for many years. I heard your name many times spoken and referred to in so many different conversations. May I call you Lexi?" he said while grabbing a pen and paper.

"That would be fine, Mr. Swede. Everyone here calls me Lexi, that is, those that knew me before my accident."

"Lexi, why have you come to see me after all these years."

I, in as best detail as possible, relayed to Mr. Swede a little about myself that he didn't know. I told him about my accident, about having no memory of anything before the accident, about Charlotte taking my son from my car and passing him off as her own; my brief memory of Joseph, my long stay in the hospital, and my searching for Joseph; and just days ago finding out about my husband's death, which is why I was here today.

"Samuel, who is the vice president of my company, filled me in as best he could. I am here today wondering if Matthew's death was an accident or foul play. I was told by Samuel that foul play could have been involved. He also said you might have more information."

"Lexi, I did think there was foul play involved at the time. However, I never had enough evidence to prove anything. I studied this case for many years. I was never quite satisfied with my findings. Your disappearance was another thing that bothered me. With first your husband's death, then sometime later you and your son just disappeared. After many years, this case was just pushed aside. With dead clues and more cases coming to light and lack of man power, it became a cold case, you might say. Now with this information about what happened to you and your son and this information you have just given me, things could change significantly."

Mr. Swede stood up and said, "Lexi, I will check into this. It may take some time. We may be able to open the case again if we find cause to do so."

I stood up, thanked Mr. Swede for his time, and proceeded to leave. Turning back to face him, I said, "Mr. Swede please don't press Charlotte too hard or she may never tell me where Joseph is. Please!"

I left knowing I had done what I had set out to do. Whether I felt good or bad about it was beside the point.

The rain was coming down rather fast. Lightning streaked the sky with its unpredictable flashes. Due to the weather, the plane was late, and my nerves were on edge. I was so looking forward to the arrival of George and David. I thought, *I can't wait until the plane touches down. I missed them so much, and I detest being away from them for any reason.*

Finally there they were walking toward me with their luggage in tow. I could almost visualize Joseph walking beside them smiling, laughing, and running to give me a hug the way David will do as soon as he spots me in the crowd. Then I whispered to myself, "Joseph, I will find you, my sweet child, I promise."

*****

The next morning started off with breakfast—omelets, eggs benedict, and coffee served in our room. After breakfast, I told George all about the board meeting. All the board members were there, which consisted of myself, the vice president, and four others whom I would introduce him to later.

I told him before I attended this meeting about my thoughts and fears of attending. Then I came to the clear, simple thinking this was my company, a business I had started many years ago. I know I have no idea what I am doing now, but it is still my company. So I will depend on the vice president and my board members, and I will learn as I go. They have done such a good job all these years, so I knew how dependable they are. They filled me in on the business, the net worth of the company, the projects that were currently underway; expenditures for the month, for the year; profits for the month, profits for the year.

After all the business talk was over, I had spoken to them candidly about my life the last ten years, the good times, and the bad times alike. I told them of the accident, the small remembrance of Joseph, and my search for him. Then I told them what I knew of Charlotte and the problems she has caused myself and Joseph, the deception, the kidnapping of my child, my memory loss. At the end of our meeting, I asked them all if they had any idea why I had left and taken Joseph all the way across the country. Before I had ended the meeting, I invited them to please call me anytime.

I thanked them for all their hard work they put into the company, and I let them know I couldn't imagine leaving my company in better hands. My appreciation and gratitude was more than any words could ever express.

George listened to all I had to say about the meeting. Then he said, "See, those fears were all for nothing. Sounds like you did a great job."

The next few days were spent going to places of interest, spending time as a family and just relaxing, laughing and just having fun.

What time I had left here in Ojai, I had to make sure I used wisely dividing the time with family and looking for important information.

So the next two weeks would wind down fast, and we would be going back home soon. I needed to find the journals that Norma Jean had talked to me about. Hopefully they still exist. Samuel had moved all my possession into storage from my house. The house was property owned by my company, which was being used for storage. There was a small apartment for out of town business guests. Fortunately for me, my belongings were still in storage. Samuel said he had thought about getting rid of it all but always changed his mind; he just couldn't bring himself to getting rid of my treasures as he called them. He told me he always hoped I would find my way back.

He would send a courier by tomorrow morning with the address and a key. I would go exploring into my past, into a world I did not remember, and this I am sure would charge my adrenaline. George and David would accompany me on this attempt to find whatever I am looking for, whether it be my journals, which may bring me closer to my past life. One thing I can say, I am looking forward to reconnecting or trying to reconnect with my past treasures. Just maybe I will find a memory.

We were up early the next morning, David and George all excited and ready for the day. I had my mind on those journals. I had to find them. I know George would support me with all the help I need in my detective work, but while he was here, he wanted also to explore Ojai.

It was so beautiful in Ojai, and it being a tourists' paradise made it even more appealing. Ojai was located in the east-west valley, east of Santa Barbara and north of Ventura, California.

George and David were planning a trip to Lake Casitas where I was sure they would try to catch the largest fish in the lake. They were also hoping to have enough time to hike some of the beautiful serene foothills and climb through the lush green mountains.

One morning, David was looking out the window at the mountains that loomed before us and broke the silence by asking, "Mom, do you think lots of bears live in those mountains and around the lake?"

I looked at David, then out at the mountains, I said, "Now, David, if you were a bear, wouldn't you want to live among those beautiful mountains?"

David's answer came without hesitation, "Oh, Mom, sure I would, oh yes!"

"Well there's your answer, David. I am sure there are many bears that roam those lovely mountains."

I did not find the journals at my old home nor did I find information that would help me with finding Joseph.

After a day of looking through boxes, reading letters, and correspondence from people I did not know, moving furniture about, looking through jewelry and drawer after drawer of clothes, I found nothing that would help me.

I found myself overwhelmed once again. The digging through letters and correspondents from family and friends was interesting, to say the least. I did find out much about my family, friends, and their relationship with me; however, they were just names to me in all that matter. After moving furniture about, I learned I must have loved antiques because most of the furnishings stored there were old, lovely antiques. I also found the same with jewelry, very lovely pieces, yet from another period of time. With drawers and closets of clothes, I found my style was a lot different compared to now. A lot of the clothes were expensive designer clothes, but what interested me most of all were all the clothes and toys that had belonged to Joseph.

I sat down and looked through all his clothes and toys one by one. I wondered how he looked in this outfit or that outfit, and the toys still looked new and almost untroubled. I wondered to myself which one had been his favorite toy?

Seeing his clothes and toys further assured me I did have a son out there somewhere waiting for me to find him. It also made me realize when I left all those years ago, I had intended to come back.

Who would leave all his clothes and so many toys behind? I don't think that would have been me.

David was here helping me and was pleased when I asked him for help in moving a box or to hand me an object that was out of my reach or put something away. He was asking me questions I could not answer about the treasures we were finding. However, I made every attempt not to leave any of his questions go unanswered. Many were answered with, "Honey, I am not sure, or I just don't have the answer to your question."

George, with his charming attitude and his charismatic personality, not to mention that gorgeous smile that he flashed around quite often, was a big bright spot in all this confusion. His smile was what attracted me to him in the first place. He was also here helping me in this attempt to try to recapture as many bits and pieces of my past life as possible.

He was standing just a few feet away, opening boxes, assisting me with whatever help I needed and encouraging me in my endeavor to find these journals. He was my support system, my helper, the person I went crying to when things didn't work out, my soundboard when the frustrations of finding Joseph became too much for me to bear.

George kept telling me, "We'll find your journals. We will keep looking till we do." He was very optimistic, and his sense of confidence and his cheerful attitude kept me encouraged and laughing.

After all our searching, the journals were still missing, and our two weeks here were winding down fast. Soon we would be boarding a plane to take us back home—home to meet my grandmother, home to asking her questions about Thomas and about the letters she had addressed to me that were stuffed in that old musty, malodourous envelope for so many years ago and finding out why she had addressed the envelope to Thomas while the letters inside were addressed to Lexi; home to finding the answers to why my grandmother had left Thomas so many years ago; home to finding Joseph!

The three of us did take two days off to just relax. We ordered food to be delivered to our rooms. We all needed a break, so we used these two days wisely and just rested. The days passed faster than I would have liked. However, as they say, time waits for no one.

With only nine days left, I must make them count. I kept repeating to myself, "Find those journals. I must find those journals!"

*****

Bonita—with her bright-red hair, hunter-green dress, big blue eyes, a huge smile—holding an armful of books, stood before me as I was exiting my office almost running her down in the process.

"Lexi, Lexi, I can't believe it's you," she said pushing past me into my office and almost dropping the books while making her way awkwardly to my desk. After dumping the books on my desk in a noisy fashion, she ran over to me, took my hands gently in hers, then in a slight British accent said breathlessly, "Lexi, where have you been? Where is Joseph? Are you moving back to Ojai?" The questions kept coming nonstop.

"And just to whom am I speaking?" I finally asked. Almost as soon as the question left my mouth, Norma Jean entered the room.

"Lexi, I see you and Bonnie have already met." Norma Jean looked from Bonnie to me, then walked over to my desk and picked up a book, then addressed Bonnie by saying, "Bonnie! I see you found them."

"Found what?" I wanted to know.

"Your journals, or diaries, of course," as they both chimed in at the same time.

"My journals?"

"Lexi where have you been?" called Bonnie's voice once again. Her voice trailed off as she handed me one of the journals.

Reaching over and taking the journals from Bonnie, I addressed her by saying, "Bonnie, I am delighted to meet you."

Bonnie let out a big outburst of laughter, then apologized by saying, "I am so sorry for laughing, Lexi, but that sounded so funny coming from you. I just can't imagine you not knowing me! Me, Bonita. You always called me Bonita!"

I strolled over to my desk and picked up another one of the journals, then looking closer, I saw my name in big red letters scrolled across the face of the jacket: LEXI.

"Bonita, where did you find these journals?" I wanted to know.

"My dear Lexi, you had stored these away in a small room just beneath your office. When Norma Jean told me you were searching for them and had not found them, I figured they could possibly be in that tiny storage room, which no one uses anymore. I liked to never found them, they were packed away so good. Well, anyway, I have found them, and here they are. I hope you find what you are looking for."

My journals...I was so excited that they had been found. "Thank you, Bonita, for finding and delivering these journals for me."

*****

David, George, and I spent the next three days exploring Ojai, and what a wonderful place we found it to be. Other than being a great place and a tourist attraction, it was an extremely beautiful area of California.

George's and David's interest for the next few days was enjoying the country, the beautiful mountains, and lakes fishing and exploring in their newest favorite area on the planet Ojai, California. Since they had heard that some of the largest bass ever caught were caught in the Casitas Lake, the Casitas became their favorite lake almost overnight. To add to the enthusiasm of fishing in the Casitas Lake, which is known for legendary bass fishing, it also has abundance of other fish, bluegill, crappie, trout and sunfish, the rainbow variety. David found out from talking with one of the hotel concierges the lake has lots of red-ear sunfish, which he informed him were good eating, and they are much easier to fillet than to scale.

I didn't accompany them on their fishing escapades; however, I did join them on other adventures, which consisted of a beautiful drive through the Ojai Valley. We took highway 150, which was such a beautiful drive, a very scenic route. We drove from Santa Paula to the upper Ojai Valley, stopping a few times along the way to have a better view of the landscape. The mountain range was astounding, majestic, or better yet, the word *magnificent* might be a better description—the foothills lush and green and in some areas, the grass or foliage was almost a yellowish mustard color, yes, and so beautiful.

The Topatopa mountain range overlooks Ojai. Along this nine- or ten-mile stretch of highway, we passed many restaurants. We let David choose where we would eat that day. He chose Susanne's Cuisine, which we found to have a European atmosphere, which turned out to be a perfect choice. The food was great. I chose salmon on a bed of sauerkraut. I wondered to myself if I would actually like that. I chose well; it was an excellent meal, absolutely wonderful.

George and David chose fish also. You can tell when those two enjoy their food. Not many words pass from either of them until they are finished. Except for maybe the words "oh yes," or "I might have to order seconds."

I enjoyed the museums and art galleries most of all. The culture of the area was so fascinating. The art galleries were filled with beautiful works of art. Our time spent there was well worth the effort.

*****

I was awakened the next morning early by the sound of my cell phone. Mother on the other end wanted to know the flight number and the time we would be arriving. She also wanted to know if I had any new information that might help me find Joseph. I talked to her every day with no substantial information to pass on to her. She so wanted me to find him.

I informed her of the journals that Bonnie had delivered to me. They had given me an insight to who I was before Joseph was born, insight on how I ran my company, my meeting Matthew, and also my marriage to Matthew; and, yes, it was true I had made a few entries every day. Some days there were pages and pages of entries.

Most of the entries were private thoughts not to be shared with anyone other than the person making the entries.

I found it strange reading about myself from the pages I did not recognize. I was also sure my fingerprints were on every page, and I could imagine a few of my tears had found their way to these pages.

It was as if I was snooping into someone else's life, prying into their most intricate personal moments. I had to remind myself these were my thoughts, my writings, and judging by the words I read, a wonderful life. However, by reading these entries, it gave me a semblance of understanding a person I did not know, myself. Me! Not the "me" in these entries. I was the Carol after the accident, not the Lexi before the accident. I must somehow merge these two because they are one—me.

My last day before our flight, which would take us back home to our normal way of life, was somewhat bittersweet. Bonita and Norma Jean didn't want us to leave, but they knew we had responsibilities we had to get back to. The main responsibility was finding Joseph.

I had called for another staff meeting the evening before our departure. I had a few things I needed to say to my staff, mainly to thank them again for all their good work and once again ask if any of them knew anything about why I had left the company so unexpectedly or if any of them had been good friends with Charlotte or were still in communication with her. All were silent and shook their heads no, but as I was leaving, the financial coordinator followed me down the hall.

"Lexi, Lexi!" she called after me. I turned to faced her, she being the woman I thought I recognized the first day upon my arrival here in Ojai.

"Lexi, I got a call from Charlotte about four months ago. She wanted to know if she could have her old job back."

"What?" I said to her.

"Yes, I am sure we were somewhat friends before she left the company."

"What do you mean by somewhat friends?"

She looked away as if in deep thought before she answered, then turning to me, she said, "Nefarious would be a good way to describe her. A friend but not a friend and someone you had to always keep an eye on."

"When did she leave the company?" I wanted to know.

"Two weeks before your disappearance."

"Was this reported to the police after my disappearance?" I asked with a serious tone.

"Lexi, there was no reason to involve them at the time. She gave a two-week notice and said she was moving away, had another job. We never thought anything about it. There was no reason to think anything was out of the ordinary."

"You were her friend back then, right?"

"We weren't close friends, but you might say friends. I didn't hang around with her. However, we doubled dated a couple of times, but that was the extent of our friendship. She called me many times asking me to hang out with her, see a movie, have dinner, or perhaps go shopping. I declined because I didn't agree with her outlook on life. Her morals were very different from my own. Lexi, I hadn't heard from her in all these years, and she just called me up one day and asked if she could have her old job back."

"What did you tell her?" I was curious. I really wanted to know the answer.

"I told her we had nothing at the time, but she was welcome to call me back in about a month, who knows there could be a position to offer you by then. She never made that call."

I asked her if she had any more information she could give me. Her answer to me was no. She wished me all the best in finding Joseph, then turned and walked away.

*****

The night before our departure, we were invited out to dinner. Samuel had made all the arrangements at one of the local upscale French restaurants. Later Bonita informed me, French food was always my favorite choice of foods, and she wanted to know if it still was. I informed her that piece of knowledge must have gone with the rest of my memory; however, while honeymooning in Paris, I fell in love with French cuisine.

The evening went well. The more I got to know Bonita and Norma Jean, the more I liked them. The evening wasn't just the excellent food. There was plenty of laughter and a few tears, interesting stories of our lives in Ojai, some business, but mostly just fun times we had had together before my disappearance. Samuel was in most of these stories too. Samuel and Norma Jean's stories went back as far as Keokee. We had gone to school together the whole time I was planning and plotting my business strategies.

Designing some interesting vases and going public with my designs, a company was born, selling them at home and abroad and hiring my two best friends Samuel and Norma Jean to help me run my company.

After drinking a few more rounds of coffee, we were forced to say our goodbyes. Bonita and Norma Jean's last words to me were, "When you find Joseph, we will be there to help with the celebration."

The plane trip back home was an enjoyable one. It was bittersweet leaving Ojai. We had so enjoyed ourselves there, such an interesting place, but we were eager to be heading home.

*****

Two days later Mother was out in the flower garden, inspecting the roses that she had been babying knowing any day the colder weather would claim their beauty, when we finally pulled into the driveway. She quickly made her way through the stoned paved path that lined the flower garden to welcome us home. She was so excited that we were back. Draping her arms around me and giving me a big hug, she whispered in my ear, "Lexi! I have much to tell you." Then she made her way to David where she greeted him with hugs then handed him one of the red roses she had picked. "David, I know how much you like to sketch, so could you please sketch this rose for me." Looking around at the beautiful roses, I thought if the words she has to tell me were as beautiful as these roses, then all will be well.

"Lexi," Mother's voice changed from loud to very soft as she said to me, "your grandmother has given me strict orders that I am not to tell you anything until she has had time to talk to you first." She smiled, and we both laughed a hardy laugh because we both knew this would be a hard promise for my mother to keep; however, she was true to her word.

As I was unpacking my luggage, the telephone rang; it was Grandmother. I was hoping I would recognize her voice, but it didn't happen; however, her voice was pleasing, soft with a slight country accent. There was also authority in her voice. She only asked me one question, "Lexi, where did you lose Joseph?"

Tears sprang to my eyes, and I wanted to run away, but I answered her as truthfully as possible. "Grandmother, I don't know, what are you talking about?"

I was shocked that she would ask me such a question, then she changed the subject. "Lexi, I called to tell you I won't be able to see you until Friday. I will be there early Friday morning, and by the way, your grandfather said to tell you hello. I'll let you go for now, love you." Silence filled my ear as the tears streamed down my face. I wondered to myself just what happened. Such a strange conversation. Then her words entered my thoughts again as her question seemed to dominate even the air that I breathe. "Where did you lose Joseph?" These hurtful words kept ringing in my ears.

"What?" I kept saying to myself. Angry and upset, I ask myself just what kind of question is this that my grandmother would even think to ask me such a question. She said "your grandfather" like it was just a normal conversation, as if my grandfather had always been here in my life, which had been no fault of his. All of this burden lay on Grandmother and her alone. I was confused. Perhaps so or maybe perhaps not, I will understand her more upon meeting with her Friday.

All that day and even into the next day, her question kept dominating my thoughts. The question made me mad, made me think, made me cry.

Mother had many questions about our trip. She had many questions about my company that I had started so many years ago, and of course, if I had found any new information, as to the whereabouts of Joseph. I filled her in on some of our adventures. We talked about the journals I had found and the journals I had not found. The journals I could not locate are the ones I needed to help in understanding what happened before I left Ojai, and the big question was why I left?

Samantha called early one morning after we arrived back home from Ojai to see if this would be a good time for her to visit. She had promised David she would be back later in the year so we all could go horseback riding together.

When I told David Samantha had called and would be arriving in a couple of days, David was so excited, and, yes, he remembered her promise to go horseback riding on her next visit. This pleased David, and he was overcome with happiness. I was sure for the next couple of days, most of David's conversations will either begin or end with horseback riding.

"As for myself, I am also looking forward to Samantha's visit. Fun, fun, fun."

Since I am a lover of the outdoors, the fresh air and beautiful scenery were always welcomed. Now I wondered which riding trail we would take. A vineyard trail with lush green rolling hills or a historical garden trail. The historical garden, which was located up in the mountains, had breathtaking views. There was also one riding trail I've heard of that followed alongside a river. That sounded wonderful. Decisions? Decisions? I thought I'd let George decide.

*****

Samantha's plane was late due to bad weather, which included rain, wind, and lightning with rain coming down rather fast when her plane finally landed.

However, she met us with her cheerful, bubbly personality along with her Louis Vuitton luggage. I always teased her about her beautiful extravagant luggage. We made our way home as the windshield wipers were doing a poor job at keeping the rain washed away. David from the back seat chattered about everything from horseback riding to the pouring down rain.

The next morning it was still raining. I thought to myself this family outing we have planned may have to be postponed to another time. By the time David got home from school the next day, the rain had ceased, and the sun was shining brightly.

David was so happy to see Samantha. They had become such good friends. This time around, Samantha had brought David a bullfight poster from Spain. He immediately took the poster to his room and hung it on the wall. Ruth served dinner in the formal dining room, and the evening meal was great. Samantha was entertaining everyone with interesting stories about her latest trip abroad. There was also lots of talk about the horse adventures that were coming up soon.

Two days later, we began our adventure with the sun beaming down on us from time to time. White clouds were scattered across the sky. The temperature was perfect—not too hot and not too cold, just about right. George chose the mountain trail with its breathtaking view. We invited Ruth, our good friend and part-time maid, to go along on our adventure. She had gone with us on our last horseback adventure in Hawaii. We thought it just wouldn't be as much fun without her.

David teased her by saying, "Miss Ruth, hold on to the reins. We don't want to lose you like we did in Hawaii."

Ruth, in her loving way, said, "Now, David, I don't want to have to get off this horse to pick you up off the ground and then help you back on your horse. Mind your manners, and hold on tight."

It was a wonderful ride; however, the horses went a little faster than I would have liked. Yes, the view was beautiful. Just like the ad said, a breathtaking view. However, I somehow missed the part that said we would be crossing a creek just before starting up the rolling hills. That was interesting. It was also breathtaking when the cool water hit us head on.

Samantha, David, and Ruth thought that crossing the creek was just the best thing ever.

George said, "Now coming down the mountain will be the best part for you all."

It didn't quite work out that way. The horses were sure-footed, I must say. However, they were a lot faster going down the mountain than they were going up the mountain.

As we were dismounting and the horses were being taken away, David turned to me and said, "Mom, I pretended Joseph was sitting right behind me holding on to me as we rode up and down the mountain." I cried.

*****

Bonita called almost every day to make sure I was okay, mainly to ask how I was, and to ask me if I had found the other journal or journals. I told her I was still looking for them. I had a good idea; if I was going to find them, they would probably be hidden in Thomas' house. Yes, the police had done their search of the rooms that Charlotte occupied. But it's a big house, I thought they have to be there, and if they were, I was going to find them.

Mother never brought up the subject of Grandmother's visit that was coming up in a few days. I thought that strange. So I decided to ask her more details about my grandmother. I told her I was a little nervous about her coming, and she would be a stranger to me, and furthermore, my conversation with her on the phone had made me anxious and leery of this visit.

"Lexi, what conversation are you talking about?" Mother asked me this question almost as an afterthought.

Looking straight at Mother and hoping for some kind under-standing of how this made me feel emotional, I said, "Mary, my grandmother, asked me the most awkward and heart-wrenching question I have ever had thrown my way." Her exact words, "Lexi, where did you lose Joseph?"

Mother, after adding a little more thought to the conversation, said, "My dear Lexi, I am sure she didn't mean that to sound so unsympathetic toward your feelings. She just came straight to the point and asked you what was on her mind."

I told Mother, "In that case, I am not looking forward to meet-ing her anytime soon."

Mother laughed and assured me my grandmother was harmless. "You'll see for yourself she is wonderful."

It was at this time Mother informed me that she had asked Grandmother and Thomas to stay the week, starting Friday. "Since they have a four-and-a-half-hour drive back home, I thought it would be nice if they just stay the week instead of driving back so soon. As for you, Lexi, you need to get reacquainted with your grandmother."

I knew it was a family responsibility, so I must step up and be cordial to my grandmother. I will sincerely try to forget this unpleasant conversation I had with my grandmother over the phone just a couple of days ago.

Furthermore, David and George would be meeting her for the first time, and on top of all that, David hasn't met his grandfather as of yet. So I would like to make these meetings the best of times, with no regrets said out of anger or sudden upset feelings. Mother laughed and took my hand in hers, squeezed it, and said, "Darling Lexi, this visit is going to be so exciting, just mark my word, and I promise you that you will love your grandmother."

I thought, I don't think *reacquainted* is the right word to use when meeting with my grandmother. I had no recollection of her. Such as it is, I would have to make the best of the situation.

When I told David of our plans, he was so excited. He had heard a lot about Thomas and Grandmother and had been anticipating meeting them. His excitement came in the form of talking and asking many questions.

*****

I told my mother one morning, "Mother, you know I haven't seen Thomas in quite a while, not since he went to find Mary. I talked to him once or twice on the phone, they were wonderful conversations about him and my grandmother."

"Lexi, my dear, Mother will fill you in on everything. It is hers to do, and I am sure you will feel better about everything once you have had a chance to talk with her."

Friday morning came around very quickly. My grandparents arrived earlier than I had expected. They had driven the four-plus hours and had arrived here by nine o'clock. I was so happy to see Thomas, but the anticipation of meeting Grandmother wasn't quite as blissful. I had so hoped to see him today. I missed what little I did know about him and wanted to hear all about when he and Mary met at the airport. I wanted to hear this story in his own words. Since he was the one who told me about the woman he fell in love with a long time ago. It seemed only right that I would get this part of the story from him.

Mother met my grandparents at the door, and I trailed behind.

Grandmother, after entering the room, walked over to where I was standing and wrapped her arms around me, and said, "Lexi, where have you been? We had no idea what happened to you and Joseph. Thank God you are found, and now we must find Joseph. The last time I saw Joseph, he was cutting his first tooth. He didn't cry very often. He was such a good baby. Lexi, where did you lose him?"

"You saw him, and you knew him?" I asked my grandmother.

"Yes, Lexi," she said as she elaborated on more details of Joseph's personality and the time she spent with him.

I repeated her words, "Cutting his first tooth." She remembers that, and I was glad. I was glad someone remembered an important event like that; however, I wish I had that event as one of my memories.

Thomas came over and stood by my side. After giving me a kiss on the cheek, he said, "Carol, I am your grandfather, but I guess you have already figured that out. Things have changed a lot since we first met in Clair's Restaurant. Maybe it was me you came to see the day of your accident. Your grandmother said she never told you about me, and your mother didn't know. This is a mystery in itself, but I feel it had something to do with the disappearance of Joseph."

I put my arms around Thomas, or should I say my grandfather, and gave him a kiss on the cheek. I told him he would make a perfect grandfather. I could see tears in his eyes, then he said to me, "We have lost so many years, we have a lot of catching up to do." Then he told me he would be honored to have me as his granddaughter. This statement was very emotional for me; I could feel tears running down my cheeks.

It was easy for me to love this man. He was so kind, and I had liked him from the first day we met at Clair's Restaurant. I thought, *Wow, I had met my grandfather that day and had no idea he was my grandfather.* This now seemed almost surreal to me now as I looked back to that day.

*****

"Lexi, my dear," my mother said as she entered the room in her soft gentle voice letting me know, "your grandmother wants to meet with you around twelve o'clock today. At present, she is taking a short nap, tired from the four-and-half-hour drive this morning, and she wants to get all this business talk cleared up as soon as possible. She wants to make sure without question this does not interfere with our week of getting to know one another or reacquainted as she called it. We'll have a quick lunch, then after lunch, you will have my mother all to yourself." Mother excused herself, and by doing so, I could tell she wanted no more conversation about her mother's inappropriate question to me.

About two hours later, Grandmother made her way back downstairs. She found me in the solarium where I was making room for some indoor plants that George had ordered.

After walking through the door, Grandmother walked around and inspected some of my assorted mums, and she kept saying over and over how much she liked the flowering maples that were just flooded with blooms, all three of them to be exact—yellow, red, and orange. I told my grandmother these three plants were my prized flowers with the flowers resembling crêpe paper. Grandmother lingered for a while looking over my prized plants and then she informed me lunch was ready and Mother will be waiting.

I lingered there for a few minutes myself, then I saw Grandmother pointing to the door. In all respect for her, I left what I was doing and hurried through the door. Grandmother joined me in the sunroom that over looked the lake.

Mother dismissed herself after bringing in a tray of coffee, cake, and croissants. Thomas would be joining Mother in the kitchen, where the two of them would dine together. They knew Grandmother had come here to talk with me, and she was eager to get this conversation over with. So, therefore, left all alone, it would be just the two of us.

"Lexi," Grandmother said as she walked around the room, "make yourself comfortable, and finish your coffee and croissant. Then I will start my story."

Not really knowing what to expect, I did as Grandmother had instructed me. I finished my coffee and croissant.

As I watched my grandmother add sugar to her coffee, I thought how beautiful she is. Before she started her story, she unfolded a picture album. She flipped through it in a deliberate fashion. Finding the page she was looking for, she stopped and carefully removed a picture. She held it in her hand then laid it down on top of the photo album. She slowly made her way to where I was sitting.

Grandmother's conversation started out by saying, "Now, my dear Lexi. I am about to tell you my story. I want you to listen and learn. I know you are nothing like me. However, anyone can learn a lesson from other people's mistakes, and, sweetie, I have made plenty."

I thought to myself once again as I sat there watching her. How beautiful she was? So charming in her movements, the way she spoke, the way she carried herself. I was sure all those years, long ago, when Thomas met her, she must have been beautiful indeed. This morning, she was dressed in such a fashionable manner. Her hair was perfect, her makeup amazing. *Wow, this is my grandmother.*

After I finished eating, she poured me another cup of coffee, then she came and sat directly in front of me and started her story.

Her story began with, "My dearest Lexi, my parents had moved from Keokee, and I was devastated. I loved Keokee and loved living there. Moving away was the last thing I wanted to do. 'What about all my friends and school?' I kept asking, hoping they would change their minds and move back to Keokee. To console me, my father would say to me, 'We still have our home in Keokee, just give it a chance, Lovely. If we find we don't like it here, we can always move back." Lovely which is what my dad always called me. That had been his nickname for me for as long as I could remember."

Grandmother told me her father had bought a piece of land with a lovely house on it, and it was about a mile from where Thomas lived now. "Dad needed help, so he hired Thomas and his brother Fred to help clear some of the land he was getting ready to farm. I remember the first time I met Thomas. My mother had cooked lunch, and I was late to come to the table that day. That specific day, she served lunch in the formal dining room. When I walked into the room, things got a little comical until I realized this handsome young man sitting in front of me was choking. He had looked up at me and started choking on food. After his brother had smacked him on the back, he regained control and started breathing again. Then my little brother, Tim, made a comment, which went something like this, 'See, I told you she was ugly.' Then Thomas started laughing and couldn't seem to control his laughter. When he finally got that under control, he left the table. I didn't see him for about three days. I was so afraid he wouldn't come back.

"As you can imagine, I was determined not to be late for lunch again. Other than enjoying the entertainment, I found him very handsome, and I couldn't think of anything but him. My life changed. I fell in love. We married, and life was great. I was so in love, we had a wonderful life together. I would call it a perfect life. We were married about five years. Five wonderful, perfect years. May I repeat this again, five perfect, wonderful years.

Then one morning, I woke up, looked in the mirror, and the person looking back at me wasn't a girl anymore. She was a woman and five years older. I had always dreamed of being a ballet dancer. Dancing was my life when I was younger. The piano also, and I was very good at both, along with being good with all kinds of sports. I was very spoiled by everyone including most of all my mom and dad, and I always got my way. Everyone had always told me I was so beautiful, and I believed them. I, under this head of blonde hair, which has sadly started turning to a nice shade of gray, knew I was spoiled but very beautiful. I dreamed of being a star and onstage one day. These thoughts became more intense as the weeks passed. Then I thought if I became pregnant, I will never be on stage and be a star. I packed my bags and left, with only a short note to Thomas. I also wrote my dear brother and my mother and father to say goodbye.

"I left with virtually no plans at all. Looking back on that day, I wonder how I could have been so bold. Luckily for me, I found a job teaching piano. I rented a small room and later started a small ballet school. However, let's go back a little, about a month after I left home, I started getting sick in the mornings. At first I thought it was a virus. I finally had to see a doctor. That is when I found out I was pregnant. I had been gone less than a month, and I had been pregnant before I left home. If only I had known then, would I have left? No, I am sure I would not have. I wanted to go back, and I wanted to go back immediately. I missed Thomas. I loved him, so how could I explain this to him. Could I say I loved myself more than him? How about ballet and piano, did I love them more than him? I loved the idea of being a star and appearing onstage one day. How foolish I had been. Could I ever forgive myself? Could Thomas ever forgive me?

"After really thinking about what I had done, I was in shock that I had been so silly, so foolish, and made such horrible mistakes. I thought I have to go back and explain all this to Thomas. I know he loves me and he will forget and forgive. We can start over. Along with being the most selfish person on earth, pride has to show up, pride that is another flaw in me. Lexi, are you listening to what I say?"

"Yes, Grandmother, I am clinging to every word," I said this while holding back tears. I was amazed at her honesty.

Again she repeated her words. "Pride had to show up. Pride!" With this said, I could see tears streaming down her cheeks, and after taking a few minutes and wiping the tears away looking straight at me, she said, "*Pride,* such a small word with so many consequences. Consequences that follow you all through your life, into your everyday world, into everything you do, even into your dreams.

I had a beautiful little girl, and she is your mother. I named her Shirley Lucille, and she has always gone by the nickname Lucy. I have never stopped loving Thomas, Never. Why didn't I write or call the man I loved in all these years? Even I don't know the answer to that. I never dated anyone else. No one could compare to Thomas. Days slipped into weeks, weeks into years, until this awful span of time was now the enemy. I never told your mother about her wonderful father. I cheated myself, Thomas, and my daughter of so much happiness. Lexi, are you listening to what I am saying?"

"Yes, Grandmother, every word."

"Thomas is amazing. After all those years of my being absent from his life, as soon as Thomas found out where I was, he came straight to me. Now is that not love? So unselfishly given, and I so undeserving."

She stopped and hesitated before she continued. Maybe she was gathering her thoughts, and perhaps thinking back was a little overwhelming for her, maybe feeling guilty for leaving Thomas in the first place. After walking around the room a couple of times, she sat back down and continued, "Lexi dear, your mother called me and told me Thomas had found an envelope with my address on it, an envelope that had been sent years ago, which he had just found days earlier. Furthermore, he was making arrangements to fly out to find me. I was very confused because as much as I would have loved to have contacted Thomas, I never contacted him. There had to be some kind of mistake.

Lexi dear, when your mother explained to me a little more in detail about this envelope Thomas had received, which was addressed to him from me, I was stunned. With the letters inside addressed to Lexi from me, I didn't know what to say. All I know is I didn't send that envelope. When I knew for sure we were talking about Thomas, my Thomas, I was overjoyed with happiness. Lexi I hadn't been that happy since the day I had married Thomas. I cried and cried, and then I cried even more. I couldn't visualize ever seeing him again.

"Lexi, your mother told me the flight number and the arrival time. Thomas had no idea I would be there waiting for him. It's a small airport, so I had him paged. He met me at a designated area. He had no idea who was waiting for him. I cannot begin to explain the moment we met at the airport. Words cannot express our world at the moment Thomas realized it was me there to meet him. Indeed I cannot express my feelings when I saw Thomas. There were no words to express such pleasure. We went straight to each other's arms, I hugged him, and it seemed as if I couldn't let go. I just could not let go. It was the same for him. We were both crying, but they were tears of joy. It seemed as if the world had stopped all around us, and we were in a world of our own. I know I never want to be away from Thomas again. May I say again? Never. I kept wondering to myself how Thomas could ever have forgiven me, but he had. He is most wonderful."

Grandmother slowly stood up and walked around the room as if in deep thought, then she made her way to the picture, the picture she had laid on top of the album. She walked slowly to where I sat, then looking at the picture once again before handing it to me. At that point, she astonished me by asking me once again, "Lexi, where did you lose Joseph?"

I didn't answer. I couldn't, and I kept silent.

"The photo you hold in your hand is of Joseph. When this picture was taken, it was the last time I saw him."

Then she handed me the photo album. Just before she slipped through the door, she said, "These pictures are mostly family. You might want to take a look at them. In some way, they may help you regain your memory." I was left alone with the picture of Joseph and a photo album which was overstuffed with pictures of people I did not know.

As I rummaged through the photo album looking for what I do not know and just barely glancing at most of the pictures because my mind was still on Grandmother and her awkward question to me, "Where did you lose Joseph?" As I stood up to go find Grandmother and make somewhat of an effort to answer this awkward question, a question she had asked me now for the third time, something fell to the floor from the photo album. I picked it up and held it to the light. I was amazed and shocked at what I saw. There staring back at me from the picture I held in my hand was none other than Charlotte.

*****

I nearly ran from the room to find my grandmother. Over and over, I kept asking myself why my grandmother would have a picture of Charlotte. I found Mother and Grandmother outside sipping tea in the flower garden under the shade of a big elm tree. I could see Thomas over by the willow trees, playing fetch with the neighbor's dog. It looked like a peaceful scene; however, that was about to change.

I went right to Grandmother's side and demanded she tell me why she had this picture in her photo album of the woman who stole my son. "Why do you have a picture of Charlotte?" I demanded the second time.

Mother realized something was wrong with me. She could see I was very upset. She stood and came straight to my side. "Lexi, what's wrong?" came her sweet voice.

"Mother, look." I handed her the picture.

"Lexi honey, what are you talking about, what has you so upset?" came my grandmother's controlled voice. Then she took my hand and said, "Lexi, what do you have here, whose picture are you talking about?"

"Grandmother, why do you have a picture of Charlotte?" I asked again in a very impatient manner. She took the picture, looked at it, and immediately said, "This is Gayle, and she has been my friend for many years."

"When did you become friends, Grandmother?" I want to know.

"Gayle worked for me about eleven years ago, after I moved to Washington. She had just moved there recently from California, and she needed a job."

"Grandmother, this is the woman that took Joseph from my car. She stole him from my car when I had my accident. This is Charlotte. What are you doing with this picture?" My voice was a little out of control. I was so upset. It seemed as if I kept repeating myself.

"Grandmother, don't you see? First she worked for my company in Ojai. This is California we are talking about. Which is far, far away all the way across the country. Somehow she was the first one at the scene of my accident and took my son from the car while I lay struggling to live. That's thousands of miles away from Ojai, and she has been renting rooms from Thomas for years. Now I find out she is a friend of yours. This isn't coincidental, it is deliberate."

For the first time, I felt like all this mayhem she has caused was deliberately planned. "Grandmother, what kind of work did she do for you?"

"Gayle ran errands for me, did light housework, and cooked some meals."

"Grandmother, her name is not Gayle. Her name is Charlotte. Grandmother, please! Her name is Charlotte," I said this loud a second time to make myself clear.

It sounded as if she has been stalking our whole family. This to me was very unnerving. I was going back to the police station tomorrow. I want to make sure they have all this new information in their records. I said out loud, "What has she done to Joseph? What has she done to me?" then I began to cry.

Through tears, I was working hard at controlling my voice and emotions. I asked Grandmother why she thought I had lost Joseph. Why she would ask me such a hurtful question?

Her answer, "How could he be there one day and just gone the next day?"

Before I thought about what I was saying, I blurted out, "Well, Grandmother, you seem to be an expert at being there one day and gone the next day."

"Lexi, that is no way to talk to your grandmother. Watch your attitude. However, you are right, and I am so sorry. I just loved Joseph so, and now he is gone." I could see tears in her eyes as she turned from me and walked away. I followed after her. I was the one with the missing child. I needed more questions answered.

"The envelope you sent addressed to Thomas so many years ago and the letters inside the envelope that were addressed to me, what do you know about them? Tell me about the envelope addressed to Thomas and the letters inside the envelope that were written months apart addressed to me."

"Lexi, I did write you many letters in the months before you and Joseph just up and disappeared. Most of them I did not send myself. Gayle took care of picking up my mail and delivering it to me."

"Gayle?" I repeated in astonishment for a second time, "Gayle!" My voice came to life as this bit of information was made known to me, and my mind began to process what I was hearing. "Her name is not Gayle. Her name is Charlotte. Now let me get this clear. Charlotte left my company after my husband's death, and a little over a month before I disappeared, she quit her job. She moved away to pursue another job, and now I have found out she went to work for you. To top this off, she, Gayle or Charlotte or whoever she is, has been renting rooms from Thomas for years, and my son is missing because of her.

"Grandmother, don't you see she had to have been using information she was getting from you against me? Or maybe she was getting information from my life to use you."

"Lexi, Charlotte worked for me for a short period of time. Now let me see as I think about it. She worked for me only a couple of months. She said she was going east. She had been accepted at one of the hospitals she had applied to. She said she had her RN degree but had taken a sabbatical and had been working for a friend for the last few years. She never mentioned the name of that company. She had written me many letters through the years, always called me on Christmas and my birthday, came to visit me a couple of times in the last seven or eight years. She was always so nice, hard to believe she could be corrupt."

"Grandmother, you had better believe it. She took my son Joseph from my car and passed him off as her own son, and now no one but her knows where he is. Grandmother, did you volunteer information to her? Now think about what I am asking you."

"Oh Lexi, I did talk to her about you and your mother. I was so proud of you both."

"Grandmother, it appears she has been using you for information. Oh no, Grandmother, I just thought of something. She knew where I was all the time, and she could have told you and my family. She kept this information away from you. Oh, my dear grandmother, she definitely was not a friend."

I thought to myself could she have caused my accident? I was convinced that she had planned it all. "Now the envelope that held the letters, addressed to Thomas, sent from you. Can you tell me about these letters and why they were sent in this fashion?"

"Lexi," my grandmother interrupted before I could finish my question to her. "I never sent that envelope. All my letters to you were sent to Ojai, California. Gayle must have intercepted those letters. Why she held them back and sent them to Thomas' address is a mystery to me. I trusted her. She was a good friend, or I thought she was a good friend."

"So, Grandmother, let me get this straight. You never sent that envelope to Thomas with the letters addressed to me inside."

"That is right, Lexi, I never sent that envelope to Thomas."

"Grandmother, how did Charlotte know about Thomas?" I asked her after taking a few minutes to control my own feelings. I could see she was stressed about the whole conversation.

"Lexi, at that time, she was a good friend. Now I see I befriended the wrong person. I did at one time tell her about Thomas, she did ask me where he lived, and I told her. I never thought twice about it. His address she must have gotten on her own."

My thoughts began to run rapidly. Could Charlotte have planned to be me? Pretended to be me and take my place? This is a question I must explore. Had she caused my wreck? Had she planned to take over my life? If so, what had changed her mind? Questions I need answers for.

"Grandmother, there was a locket in the envelope. What do you know about that locket, and what is the significance of it?"

"A locket?" Grandmother questioned. "What locket are you talking about?"

"There was a locket inside the envelope with the letters, a beautiful gold-cased locket. The locket contained a lock of blonde hair tied with the tiniest little blue ribbon," I said to her as I watched her face cloud over.

"Lexi my dear, if that is my locket, it contains a lock of Joseph's hair. Where is this locket you are talking about? Lexi, do you have the locket with you?" My grandmother wanted to know, as she reached and took my hand in hers.

I looked directly at my grandmother and said, "I thought it must be Joseph's hair, so I kept it close to my heart." Pulling it from beneath my jersey, I handed it to my grandmother.

Upon taking the locket and carefully inspecting it to make sure it was indeed hers, my grandmother said, "Oh yes, this is my locket, and this is the only physical evidence we have of Joseph. So this is what happened to my locket. All this time I thought I had misplaced or lost it. It has been a long time since I've seen it and now that we have found it, we must find Joseph." She handed the locket back to me and said, "It is yours now, Lexi. Keep it close to your heart."

Grandmother's voice was flawless as she said, "Lexi, my dear, I will help you all I can, I promise, and I will do all I can to help you find Joseph." Then she gave me a kiss, turned, and walked toward the house, and just before entering, the door, she turned to me and said, "Lexi, I'll see you at dinner," and bade me good evening and made her way to her bedroom.

*****

Tomorrow David will arrive early. He will be meeting his grandparents for the first time. I want everything to be perfect or as perfect as could be expected when he arrives. David had spent the night with Aunt Julia and Uncle Craig. I thought it would be better meeting with Grandmother and getting all this talk over with before presenting David to his grandparents. I had told David they were coming for a visit, and he was elated, yelling, "Yes, yes!" Jumping up and down being a very excited eleven-year-old boy.

We would have family time with introductions, and the next few days would be filled with happy times—cookouts, games, walks to the lake, and with snow in the forecast, some snow activities if David has his way.

After dinner, I decided that I needed to talk to Mom, so I made my way to her room; and after realizing she was taking a nap, I thought, *Well, I will come back later.* I grabbed my coat and a scarf and decided to take a walk, so I headed for the lake. The weather was warmer than I expected, although there was a breeze coming off the lake. Sometimes I just need to go outdoors take a walk and clear my mind. With all the things going on—my grandparents here for a week, David meeting them for the first time, with me making sure everything ran smoothly—I wanted this to be a good time for all concerned. However, life became so busy, and I found my life consumed with all the plans going forward. I found myself feeling guilty, guilty for enjoying myself while Joseph's whereabouts were still unknown to me, guilty for not trying harder to find him. I tried to clear my thoughts and keep a positive attitude, so I lingered by the lake for a while, watching the fog settle in over the water, then I started my walk back toward the house.

Upon returning from my walk, I found Mother in the kitchen filling pastries with her special recipe for strawberry-cream filling. After sampling one of the perfectly filled pastries, I informed her I had come to her room earlier because I needed to talk to her but found her sleeping, so I decided instead to take a walk down by the lake.

Mother set the pastries aside that she had been working on and took my hand in hers. She directed me to the sitting room. Then, addressing me she said, "This is as good time to talk as any. So, Lexi, what's on your mind? Better yet, what is troubling you? You seem down, not your normal cheerful self."

"It's Grandmother!" I blurted out.

"Grandmother," she repeated my statement. Then looking directly at me, she said, "What do you think of your grandmother, Lexi?" Even before I could answer her, she said, "See I told you your grandmother was harmless."

"Well, Mother, I could have done without the one question she asked me."

"What question was that, Lexi?"

"She asked me more than once, 'Lexi, where did you lose Joseph?' She said it like I lost him on purpose, almost accusing. It was a shock to me that she would ask me such a hurtful question. Mother, why did she ask me that question?"

Mother responded by saying, "My dear Lexi, you will have to ask your grandmother. It is as simple as that."

I responded to this negative answer by saying, "Nothing seems simple when it comes to Grandmother. Mother, I did talk to her about it, but the hurt is still there. I so worry about Grandmother's attitude about my ability of protecting and taking care of Joseph. The real reason I wanted to talk to you, Mother is a question I ask myself over and over. One that is ever present on my mind. So, Mom, here it is: do you think we will ever find Joseph? I mean really find him, am I deceiving myself, it has been such a long time since the accident and his disappearance." I asked her this question as pain gripped my heart.

"Yes, Lexi, if he is to be found, I believe you will find him," she said this as I saw tears run down her cheek. Her words were a small bit of encouragement, but some encouragement is better than none.

*****

As I was making my way upstairs, I passed George and Thomas in the living room with the chessboard sitting on the table between them. Thomas with his head bowed, pipe in his mouth, and George tap, tap, tapping his fingernails on the surface of the table, both appeared to be in deep thought.

The game of chess seemed boring to me, just downright boring. George loved the game, and he took the game very seriously. Now whether Thomas takes the game seriously or not, I don't know; we had never had that conversation. I stood there a few minutes watching them, seemed as if Thomas is winning the game. "Check," I heard the words coming from him, then the word *check* coming from George. To me I thought this was funny, and I laughed out loud. They both looked at me as if to say, *I'm trying to think here.* I smiled and giggled under my breath and continued on my way upstairs.

Saturday morning finally came, and Julia and Craig were on their way here. They were bringing David home where he would meet his great-grandparents for the first time. Mother and I had been watching for them to arrive, and through the picture window, we could see the snow coming down. It seemed to be a wet snow with the snow clinging to the strong, sturdy evergreens. Cardinals with their bright-red color seemed to be enjoying the snowfall as well. With blue jays flying about making their whereabouts known, I always thought of the blue jays as domineering birds or to say boss of the little birds.

As we waited for David, Mother took some time to tell me about her beloved Keokee stories from early spring to winter, like how in early spring the snow lingered on the mountaintops. As the sun came up and made its way through the thick clouds and shined upon the snow-covered mountains, it created a kaleidoscope of brilliant colors—colors from light pink with tones of orange and whites to multi shades of a grayish-blue hue.

Then she told me how spring progressed in a slow manner melting the snow away bringing with it the blossoms of mountain laurel, wild dogwood, and redbuds, which dot the mountain landscape with a pallet of stunning colors. Summer catches hold of spring, which is flourishing with all the new born hatchlings bringing sweet sounds to the mountains—rabbits nestling their young beneath the thickets and underground burrows, a new litter of baby kittens can be found in and around homes and farm yards, calves just days old out in the pasture near their mothers while mothers graze almost silently for the most part on fresh green grass.

In the summer, the mountains are a beautiful green, with many varieties of trees, the foliage varying in colors from dark green to light and all kinds of eye-catching colors in-between. The streams that flow from these mountains are teeming with life—fish, deer, fox, rabbits, and occasionally mink, and you can spot a mother bear with her baby cubs from time to time. Then flowers that just weeks before painted the landscape with beautiful colors, now faded, wilt; and the lush green landscape takes on a new look.

"Lexi, in Keokee, with fall comes the most incredible colors." Mother made a declaration and called my attention to the mountains around Keokee and how fall robs the lush green foliage of its color and replaces it with colors so incredibly beautiful. I noticed as Mom made her way through the seasons her eyes sparkled, and I could hear the excitement in her voice.

"Lexi, the snow this morning makes me think of how special Keokee is in the winter. When a big snow covers the mountains and the tree branches are covered with white powdery snow, and everything is so quiet in the mountains, and if you stand still, close your eyes, and just listen, sometimes all you hear are the snowflakes falling, and with the air so cool and silent, it is almost magical."

Mother stopped her story here after a few minutes of silence. She seemed to be deep in thought. I took over the conversation.

"Keokee sounds wonderful, Mother. I wish I could remember all the seasons as you have described them."

Mother changed the subject a little by saying, "Lexi, we need to take a two-week trip and go to Keokee. It is your home. It is where you grew up, and you need to go back. Yes, back home. That is where you need to go. Going back home to Keokee might activate your memory. I think it would be a good thing for you to consider. In those wonderful mountains of Keokee, I've seen many miracles occur in people's lives."

"Mother, I would love to take a trip and go to Keokee, sounds like a lovely place, a place that I would enjoy. However, Mother, I will give this a lot of thought, but right now, I cannot entertain the idea of going away until I find Joseph."

Mother answered me by saying, "Being there and seeing your hometown could jog your memory. This indeed could be a good thing. Please, Lexi, consider what I am saying, give it a lot of thought," she said as the front door opened and David burst into the room calling in an excited voice.

"Mom, Mom, it's snowing outside." With a great deal of excitement, David took himself strait upstairs to tell his dad about the snow.

I heard George calling from upstairs, "Is that my sister Julia? Please, Julia, don't leave. I need to talk to you. How's the snow, Julia?" George asked as he descended the stairs.

It is true George seemed to always miss his sister's visits, and with his schedule at the hospital, he was in and out of the house more than most.

"Dad, did you see how fast the snow is coming down?" This coming from David with much excitement in his voice as he trailed right behind his dad's footsteps descending the stairs.

"George, the snow is coming down rather fast," Julia answered him as she brushed snow from her coat and hair. George took his sister's coat and scarf and gave her a kiss on the cheek, then stepped forward, and greeted Craig with a friendly handshake. "There, sis, you and Craig sit by the fireplace and warm yourself." As they made themselves comfortable, George said, "I'll make some hot tea as he placed a log in the fireplace."

"Dad, I want to go out and make a snowman. You want to come help?" David said with much excitement in his voice.

"Yes, David, I'll help with the snowman," he answered, "and, David, if it keeps snowing like this, we will be snowed in for a week. David, the snowman will have to wait a little later right now. I want to talk to my sister that I rarely see. She and Craig can't stay but a little while. They'll have to be on their way or they will be snowed in. Then we will all be throwing snowballs together for a while."

David laughed at that and said, "The more the better."

*****

"Is this my grandson?" I heard my grandfather's voice as he walked into the room, then he held out his hand for David to shake. I watched David in his own cool manner take his grandfather's hand in his and gave him a good, strong handshake. I laughed as grandfather scooped up David and threw him over his shoulder.

"Awesome," David kept saying. Awesome!

Then he put David down and said, "George and Lexi, a fine young man you have here." From that moment on, they were the best of friends, and of course, Grandmother was there ready to bestow hugs and kisses on her newly found grandson.

Mother was sitting back watching all the excitement in the room, so I joined her. It was so nice to watch my grandparents with David. They talked for hours, first David with his questions, then my grandparents with theirs. In all the excitement, David forgot about the snow, for the morning anyway.

As the evening progressed after David and George had made a huge snowman on the front lawn, I decided to venture out into the snow. George had gotten a call from the hospital and had to leave. Mother was watching her favorite cooking show, and my grandparents were in the solarium watering some of my seasonal flowers. I asked David to come along with me.

The snow was coming down rather fast when David and I exited the house and made our way outdoors to play in the snow and roam around the lake. I told David if the snow doesn't let up a little, we wouldn't be able to stay out long. As we came upon the lake the snowflakes became larger and larger, and the snow was coming down much faster.

Remembering my conversation with my mother only this morning, I stopped, closed my eyes, and listened to see if I could hear the snowflakes fall; but with the sounds coming from the lake and sounds of birds seeking cover from the snow, and of course, Blondie the neighbor dog, I could not hear the snow fall.

I thought to myself when we find Joseph, we will all take a trip to Keokee. Mother had me so interested in the place I grew up. I must go explore, and definitely, if I were there in the winter, I would listen for the snowflakes to fall.

David and I threw snowballs for a time at each other, then made snow angels and even made a large snowman, David's second snowman of the day. One was on the front lawn, and the second snowman was down by the lake. The wet snow made it easy to make a big snowman. David used twigs from a nearby bush to make the arms. A small pine cone for a nose, stones for eyes and the lips David weaved from pine needles. Big green lips looked funny on a white snowman. We laughed and laughed about that.

As we were walking home from our evening out in the snow, David stopped walking and said, "Mom, I want a horse for Christmas."

"A horse," I said quite shocked, "where would we keep a horse?"

He replied so quickly, which led me to believe he had been thinking about this for some time, "Mom, we can build a barn, and there is plenty of land. We can put up fences to keep him or her in."

David was silent for a while as we walked through the snow back toward the house. Just as we entered the house, David stopped walking and said, "Mom, the other day I told you I wanted only one present for Christmas this year, will it be okay if I change my mind? I know Thanksgiving is coming up, and it's still over a month till Christmas. Please I'll never ask for anything else. Please, Mom! I want this so bad."

I thought to myself he must want a saddle too. "Sure, David, of course you can have more than one present. However, David, before you say anything more about this horse you want so badly, remember I haven't made a promise yet that you can have a horse. So tell me, David, what else would you like for Christmas?"

"Well, Mom, I told you I wanted a horse, but actually..." then he hesitated for what seemed like an awkward space of time, he started to say something else, which was followed by another pause. After he fumbled with his jacket zipper, he started again, "Well, actually, Mom, I want two horses."

"Two horses!" I said almost laughing. "What would you do with two horses, David?"

"Mom, I want a horse for me, and I want a horse for Joseph so we can go riding together. Please, Mom, it would be so much fun."

Tears suddenly sprang to my eyes; I just couldn't hold them back. After a minute or so, I got my voice to utter the words, "That's a good idea, David."

I was glad we were near the entrance of the house. I was crying, and I didn't want David to see me cry, so I removed my boots and ran to my room, not able to hold back the tears.

*****

Thanksgiving was just days away. Mom and Grandmother were already planning the meal—prime rib, ham, and shrimp. Wow, does it get any better?

I heard Grandmother telling Mom, "The turkey shoot is coming up soon, so we won't need to buy a turkey."

Mom said, "Are you so sure George or Thomas are that good of a shot to win the turkey?"

"Well," my grandmother said, "I don't know how good of a shot George is, but I know Thomas, and he will bring that turkey home." I laughed to myself. This was such a funny conversation.

The next few days were wonderful. My mother and grandmother had declared they were going to do all the cooking for the next week. They both loved to cook, and they both were at their best when they were in the kitchen. Both my mother and my dear grandmother were looking forward to this time together. With Mother living in Keokee and Grandmother living in Washington for the last two years, they hadn't had much time together. Mother said cooking was something they always did together when she was growing up in Keokee. My mother added, "And those were wonderful years."

David was bursting at the seams with excitement. He was going on a turkey shoot with George and Thomas tomorrow. That was all he wanted to talk about. All the talk of cooking and Thanksgiving coming up and the turkey shoot tomorrow made for a very animated conversation at the breakfast table.

I had gotten up early the next day, and after a delightful breakfast, I was getting ready to take my four-and-half-hour trip back to the police station where I would once again go in and have a confrontation with the chief of police, once again trying to get in to talk with Charlotte. As usual his answer would probably be no.

It had been an enjoyable drive, and to my surprise, the traffic was light. Upon entering the police station, the first person I encountered was the chief of police, and he shook his head. I got a no even before I asked any questions. He knew why I was there, and he was getting used to my routine. However, I asked him anyway the question he didn't want to hear. "Please, can I have a meeting with Charlotte?"

"No," came his firm answer. With great resistance of being bombarded with any more questions from me, he turned to walk away. Following behind him, I asked if I could look one more time at the items in the box that had been taken from Charlotte's living quarters, items that belong to Joseph and me. He turned to face me and looked at me with an attitude I couldn't quite explain. Disgusted, maybe?

Surprisingly he lead me himself down the long flight of stairs and into a huge room lined with boxes lined up all the way to the ceiling. Wow, so many boxes. Some small, some large. I guess if all these were filled with evidence, then some cases had very small evidence. Large boxes must contain a mountain of evidence.

My box of evidence against Charlotte was here with mine and Joseph's few belongings that she took from the car the day of the accident. Hopefully my journals were here.

Another officer entered the room, and the chief of police gave orders to the details of what I was looking for. The chief of police made his way back upstairs as my box was pulled off a shelf and carted to a room across the hall. This time, to my surprise, everything was dumped on the table. There were no journals there to be found. Heartbroken, I made my way back upstairs, and just as I was making my exit from the police station, the chief of police yelled my name. He told me he had to be in court in fifteen minutes. The courthouse is next door, so that is where I'm headed. "Walk with me," was his invitation, "and we will talk."

The chief of police started the conversation, then he hesitated. He was silent for a few minutes, then gradually began talking again. "This morning I talked to Charlotte, and she told me she would like to talk with you. She said she will not have a conversation with you until after Christmas."

"That is a little over a month," I said. "And are you sure she won't talk to me sooner?"

"That is the best I can do," he assured me. "Unless your lawyer objects or her lawyer objects, then after Christmas, you should be able to meet with Charlotte."

Before he left to go into the courthouse, he warned me, "Most of the time, these meetings go nowhere. Don't get your hopes up.

People like the one you're dealing with prefer to squash their victims instead of giving them any real information that they could use. Just you remember, don't put too much importance on this meeting."

As he turned to walk away, I told him, "I will try not to, and I'll see you after Christmas." He nodded his head and kept walking.

As I made my way back to my car, I felt there was some hope here. I thought to myself there must be a reason she has agreed to talk with me. Just maybe it will be the whereabouts of Joseph.

My drive back home this evening would be more enjoyable than all the previous trips to the police station. I'll just think positively that she will tell me what I need to know. "Just think positively," I kept telling myself.

It was late evening when I finally arrived back home. There was still lots of snow on the roads, which made the drive longer than I had expected. Mother made her way downstairs when I entered the house. Dinner had been over and forgotten hours ago. She made her way to the kitchen to warm my food and see how my day had gone. Mother was almost as surprised as I when she found out Charlotte was going to meet with me after Christmas. She was so excited with the anticipation of what might become of this meeting.

It was late, and David was asleep when I went in to check on him. George was still on call at the hospital, and my grandmother was upstairs planning a wedding, I was informed by Mother.

"What wedding? Whose wedding?" I wanted to know.

Mother didn't tell me who; she just kept fumbling with the dishes in the sink. "Grandmother is the one making the plans, Lexi my dear, I am sure you will get an invitation." I thought to myself as I went to my room to retire for the night, must be wedding plans for one of my cousins that lived in Keokee. Grandmother was good at planning things, and I was sure it would keep her busy.

*****

David was up and out the door early the next morning before the sun came up, all dressed in camouflage, right down to his socks. You would think he was going on a big hunting expedition. It was only a turkey shoot, but it was a big deal to him. Yesterday David and his grandfather had spent time at the Bass Pro Shop looking for the outfit he was wearing. Grandmother had been telling him all morning how handsome he looked in his camouflage threads. David's face turned a little red each time she made this statement; however, he seemed to be enjoying the attention.

When my grandmother left the room, David whispered to me, "Mom, what are threads?"

"Threads is just another name for clothes," I whispered back to him.

David laughed. He was at the age that he laughed at almost everything. "Threads," he kept repeating. "Threads!"

I overheard David talking with my grandfather just before they left for the turkey shoot. He wanted to know if my grandfather had ever been to a turkey shoot. David's second questions was, "Do they shoot real live turkeys?"

Grandfather took his time before he answered, "David, I have been to many turkey shoots. The first one I went to was before I met Mary. It was just Fred, my twin brother, and me. Boy, did we have fun. Everything we did each always tried to outdo the other. We were both pretty good shots with a .22, and we were always in some type of competition. Fred was really the best at hitting the target. He knew this and so did I. We brought a turkey home that year, and to this day, I said that was the best turkey my mother ever cooked. Now to your second question, do we shoot a real turkey? No, David, frozen turkeys are given away as a prize when the paper turkey or other target is hit in the right spot."

I heard David say, "I sure am glad it is a paper turkey and not a real live turkey we will be shooting. Because turkeys have lots of feathers. I was thinking I would feel really sorry for that turkey, and there would probably be feathers flying everywhere."

I laughed to myself; I thought what a strange statement. Their conversation ended just as George pulled the car around front to pick them up. Then they were off to the turkey shoot. I thought to myself I know what this evening and tomorrow's conversation will be about.

Then I laughed. If they hit the target and win the prize, there will be another meat added to Grandmother's Thanksgiving menu.

I was right. The next morning, David was up early, and all he wanted to talk about was that darn turkey shoot. After breakfast and a game of chess with his grandfather, David made his way to the kitchen then straight to the cookie jar, where my mother and I were making out our grocery list.

David reminded Mother and I we didn't have to buy a turkey since they had brought two home from the turkey shoot. "Two turkeys. How did that happen, David?"

"David," my grandmother said as she put the lid back on the cookie jar. "Since you are here and before I forget, I need you to do something for me."

"David, tomorrow is Thanksgiving," Grandmother said as she handed him a pen and notebook. "David, how about making me a list of ten things you are most thankful for."

Mother chimed in about that time by saying, "I had to make those lists also as a child. It's a tradition in our family, and, David, your mom did the same as a child. Lexi always did this with great enthusiasm, and her list of ten items sometimes took up pages. I always loved reading them. Some were even funny but heartfelt. I remember one time when she was about your age, she said she was thankful for Pugie who lived in our barn. She went on to write about how cute Pugie was. Earlier in the day, she had found a blue satin scarf and made for Pugie a ribbon to wear around her neck. Then she went on to say Pugie couldn't talk, but she enjoyed her company anyway."

"Naturally, I became curious, very curious. So when Lexi was at school the next day, I went to the barn to explore. Upon entering the barn, I heard a lot of commotion, a scratching sound, which took me a few minutes to locate where all the noise was coming from. To my surprise, Lexi had taken an oversized dollhouse that she had quit playing with a couple of years back and turned it into a house for a rat. Not a cute little rat but a big ugly rat. She had secured the windows and doors with plexiglass and strong wire to keep the rat from escaping. To me, that was an ugly rat staring back at me with those big ugly beady eyes."

Mother laughed as she told the story. Then she said, "The day I found Pugie, that ugly rat, I said to myself, 'I know how this is going to end.' I with great caution, bent over very slowly, opened the door to the dollhouse, and ran!"

"Mother!" I said, "you did what?" Then I began to laugh. Before all was said and done, we were all laughing.

"Grandmother, what happened next? Where did the rat go?" David asked his grandmother with great curiosity.

"David, in all sincerity, I don't know. I never looked back. All I could think of at the moment were those big ugly beady eyes, and those sharp little teeth as I opened the door and planted my feet on safe ground."

Mother asked me if I remembered anything about Pugie. No, I told her, but it was an interesting story all the same. Truly I had no recollection of this lovely event. Another event erased from my memory; however, I can visualize this little bit of excitement I must have had as a child.

David was excited and wanted to know if my mother had any more great stories like the one she just told. Mother told David she had plenty stories, and his great-grandmother had even more. "But now I want you, David, to go and write down ten things you are most thankful for. Keep in mind this is Thanksgiving when we all should reflect on things we are truly thankful for."

My grandmother spoke up and said, "David, we will expect your list by dinnertime, so move along and get your mind to working on this list."

I thought, Thanksgiving, and we have my grandparents and Mom to share the holidays with this year. Such a big change from our previous years when it was the three of us, David, myself and George. And for this I am so very thankful.

Grandmother's visit was a lot better than I had anticipated. She was energetic and caring as well as a lot of fun. David loved her too that made it all the better.

Thanksgiving Day went by fast, with all the food preparation, eating and laughing around the table. Much of the conversation was about the turkey shoot and revisiting the story about Pugie, which David begged my mom to tell again and again. Before the sun had set that day, we all, including my mom, dressed in our warmest clothes and went out to play in the snow. Except for Grandmother, she sat on the porch wrapped in heavy winter clothes, sipping hot chocolate while laughing at the rest of us who were slipping and sliding and getting pounded with snowballs. What fun we had, laughing at one another as the snow continued to fall.

I thought Thomas had the most fun. He was so happy, so very happy. I know this happiness was mostly contributed to finding Mary, the love of his life as he called her, finding her again and falling in love the second time.

I ran this thought through my mind again. I started this search to find Joseph; however, he was still missing. But now because of this search, I had found Lucy my mother, Thomas my grandfather, and Mary my dear grandmother.

*****

Now that Thanksgiving was over, Grandmother and Thomas left early the next day in the wee hours of the morning. They were heading back home, to the same home that was once filled with joy, love, and laughter. Now it was such a pleasure to witness the warmth, love, and happiness that beams from both of them. I am sure all those lost years while they were apart from each other were very lonely years for the both of them. Now they are living a true dream, a dream of finally being together again.

Before they left, I had promised my grandparents I would drive over to see them sometime this week. I had already ask them if I could do an in-depth investigation of their house to see if I could find my missing journals. Charlotte might have hidden them in other parts of the house, somewhere beyond the rooms she had rented from Thomas. I hoped against hope that Charlotte had hidden the journals somewhere other than the rooms that the police had already searched. However, I would search the ones the police have already dug through. Just maybe they had missed something. I couldn't let myself entertain the idea that she could have possibly destroyed them.

The police had searched the area of the house Charlotte rented from Thomas, which consisted of two rooms, a full bath, and a small room she used only for storage. Now it was my turn to search. I was sure I was not allowed to, but this I will ignore. Hopefully they hadn't padlocked the rooms. I was going in there and search no matter what!

The next day, I talked to George about the horses David wanted for Christmas, two I informed him! Yes, he wanted two.

George said, "It is a good subject for conversation."

Having grown up with horses, George knew all too well how much work was involved in feeding and taking care of horses. After walking around the room a couple of times, George said, "I'll think about it. I am sure David would love having a horse as much as I did when I was a young boy. With only about a month until Christmas, finding the right horses will be no easy task. I'll make some calls. I won't rush this, Carol. I do, however, know some people that have horses that I can talk to.

"Probably this is how all this horse business will work out. Give David six months or so of riding lessons for Christmas, and if we decide yes on getting David a horse, we can go ahead and choose a saddle." George looked at me a few minutes as if studying my face, then he said, "Make that two saddles. However, he will have to wait on the horses until all the riding lessons are over.

"In the meantime, we will look at having a barn put up and, of course, a fence. Glad we have some extra land for this use." George paused then continued, "If we choose this route, because, Carol, we still have to decide if this is what we want to do. Furthermore, David might decide he doesn't like horses as much as he thought he would. So riding lessons first. I think he will be fully satisfied with that for the time being." Then George asked me, "Carol, what do you think about what I just told you? About my thoughts on the horse business."

"George, I think it's perfect. You have a way of making everything seem less complicated." On that note, Mother walked into the kitchen and announced dinner was ready.

When dinner was finally over, and as I filled the dishwasher, I kept thinking about the trip I would be taking tomorrow morning. Heading back to my grandparents' house, back to search through possessions this time that didn't belong to me, thinking maybe I will find something the police hadn't found.

I was so excited; sleep didn't come easy during the night. I just couldn't get this trip off my mind. My mind kept racing with so many thoughts, and when I finally slept, Pugie that ugly rat Mother had told us about kept showing up in my dreams.

*****

Needless to say, I was up early the next morning because I wanted to get an early start, and half an hour later, I was speeding down the road excited about what I might find.

The weather was rather chilly. Snow still lay on the ground from the last snow, and by the looks of the sky, there may be more snow coming our way. Making a stop at the *Gazette* to say hello to Noel and to see if she had any more news for me was my first stop of the day. Usually I talked to her every day, but with the holiday season upon us, it had been a little harder to find the time to call.

Main Street was really busy, especially for this time of morning. A Christmas bazaar was being setup, and crowds were already gathering. In front of all the buildings located on Main Street were huge red striped decorative candy canes, and all the side streets were lit up with colorful lights, which were also draped with holly and stunning red and gold ribbons.

I made my way through the crowd and finally to the *Gazette* where Noel was helping to hang a Christmas wreath. She greeted me with her cheerful, almost contagious smile.

When Noel was finished hanging the wreath, she poured me a cup of coffee. Seating herself, she looked straight at me and said she did have some more information she had gathered just last night.

"Sit down, drink your coffee, then we will talk," she said. She politely waited till I had drunk all my coffee. "Carol, I went to see Charlotte yesterday. This was at her request. I was very surprised that she wanted to talk to me. I went immediately hoping she wouldn't change her mind. She told me she was going to have a meeting with you after Christmas. She kept saying Joseph was gone. Charlie was gone. She seemed to be very frail and almost in her own world. Carol, having met Charlotte only once before, it was hard to judge her health. However, my guess is her health is not very good by the looks of her. It seems jail doesn't agree with this mischievous kidnapper."

I thought to myself *mischievous kidnapper* was a mild description of this devious, horrible nightmare of a woman, who has been hiding my son for such a long time.

My heart almost failed me as I sat there. I could not wish her ill or bad health; she was the only person who knew the whereabouts of my son. I was at a loss for words, so I said nothing. Noel kept talking. I kept up with her part of conversation, but still I was at a loss for words. I kept thinking to myself I must stay strong. I must continue on until I find Joseph.

I sat there until I had my emotions under control, said my goodbyes, then I made my way to the car, where I cried for a better part of an hour. After saying a prayer, and with much hesitation, I got back on the road making my way to the house Charlotte had lived in while deceiving so many.

Grandmother met me at the door. "Come with me, Lexi," she said, pointing to the stairway as she hurried me along. "Lexi, I took care of those locks for you."

"You did what?" I asked her, but she didn't bother to answer.

She just said, "Go! Go!" and kept pointing toward the stairs.

As I entered the door to Charlotte's living quarters, I saw lying on the floor the locks, and yes, they had been cut. I didn't asked, and she didn't tell, but I smiled inside at the thought of what she had done. By the looks of things, she had probably already been searching through Charlotte's belongings, searching for evidence as she called it.

"Where is Thomas?" I asked.

"He had a doctor's appointment, so I took advantage of his being absent, and, Lexi, I thought I would get a head start, and just maybe I would find those journals before you arrived."

"Did you have any luck?" I asked.

"No," she answered, "but I did find something else." Walking over to a small table in the corner of the room, she picked up a metal box and handed it to me.

"What is this?" I asked as I took the box from her hands. "Where did you find it?"

"Well, as for where I found it, it was hidden in a concealed cavity in the wall. I would have never known it was there, except Thomas told me when this house was built in every room, they had built a hidden space somewhere in the wall, and believe me, it was hidden well. Now whether this box has anything to do with Charlotte or Joseph will be determined by what is inside this locked box. As soon as Thomas gets back, we will ask him if he knows what is inside or if he knows the whereabouts of the key."

I picked up the metal box and looked it over. I wondered if Charlotte had hidden her dirty deeds inside this box, then Grandmother took the box from my hands and set it down.

My search started where she set the box and continued till the whole room had been carefully searched. Nothing there to help me in my quest to find answers, so on to the next room. This room was set up in an awkward manner, a bedroom nonetheless. At the foot of the bed was an old wooden trunk. I stopped where I stood, closed my eyes, and said to myself, *Just take a deep breath and just breathe.*

I stooped down and opened up the trunk. It was empty; however, this must be the dark, musty trunk that Joseph's pictures lay hidden inside for such a long time. What a strange feeling I had about this trunk. It had housed my son's baby items and preserved them, and yet this trunk had held secrets—yes, secrets of Joseph's past. As I continued my search, I began to lose hope.

The storage room began to show some promise. I found one journal then another hidden beneath some boards in the floor. The boards weren't even loose; however, they looked just the slightest bit different from the other boards. I was amazed that I even noticed or should I say spotted this difference. The police had missed this, and I could understand why there was just the slightest color discrepancy.

Grandmother was there by my side through all the digging through boxes, shoes, and clothes; and upon finding the journals, we became ecstatic. We both cried a little and then cried with joy.

I took the journals in my arms and held them close. Somehow they made me feel closer to Joseph. I sat down right where I stood, with great excitement and an overwhelming anticipation of what I might find written inside, I opened the first journal.

Here I was again feeling as if I was invading someone else's life. I had to keep reminding myself this was my life. There were so many entries about Joseph, and I read each one as if I was living it for the first time. I had written about Matthew. Wow, the love we had for each other. Many entries were about the company and the employees who worked for me. Entries of Bonita and Norma Jean filled a great many of these pages, all the good times we had together. I laughed through most of those entries.

A conversation I had recorded between myself and the vice president stood out as odd. I kept reading. It was a conversation about Matthew and how one of the coworkers was making trouble for him. We had been working hard trying to figuring out which coworker or coworkers were involved.

In an entry a week later, the coworker was named. The entry read, "Matthew just told me today someone seems to be sabotaging his work. 'This is serious,' he said. The coworker was Charlotte!"

The entry the next day said: "It seems that Charlotte doesn't like you either, and I don't know why. Lexi, we have to get to the core of this matter, and again I say, Lexi, this is serious."

The word *serious* somehow startled me.

I immediately got on the phone and called Samuel. His secretary informed me he was not available, but she would get the message to him, and he should be calling me back very soon.

The call took longer than I preferred; however I caught him before he left for a two-week vacation. "Samuel, I need to know again exactly what job Charlotte performed at my company in the months before my disappearance."

"She worked mainly in construction. She had a lot of leeway as far as the company goes. She made some decisions about the construction that went on here and again all the decisions that were made by her had to be approved by me. Then, Lexi, you had the last say." Samuel brought me up-to-date on this information.

"Interesting," I told him, "but I still have a few more questions."

"Sure," he said.

"Samuel, did Charlotte have any family that lived in the area or anywhere else that you know about?"

"Yes, Lexi, I overheard a conversation she had, didn't mean to hear the conversation, but sometimes it just happens. She was talking on the phone, and she was telling her brother to apply for a job here, which was fine, until I heard her say, 'don't tell them you have been in any kind of trouble.' She informed him she would let the hiring department know he was coming to apply for a job. I felt bad, but after hearing that conversation, I had to do my job. Therefore, I could not allow him to be hired into this company."

"Do you remember or can you pull the files and see if Charlotte made any attempts to bring another architect in other than Matthew?"

"Lexi, it may take me a day or so, but I will get that information for you," then he added, "if I remember correctly, it seems like she did try to hire another architect. I could be wrong. I'll have to check this out. I'll get this information to you as soon as possible. I will call you in a day or two, when I get to my vacation destination." Then the phone went dead.

With this information running through my mind, I took the journals downstairs. I had been so interested in what was in these journals, I hadn't missed my grandmother.

Where did she go? I wondered.

*****

Entering the kitchen, I could see Thomas was back from his doctor's appointment, and my grandmother was removing a fresh loaf of bread from the oven, which smelled heavenly.

Thomas greeted me with a kiss and asked me if I had found what I was looking for. "Yes," I answered while surveying the freshly baked bread and moving over to where Grandmother was slicing the bread.

"Thomas, here are two of my journals. I still haven't found what I am looking for, and I am half through the first journal. I came down to look for Grandmother," I said while taking a piece of bread Grandmother had buttered before handing it to me.

Grandmother said, "Lexi, when I saw you found some of your journals, I decided to come on downstairs and let you go through these personal writings on your own." Giving Grandmother a kiss on the forehead, I went to find a comfortable seat.

I made my way to the bedroom I would be sleeping in while staying a couple nights with my grandparents. I fluffed up some pillows and made myself comfortable. I opened the journals, found my place, and continued my search.

I was awakened the next morning with a start. I had fallen asleep while reading my journals, and it was morning. Looking at the clock, I realized it was late. I was almost always an early riser; this was very unusual for me to sleep late. However, it was a good sleep, and I was sure it was much needed. I was just about to drift back off to sleep when the telephone rang. It was Samuel with the information I had ask for just yesterday.

"Lexi," he said as I answered the phone. "Yes, to your question yesterday. According to my secretary, after looking through the files, Charlotte did try to hire another architect."

"Was another architect hired?" I asked as I managed to pull myself out of bed and annoyed at myself for oversleeping.

"No, Lexi, at that time, no other architect was hired. However, after your husband's death, his job would have had to be filled."

"Who took that position?"

"One of Matthew's top employees was hired in his place. Rob is a very nice guy. He still works for us from time to time. Matthew trusted him explicitly. Matthew would have approved. Lexi, may I ask why you need this information?" Samuel asked candidly.

"Samuel, no precise reason, just trying to figure some things out." Then I wished him a nice vacation, and we said our goodbyes.

I was thinking to myself of how Samuel and Norma Jean had described our lives together in Keokee. We three had been friends while we were growing up in Keokee. I so wish I could remember these friendships back then, but like so many other memories, they were just not there.

Now back to the reading of these two journals. Let me find what I am looking for within these written memoirs of my past. As I was reading, I kept asking why I didn't write more. I need more clues to my past. By the time I had finished reading the last entry, I had become more troubled; however, I tried to keep myself motivated. I told myself I had to stay strong and focused.

At this point I decided, to search the whole house, so my search continued. There were about three more rooms on this floor, then the attic. However, I stopped in my tracks as I spotted the box my grandmother had found hidden in the wall.

I had almost forgotten about the box. I had been so busy searching for and scanning the journals for clues. I grabbed the box and made my way downstairs looking for my grandfather. I found him in the room he had built for my grandmother. He smiled at me when he saw me entering the room. While walking toward me he asked, "What are you carrying in your arms, Carol?"

Holding the box up higher so he could get a better look at what I was carrying, I told him Grandmother had found this box hidden in the wall and given it to me. "So, Thomas, do you know what's locked away hidden inside this box?" Thomas lifted it from my hands and set it on the table next to where we were standing. He took out the handkerchief from his pocket and wiped the dust away.

Then looking straight at me he said, "No, Carol, I have to say I have no idea what's inside that box. I haven't seen or held it in years. However, Charlotte did know about the secret place in the wall. She found it years ago. As far as I know, this box is the only one she knew about."

My next question to Thomas was, "It's locked. Do you know where the key is?"

"I knew where it used to be." Then he reached for the box, turning it over and removed one screw, and the key fell out of a little secret compartment. *Oh how cool*, I thought.

Thomas handed me the key and said, "Carol, it is your search. Now you open it."

Before I turned the key, I asked, "Thomas, do you think Charlotte hid anything in this box?"

To which he said, "Carol, you are about to find out."

The key worked the first time, and upon opening the lid, I saw another one of my journals. Lying in the bottom of the box was a chain attached to a key. I took the key and draped it around my neck. I thought to myself I don't want to lose this key; it could be very important in my quest to finding what I am looking for.

I was excited once again. I thought to myself if she hid this so good, there must be some important information written within these pages. Thomas left me to my task as I opened the journal and started scanning the words I had written so long ago, and important information began to spill from the pages.

One of the first entries I came across in my journal was the conversation that Norma Jean had first mentioned prior to my husband's death. Norma Jean had no details of this conversation other than clueing me in that there was a problem. Bonita knew the story, which she told me about, and now here it was written in my own handwriting written over ten years ago.

I read from my journal.

> Today, I was given some disturbing information from my husband's secretary. She told me someone had broken into Matthew's office and had stolen some important documents and had reprocessed them, which made it look like Matthew had not gone by the codes that were set by the state of California.

A later entry the same day, written by me, said, "I know my husband would never have built or designed anything without going by the codes just as they were written. Never."

Three days later, another entry written by me. "Charlotte is the one that had caused my husband so much grief before his death."

I was going through the journal rather fast hoping to find some of the last details of our lives before the accident. When I came across this entry: "Met with Charlotte today, in her office, I went there to terminate her position at my company."

An entry later that day, read, "I left Charlotte's office that same day without terminating her position."

What? I did what? Why would I have not fired her? I wondered. No more information why had I changed my mind and not fired her. Over and over, I asked myself this question. I read with much inquisitiveness but found no more on the subject.

"Why hadn't I written more? Why?"

I was frustrated with myself, and I needed more to go on. I continued searching and reading with no more clues on the subject of my firing Charlotte. They were mostly just inserts about the business in general: "Two new large vases I had designed for a company in Sweden, they were to be used as showstoppers at a house being built for some dignitary."

Entries of small talk seemed to dominate the pages until I got to the last page, and at the very top of the page it read, "Flying out tomorrow. Going to find my grandfather. Can't get Grandmother on the phone. Mother is somewhere in Paris. This will be Joseph's first plane flight. I am so excited!"

That was it; there were no more words written inside that journal. I held my breath. I need more I thought to myself. I sat there just pondering on all that I had just read. As I closed the journal, I noticed written on the back cover as almost an afterthought was scribbled in red ink. "Charlotte gave a two-week notice today. She said she is moving to Washington State. She has found a job there."

There was also a date and time it was written. It appeared to be five days after the day I had gone to her office to fire her. This was good a little more information, but how strange, I thought. There were two cards secured inside the pages of the journal. I had taken them out and laid them on the table before opening and reading the journal. I had almost forgotten they were lying there. One was from Charlotte, the other one from my grandmother.

With a big sigh of relief, I reached for the two cards. I thought these cards could be very important. I opened Charlotte's first. "Lexi, you have a grandfather who needs you, you must go immediately." Thomas' name and address were printed in big bold letters. Signed by Charlotte and nothing more.

There written in the letter in front of me was Thomas' address. I recognized it immediately. The writing appeared to be the same handwriting that was on the envelope that had been sent to Thomas all those years long ago. I stopped for a minute thinking this journal was with me the day of my accident. By the postmark on the envelope, it had been sent two weeks after Charlotte had given her notice of terminating her job. So she had been gone two weeks, give or take a few days, to allow for the postal system to perform their job of delivering this letter.

I was so thankful for this one journal that has shed a lot of light on the shadows of my past. Now I know Joseph and I took a plane flight to find my grandfather, and no one knew except Charlotte, or so it seemed. I began to question myself, where did I get the car that had almost claimed my life? Not able to answer that question. I thought to myself just another question I did not have the answer to. However, some of the questions answered here were answers to questions I had been looking for, for a long time. I was sure I will never find all the answers to this complicated past life of mine. However, the answers that help me find Joseph were the only ones I really cared about.

Charlotte must have known I was trying to find out more about my mother's family. Or was I? There was no evidence of that. What was her reasoning for this interference in my life? This was mind-boggling to me. Charlotte helped me find my grandfather. Why was my question? This all seemed very strange to me.

I opened the card that was from my grandmother. It was a beautiful birthday card, and the salutation seemed to be written with such love from a grandmother to her granddaughter. The card was sent the first day of June, so therefore, I had learned one more thing about myself. My birthday must be the first part of June. I thought to myself, I don't know the date, but I do know the month. This was very much pleasing to me. I must remember to ask Grandmother the date.

*****

From Thanksgiving until Christmas, time seemed to pass very fast. Mother wanted to be in charge of decorating the house for the Christmas holiday, and she kept herself busy doing just that. David by her side when not at school or out playing cops and robbers, or let's not forget playing in a tree house with Artie and Michael. Before all the Christmas decoration were done, the tree house sparkled gleefully with lights of green, red, and blue. There was even a Charlie Brown–type Christmas tree attached to the top of that tree house.

I was a little surprised when my grandmother called and asked me to be her bridesmaid at her wedding. I knew she had been planning a wedding, but I had no idea it was a wedding for her and Thomas. She informed me renewing their wedding vows was something they both wanted to do. Oh, I was so very happy for them.

It was to be a small wedding, and no more than thirty invitations had been sent out. The wedding was to take place the twenty-third day of December. Poinsettia and spider mums were her choice of flowers for this Christmas wedding. The wedding would take place in their home, in the room that Thomas had built just for Mary—this beautiful room built with so much love for her and hope that one day she would return, making this room the perfect place to renew their wedding vows and their commitment of love for each other.

Mother was to be her maid of honor and was already planning on this big event that would take place soon. Craig and Julia would sing the wedding song with their voices blended so beautifully together. Tim was to be Thomas' best man. I was really excited when I heard this. Couldn't wait to meet Tim, Grandmother's little brother—Grandmother's mischievous little brother as she often refers to him. I was sure he wasn't little anymore, but I've only known him from the stories in which both my grandparents had told me. Couldn't wait to meet him. In my opinion, this wedding was going to be so much fun.

Thomas and Mary will spend Christmas Eve and Christmas at our house with family. The day after Christmas, they will fly to Florida where they will leave on a slow-moving boat to the Caribbean on their second honeymoon. To me they both seem much younger than they actually were. Both were very active, outgoing, and so much fun to be around. Now that I had gotten over this hurtful feeling Grandmother imposed on me, I do find her wonderful, just as Mother said she would be.

Christmas dinner was to be at our house with Mother and I planning the food and all the Christmas festivities. Mother had been making candy for what seemed like weeks now. "Don't know what we are going to do with all that candy," I told her one morning as I scrambled eggs and burned the toast.

"Now, my dear Lexi, some candies will be served at the reception after the wedding. Other plans for these delectable, assorted candies are to be sent in a nice, colorful Christmas tin home with Artie and Michael. Of course, a few tins of candy will be delivered to our closest neighbors.

While mother was getting her plans all squared away, I was busy with my own planning our Christmas menu. Of course, we would have all the traditional foods. I always tried to find one unique recipe that I had never served before and introduced it to the family on Christmas Day. Most of these dishes had turned out pretty good through the years. However, there was always one.

Most of the Christmas decorations had been taken care of except the Christmas tree. Mother and I still had lots of shopping to do. It was such a busy time of year, especially with the wedding so close to Christmas. We found ourselves racing against time to get everything done. However, with all "the racing," we made sure we enjoyed ourselves. We planned our days well and took out time for ourselves. We worked at keeping it a merry Christmas. Christmas shopping seemed to be an ongoing event.

David loved going to see the live nativity scene. We usually go and view this two or three times the week before Christmas. David loved being there and loved hearing the story of the birth of Christ that went along with the nativity. Such a wonderful story the birth of Christ.

George, David, and I usually take a horse and buggy ride through town at night and with the streets lighted with lights and decorations; it was so lovely. I really enjoyed this, and I liked it even better if there was snow, the white snow seemed to make the whole experience so peaceful. This and the nativity scene were two occasions we partake together every year and try never to miss. I spent the rest of the morning with George who was so caring and always ready to come to my rescue. He made everything seem all right. I rested.

*****

It was only five days until Christmas, and everything including the wedding was coming together nicely. Mary and Thomas came to spend a few days at our house before the wedding.

Finally it was time to get the Christmas tree. This year, we were getting a live tree, and with all the woods near and around the lake, there were plenty of beautiful live trees to choose from.

George, David, Grandfather, and, of course, Blondie the neighbors' blond lab, took off together down by the woods near the lake to cut our Christmas tree. They were so enjoying one another's company, talking, laughing, just goofing off as they strolled off toward the lake. Mother called it bonding. Grandmother said, "I will call it when I see them dragging that Christmas tree up from the lake."

Mom and I looked at each other and she said, "What a strange statement."

Grandmother said, "I heard that," and we all laughed.

I brought all the Christmas tree decorations down from the attic and untangled the lights in preparations for decorating the

Christmas tree. We had everything ready but the tree. Mother asked, "What could be taking them so long?"

Grandmother said, "Yes, and while they have been gone, I have wrapped most of my Christmas presents. However, I am glad that fun job is done."

"Where are they? They have had plenty of time to cut a Christmas tree and get it back here," Mother said in a very soft voice.

I looked at the clock and thought, *How long does it take to pick and cut a Christmas tree?* Thirty more minutes went by, and I really started to get worried, and furthermore, it was getting dark outside.

I slipped a coat around my shoulders and walked to the front porch with Mother trailing right behind me. I listened to see if I could hear or see any sign of them or the tree.

To my relief, I could hear David laughing and talking and the dog barking. Then I could see them off in the distance. Grandmother joined us on the porch, and her first question was, "Well, where is the Christmas tree?" I took a closer look, and there was no tree.

"Wonder what happened?" I said mostly to myself.

Then I smelled something. It seemed the closer they got, the stronger the smell. Then I heard Mother say, "That smells like a skunk."

I heard myself say, "Oh no, they have been sprayed by a skunk." Then I snickered out loud.

Grandmother thought it was so funny at first till she saw the dog running straight toward us. Then her voice got somewhat louder as she said, "Hurry, get into the house." However, the dog got to us first before we could get across the extended porch and back into the house. Wouldn't you know Blondie was a sweet, loveable, friendly lab, so the first thing she did was run straight to us. Before it was all over, we were all wearing the pungent fragrance of that skunk.

Well, that ended our evening of decorating the Christmas tree. Instead of gathering around and decorating the Christmas tree, we gathered around the kitchen mixing hydrogen peroxide, baking soda, liquid dish soap, and sure enough, all the canned tomatoes we had in the house doing our best to get rid of that horrid pungent smell. Needless to say, all of our efforts paid off. Well, almost paid off. The next two or three days, every now and then, we would get a slight hint of that horrible, overpowering smell.

The next day we were up early with the whole family together and bacon and eggs frying in the kitchen. There was no school, and George was off work for the next two days.

David was also up early in the kitchen with Mother and Grandmother. They were laughing and talking as I entered the cooking area. David liked to help in the kitchen, especially with Mom and Grandmother. He liked helping with the food as well as all the attention he was getting.

As I poured myself a cup of fresh-brewed coffee, David quickly gave me a weather forecast for the day. He informed me he had already been outdoors to measure how deep the snow had piled up during the night. "Mom, guess?"

"Guess what?" I asked David in a teasing way.

"Guess how many inches it snowed last night?"

"Can I look outside first?"

"No," came his answer.

"I'll guess ten inches."

He laughed then said, "No, guess again."

My second guess was, "Nine inches."

"I am glad it is not that deep," George said as he entered the kitchen, making his way to the coffee pot.

"Mom, do you give up?" asked David once again.

"Yes, I give up. How deep did it snow last night?"

"Six inches! It is deep enough for me to go sleigh riding, and I was thinking about trying to build an igloo. Guess what else, Mom?" Before he gave me time to answer, he blurted out, "It is not so deep that we can't get a Christmas tree today."

"Oh, so you want to try that tree thing again so soon?" I asked as I looked at George as he sat there sipping his coffee.

I heard Grandmother call from the dining room, "Watch out for a little black animal with a white strip down his back." Then I heard Mom and Grandmother giggling off in a distance.

"Mom, okay, it snowed six inches, and the guys have already talked about it. After the snow plow does its job in clearing the roads, we are going to go pick out and buy a Christmas tree," David said as we made our way to the dining room where breakfast was being served.

After a wonderful breakfast cooked by the two new chefs of the house, David did just as he had planned. His friends, Artie and Michael, came by the house pulling their sleds. Artie said in his playful attitude, "We are headed for the biggest hill/slope down by the schoolyard."

I asked, "Isn't that quite a long walk?"

"Yes, Mrs. Wainwright, but this is going to be so much fun." With that said, they were out the door.

Mother joined me down in the solarium. She loved flowers almost as much as I did, and with it being close to Christmas, my Christmas cactuses were in full bloom, and my poinsettias were in deep-red color. Growing flowers was one of the things I loved to do. I babied my indoor flowers and was always happy when they started showing their beautiful colors.

Beside the ones in the solarium, George knew how much I loved flowers, so every Christmas since we had been married, he had brought in at least a dozen poinsettias, placing them in different areas all through the house. Along with these, he would bring in a few Christmas cactuses. With all the bright-red plants all through the house, it was such a beautiful sight. It gave it a feeling of Christmas.

It was nearly noon when the boys came pulling behind them their sleds. They were all cheery and red-faced. These were active growing boys, so they were hungry. Mom and my grandmother came to their rescue. To start with, my mother served hot chocolate. It seemed like hot chocolate was always the perfect drink on a beautiful snow-white day.

As soon as lunch was over, they worked on making an igloo, and actually it turned our pretty nice, small but well done. It even consisted of an open window and a makeshift door. Pretty cool, I thought. I was so happy to see that this week was going better than I had anticipated.

Dinner consisted of all kinds of appetizing, mouthwatering foods Mother and Grandmother had put together and David with stories of all the excitement of the day's adventures being told with much enthusiasm made for a very enjoyable and cheerful dinner time.

The men had planned another adventure for the evening, which consisted of finding a Christmas tree, but David had fallen asleep on the couch, tuckered out after a hot meal, and from all the entertainment created by the snow activities. So the Christmas tree hunt would have to wait for another day.

I was suddenly awakened early the next morning with a lot of commotion downstairs. I could hear George calling my name: Carol. Then I heard David's voice calling, "Mom, Mom, come see the Christmas tree," as he ran up the stairs two at a time. I realized they had just came home from some early morning expedition.

Looking down from the top of the stairs, I could see a beautiful live eight-foot Christmas tree waiting to be decorated.

I lingered upstairs for a while thinking just what does Christmas mean to me. After pondering on this for some time, I got myself ready for the day and went downstairs where the smell of coffee, bacon, and eggs let me know Grandmother and Mother were in the kitchen.

After breakfast was over and all the dishes had been cleaned and put away properly, the decorating of the Christmas tree started. After all the lights were placed on the tree, we started hanging the ornaments. Thomas brought into the living room a small box, a box he had brought with him from his house, set it on the table near the Christmas tree, and proceeded to open it. The box was filled with Christmas ornaments, all delicately wrapped. He turned to my mother and me he asked if he may place these ornaments on our Christmas tree. He said these were very special ornaments, and with each one, he had a little story to go along with it. The first ornament he unwrapped was one he had made for Mary out of stained glass all those years long ago when they were first married. This being their very first Christmas together. The ornament was made of the colors of green jade and a beautiful aqua blue. He described the colors of choice for this ornament, which were the colors Mary was wearing the first time he saw her. As he placed it on the tree, I thought to myself, *This is the most beautiful ornament I have ever seen.*

All were done in a different styles—one for his brother Fred, one for his loving mother, and, of course, one for his dear father, all very beautifully done. He elaborated on each one by giving a theme or better yet a story for each of the ornaments he placed on the tree.

Then he carefully took one jeweled ornament out of the box for my mother. Again beautiful. As he gave it to my mother, he said he had made all these ornaments the first year he and Mary were married. He had made some for his children and his grandchildren that he had planned for. He had packed them away knowing after Mary had left that dream was over, with no children and no grandchildren. Then he said in a humble way, "Standing here in front of all of you is the first time this box has been opened since I put them away all those years long ago. Years that as of now have faded into this moment in time. Now knowing with pride I have a beautiful daughter named Lucy, a granddaughter Carol, or should I say Lexi, and two great-grandsons David and Joseph. Let it be known I had planned for you all those years long ago."

As I stood there looking at my grandfather, I once again realized what a wonderful man he was. The years must have been very lonely for him, yet he had been faithful to the one he loved. I know there were tears in my eyes, and "Oh my," Mother was crying out loud. It was an emotional time. Lots of love there in that room as it should be.

Mother went over to Thomas and gave him a big hug. Taking his hand in hers, while looking up at him, she said, I have never been able to say these words before. Now that I have found my father, I can say them. Father, I love you."

David interrupted by saying, "I am sure glad all these tears are happy tears."

Looking up at me, he said, "Mom, I hung Joseph's ornament right beside mine on the Christmas tree." Sure enough, there hanging right beside David's ornament was Joseph's, both so beautifully done—one a sleigh and the other a horse, both representing two young boys.

I thought to myself Joseph's ornament was hanging on our tree. My grandfather said he planned for his children and his grandchildren all those years so long ago. This I considered amazing.

Grandmother, in her gentle motherly way, said, "Anyone want hot chocolate or spiced apple cider?"

"Yes," almost in unison, we were all in for that.

My mother came over to me and said, "I have dreamed of a Christmas like this all my life. God truly does work in mysterious ways." I gave her a big hug and a kiss on the cheek and handed her a cup of hot chocolate. We sat for a while just relaxing and listening to the conversations going on about us.

*****

Tomorrow a professional group would show up early at my grandparents' house to decorate for a Christmas wedding. George, David, and I would arrive a little later in the day where we would add our own special touch too or make any changes before the wedding, which would take place the next day.

Exciting, yes, it was a very exciting time for us all—Christmas and a wedding. The wedding cake, my grandfather had taken care of that. It was also to be a surprise for Grandmother. Can't wait, the excitement was overwhelming.

I was awakened earlier than I had hoped the next day with the sun shining through my window. Snow was in the forecast for the day, so I knew the sun probably wouldn't stay around long. I made my way to the front porch as I normally do every day to check out the weather. Very cold this morning, I thought to myself with snow still lying on the ground from the last snow. I hoped the snow would wait for another day and that the sunshine linger on into the evening.

My grandparents and Mother left early. George, David and I were to follow a little later in the day. This was going to be a wonderful wedding, a Christmas wedding. Tomorrow my grandparents would be repeating their wedding vows—the same vows they had made so many years ago. As I sat there thinking about all the years they had missed being together, I became weary and sad. They had been apart for such a long time.

Then my mind went to Joseph. Ten years of being without my son, make that eleven and a half years now. It has been almost one and a half years since the day I remembered I had a son. How could this be? How could time pass so fast? *Gone* and *time* were two words with meanings I prefer to ignore.

David, every fifteen minutes, ran up the stairs two at a time, wanting to know if I was ready to go. George was just now putting away the last few items in the car for our trip.

David was excited, and when he got excited, he is very talkative. This morning was no exception. His conversation of choice this morning was riding horses with Joseph and a couple of saddles that he and George had been checking out, and of course, the wedding. He has no idea he will be getting six months of riding lessons for Christmas. This he will love I was sure. I was so looking forward to this exciting time—the wedding and Christmas—and I don't want to rush any of it, but I want to enjoy all these events as they come about with family.

However, I was counting the minutes until I can meet with Charlotte. I just know she was going to tell me where I can find Joseph. I just know it. The drive to meet my grandparents and my mother was pleasant. David, after being up all morning, was now in the back seat sound asleep. George, wonderful as usual, was a perfect companion for this trip. With the feeling of love and happiness, I actually sat back and enjoyed the scenery. Such a beautiful day with snow on the sloping hills and the sun shining brightly with big beautiful cotton-like clouds dotting the blue sky. The air was crisp and cold with a very mild wind. No new snow so far, I thought.

My mind drifted back to the stories Mom had told me about Keokee and the beautiful snowcapped mountains in winter. I found myself longing to go there, to go home, as Mother and Grandmother put it, in their own words—home.

It was as if I was being pulled there by an unknown force. I found myself wanting to take a trip and go explore my past. *Keokee,*

Keokee, I kept saying the word. Such a lovely name for a small town, a town I should know well but I don't.

Our arrival was very eventful with Thomas waiting outside where more wedding and Christmas decorations were placed in the order intended, and yes, the decorations were very beautifully done.

The house was decorated exquisitely for the wedding. The room where the wedding would actually take place was the room Thomas had built just for Mary. This room was decorated in the same jade green and a stunning aqua blue. These colors were used throughout the house in all the decorations, along with the red-and-white poinsettias made the decorations spectacular.

We were all invited to a dinner party the evening before the wedding. It turned out to be really nice, with my grandparents the honored guest. After all the food was served and the music began to play, one after another began to approach the dance floor. George and I danced the first couple of waltzes together, as did my grandparents. Then my grandfather stepped forward and made a toast. "This toast is for much happiness in the wedding that is coming up tomorrow." Then my grandparents made their exit. With lots of well-wishes following them.

David left early with my mom. She had a few things she needed to take care of before the wedding tomorrow, and she wanted David's help.

George and I stayed for a while listening to the music and just enjoying ourselves. It was a perfect opportunity for us to be together and just relax and have fun.

*****

I set my clock to wake me at five o'clock the morning of the wedding, I wanted to make sure everything was in place and perfect for my grandparents' wedding. The reception following the wedding was to be held at the country club.

The cake, yes, the cake. I was still wondering about the wedding cake. Thomas said he was in charge of it and not to worry. *Interesting*, I thought to myself.

Then I caught myself laughing. However, I was a little worried. David was to be the ring bearer, already dressed in his tux and looking quite handsome. George and David were by my side greeting the wedding guest as they arrived.

Most of the morning Mother and I had spent with Grandmother, and since I was her bridesmaid, I had lots to do. The dress she had chosen was beautiful. It was white with light hints of red woven into the dress. This was to keep with the theme Christmas wedding, which was stunningly beautiful with the red poinsettia and white mums she had chosen for her flowers. Such a beautiful bride. Her hair and nails had been done earlier in the day. Her makeup she preferred to do herself.

Only thirty invitations had been sent out, and all thirty guest were attending the wedding. Some of my mother and grandmother's closest friends and family were attending from Keokee. This was very exciting for me.

Thomas, having lived here since birth and had many friends in the area, these were the people he chose to invite. They were the ones that were still around who had known both my grandfather and Mary from days gone by.

The wedding went great. I cried as did my mother. As all weddings go, there seemed to always be some mishap, some more or less. However, this wedding, it happened to be the wedding rings. Customarily the best man hands the groom the ring to be placed on the bride's finger and then the maid of honor holds the ring for the bride till she is ready to place it on the groom's finger. However, Grandfather had different ideas, and of course, it was his and Grandmother's wedding, so they can do as they please.

This was something they both wanted for their wedding. They wanted David to carry the rings. They wanted this to be a special memory for David in years to come. David had tried on Grandfather's ring during the wedding ceremony. *Of all times*, I thought to myself. However he dropped it in all the excitement and hadn't realized it was gone. Or so I thought.

Just before the placing on the rings, I noticed David being fidgety and looking around on the floor. He glanced at me a couple of times as if to say help. I was thinking to myself, *What is he doing?* Then I realized he probably has lost the rings or ring.

The ceremony continued. After Grandfather had placed the ring on Grandmother's hand, then it was Grandmother's turn, I watched closely to see if indeed the ring was gone. Grandmother took something from the pillow and placed it on Grandfather's finger and continued with the ceremony. I thought to myself I was wrong; he didn't lose the rings.

As the crowd began to disperse, I noticed David, and he appeared to be looking for something. What has he lost? I wondered to myself.

I went over to the newlywed couple and gave them both a kiss, congratulated them both and telling them what a beautiful couple they made. Then I asked, "Do you know what David was looking for during the wedding?"

Grandmother said, "He was looking for your grandfather's ring."

"What? I don't understand. I thought you put the ring on Grandfather's hand."

"Lexi, honey, I didn't want to embarrass David in front of all the guest, so I did what I had to do. I pretended to place a ring on Thomas' hand."

Grandfather laughed, then pointed to David who was still looking for the ring. As I made my way over to help David on his search, an older man walked up to David and held out something for him to see, and I heard him say to David, "Is this what you are looking for?" David, not saying a word, just looked up and nodded his head. Then the man handed the ring to David.

David immediately ran over to Grandmother and handed her the ring. Then he took a seat, saying nothing as if relieved this ordeal was finally over. Grandmother, upon receiving the ring from David, with no hesitation moved near to Grandfather and placed the ring so lovingly on his finger.

I was curious of two things: one the wedding cake Thomas had been in charge of, which I had not seen as of yet, second would be Tim, Grandmother's brother. I was so looking forward to meeting him. I hadn't had the opportunity of meeting him before the wedding. His plane had been delayed, and he arrived only hours before the wedding. He was here as the best man for my grandfather. As I watched them standing there waiting for my grandmother to come down the aisle, my mind imagined them as young boys as my grandmother walking into the dining room, where these two mischievous boys sat. One with a playful sour mouth, and the other one falling in love at first sight, and of course the young Mary enjoying every moment of their attention. I couldn't wait to actually meet Tim and talk to this interesting person.

After entering the country club and making our way to the ballroom where the reception was held, I realized my curiosity was getting the better of me. I still hadn't met Grandmother's brother, which would make him my great uncle. Grandmother had told me he was still a jokester. She gave no more explanation. I thought to myself, *Jokester, how do you explain that portrayal of a man?*

After a lot of talk and pleasantries among the guests and the newlyweds, we were seated in a large dining room for a delightful dinner. This room was stunning, so well decorated, still with the theme of Christmas wedding. There were lots of exquisite bright-red poinsettias and bouquets of yellow roses and white spider mums, which were placed around the room in a splendid fashion. The room looked like a picture from a magazine.

David got excited over the place cards, looking for his seat and finding mine and George's alongside his; he was happy. As George, David, and I were being seated, I noticed a place card beside Grandmother's plate. Tim, it read. Saying out loud mainly to myself, "Can't wait to make his acquaintance."

Just before the food was served, Tim showed up and took his seat beside my grandparents. He introduced himself to George, David, and I, and then the fun began. I kept thinking of him as this rowdy teenager who was always taunting his sister. So this was Tim; I was impressed. He definitely was a jokester, as I had heard Grandmother call him many times. So very funny, he kept David entertained. He kept us all laughing, and yet he was such a gentleman, so kind and attentive. He definitely stole the spotlight from the newlyweds. However, it didn't seem to bother them; they were so in love and so happy to finally have the life they had always wanted.

The food was delightful. Seven courses were served, making the dinner very interesting indeed. Once dinner had been served, it was time for cake.

Grandfather brought in the tiniest cake I had ever seen. This cake was about two inches by two inches, sitting on a tiny crystal plate and decorated so beautifully. *What?* I thought to myself, *There has to be more to this than what I see before me. What is grandfather up to?* He made his way straight to my grandmother, not taking his eyes off her and presented the cake to her along with a kiss. While everyone was silent, probably thinking the same thing I was thinking. "No cake for us," I said, laughing to myself.

Then I heard a commotion, and looking around, a magnificently large wedding cake was being carted in. I could hear the guest whispering. Oh look, there is cake for us. *Funny,* I thought.

After the cake was served and in-between bites, people started asking the question what was the significance of the little cake? At this point, friends and family went to talk to Grandmother only out of curiosity, I am sure. You know how curiosity is sometimes; it just doesn't go away until you get the whole story.

At this point, Grandfather stood and gave a few words concerning this special day. When he was finished, my grandmother stood and only said four words, "The cake was wonderful," smiled, and at this point she held out her dainty hand for all to see.

Nestled there on her ring finger was a beautiful three-karat solitaire diamond. After all, the *ahh*s and *ohh*s were finally uttered by envious people who loved her dearly, my grandfather took her by the hand and waltzed her to the center of the room where the music began to play. They danced the first dance alone, then everyone else joined in when the second song began to play.

After the reception, my grandparents retreated making their way through bubbles, confetti, lots of cheering, and well-wishes back to their home, a home that Thomas had lived in since Mary had left him and built a special room while planning for her return. Mary was returning to a home she had always wished she had never left.

They would join us for Christmas Eve and Christmas, then the day after Christmas, they would be leaving on their second honeymoon. "Dreams do come true," Thomas had said this to me many times during the short time I had known him.

The air was crisp, and snow began to fall as we made our way back home. I loved the snow. It seemed to soothe the soul. George and I talked a lot mostly about the wedding and how every detail went off as planned with the exception of the ring, which we laughed about.

Christmas music was playing softly on the radio. George was driving unhurriedly through the falling snow. It was such a lovely end to a Christmas wedding, I thought to myself, just before falling asleep.

Tift-Tift, our cat, met us at the door. She was such an affection-ate cat, always ready for one's undivided love and attention. Her long white hair and blue eyes, along with her charming cat personality, made her irresistible to everyone who entered the house. Picking her up and loving her was a must. She had been with me the night I had remembered Joseph. As those thoughts raced back through my mind once again, I thought about this meeting I would be having—a meeting with Charlotte after Christmas. I was so ready for this meet-ing, I thought to myself as I picked up Tift-Tift and made my way to the couch for some cat loving time.

David was awake, and after hours of sleeping in the car, he was full of energy. While playing with Tift-Tift, he said, "Mom, I have a question to ask." After setting the cat down and walking over to the table where Joseph's pictures lay, I said, "David, and what question might that be?"

"Mom, somehow I didn't get the meaning of the little cake. Why did Grandmother get such a little piece of cake?" I laughed, then apologized.

"David, did you see the dazzling ring Grandmother was show-ing off, the one that everyone was looking at?"

"Yes, Mom," David said, "and everyone was talking about how large the diamond was."

I smiled to myself as I thought of the dazzling ring and her pleasing smile. "Yes, David, they were and rightfully so. The ring was a gift from Grandfather to his lovely bride. The ring was hidden in the little cake that he gave to her. It was just a fun thing Grandfather wanted to do for Mary, and I think it was divine."

David laughed, then said, "Mom, that is a great idea. I will have to remember that one." Then I laughed!

*****

Tim showed up early Christmas Eve carrying an armload of Christmas presents. He handed them to David, and in an authoritative yet playful voice asked David if he could put the packages under the Christmas tree. After David finished arranging the packages in an orderly manner under the Christmas tree, Tim asked, "David, have you had any good snowball fights lately?"

David circled the room, then answered, "No, but I am ready if you are?"

Grabbing their hats, boots, and coats, they were out the door faster than you could say snowball fight.

I heard my mother behind me laughing. "You can say two things for Tim. He loves kids, and he loves the snow."

My grandparents showed up during the snowball fight. Grandmother said as she entered the house that she had escaped the snowballs. However, Thomas wasn't so lucky. After being hit a few times, he decided to watch as David and Tim pounded each other with snowballs. He said he just couldn't let a good snowball fight pass him by.

We had a Christmas tradition at our house. On Christmas Eve, I always serve a baked ham and homemade yeast rolls. I also serve shrimp cocktail, a variety of finger foods, along with hot chocolate, chess pie, and this year all the other desserts Mother had been baking for what seemed like weeks. I tried to keep this meal light because it is served later in the evening, but it doesn't really work out that way. We invited some of our dearest friends over, and George's parents were always here this time of year.

George's mother was an excellent piano player. They always show up on Christmas Eve, and as usual, she was at the piano playing Christmas carols. I loved how she chooses her songs. She always starts out with "Silent Night" and ends the evening with "Silent Night." All the music in-between was so cheerful and beautifully played. We sang loud and long up into the night. Partying, you might say. We sang old and new Christmas songs, hymns, and Christmas carols. My grandfather even got out his harmonica, which I must say energized and added a new sound to our already dynamic songs.

We took a break somewhere along the way and opened a few Christmas presents. The rest were reserved for Christmas day. I usually have extra Christmas presents under the tree for friends or unexpected guest that might show up during the holiday season. This I found was so much fun, seeing the expressions on their faces when given an unexpected Christmas gift was worth the trouble.

All the guests were gone by one o'clock. With my mother being a night owl, she was still up fidgeting around in the kitchen. I stayed there with her for a while, taking care of a few last-minute details before telling her good night and going upstairs to listen for those reindeer hoofs on the roof.

Christmas morning, we were awakened early with a sudden sound of an alarming ear-piercing bell. It sounded to me like a cow bell, and it was over the top as for being loud. We were all startled. Everyone ran downstairs to see where all the commotion was coming from. David was running around all through the house looking for that bell, with no luck. No bell was to be found, and no one fessed up.

I came running down the stairs half asleep trying to figure out where that loud irritating noise was coming from. My grandfather said it must have been the man with the red suit and a white beard. That made me laugh, and it made me think it was him that made all the noise. Maybe, if it was him, it was to get us all downstairs early and at the same time, but when I was making my way down the stairs, I could have sworn I passed him on the stairs going down.

It wasn't George; he was coming down stairs the same time as I. Grandmother came down last of all, so it wasn't her. Mother, no, couldn't have been her; she was just ahead of me. George's parents were standing at the top of the stairs. Tim the jokester had left with the rest of the guests last night.

Well, I guess we will put this mystery on hold for the time being. It looked like my grandfather was handing out the presents. Grandfather, holding a bright-red package in his arms, said, "Here, Mary, you get to open the first Christmas gift," as he gave her a kiss on the cheek. After he moved a few presents to the side, he then turned to David and said, "Here, David, open this one first." It was a huge box wrapped in bright red-and-blue-stripped paper with all kinds of frills for decorations.

I thought, *I have no idea what is inside this present. I know it isn't one of the presents I had wrapped.* I watched carefully as David ripped the present open, with all the excitement of a young boy. I couldn't begin to explain the deep love I had for David, watching his expressions. The excitement that beams from him was so real. David loved receiving presents, but he also loved giving gifts and he also took it very seriously.

Once the present was opened, David looked somewhat puzzled, then he reached to the bottom of the box. He pulled out an envelope, opened it, and began to read.

"David read it out loud," said my grandfather.

David read it to himself first then, with a big smile, read it out loud for all of us to hear.

"Six months riding lessons. Location: Horse and Equestrian Center, Sparrow Drive."

Excited would have been a good word trying to describe how David felt about getting riding lessons. *Ecstatic* might have been a better word.

I don't think I had ever seen David so happy. He was jumping around and yelling with sheer joy.

Mother brought out a tray of hot chocolate along with hot spiced cider and set it close at hand as the presents were being opened.

David also got the saddle that he had wanted so badly. When he saw the saddle hidden at the back of the Christmas tree, he burst out by saying, "Dad, Dad, does this mean I am getting a horse?"

George grinned at David and said, "Well, now, David, you can't very well ride a saddle unless you have a horse under it." Then they both laughed. David's face beamed with joy as he ran and gave George a big hug. "However, David, six months of riding lessons first, then on to the horse business," George said this as he and David inspected the saddle.

It took up most of the morning opening presents and thanking each other for the wonderful gifts they had received.

After all the presents were opened and when it seemed like all the Christmas wishes had been fulfilled, we all retired to our rooms to get ready for the day. However not before David asked everyone once again, "Who had rang the loud bell, and did anyone know where the bell was?" A second chance for the guilty party to fess up, but no one did.

That was my question also. "Where is that loud bell, and who rang it? No answers and no clues."

Most of the prep work for the Christmas dinner had already been taken care of. With Mother and Grandmother here yesterday, things were going smoothly today, as planned. Tim will be preparing the prime rib. Grandmother said, "Tim knows how to prepare and bake prime rib, and it seems to come out perfect every time."

George will be carving the turkey as David watches eagerly. After thanking God for all of our blessings and all the food set before us, we enjoyed the food and the company. As the evening passed, we sang a few songs together and retired for the night. My grandparents would be leaving early in the morning, off on their second honeymoon. "How sweet is this?" I asked myself just before falling asleep.

Upon returning home after seeing my grandparents off, I decided to rest and just enjoy what was left of my early morning. I pulled up a good book I had been wanting to read for some time now and went to my room. I propped my pillows up, relaxed, and began to read knowing full well I would probably fall asleep before the second chapter was finished.

With Christmas behind us and the New Year fast approaching, life had begun to slow down somewhat. As for me, I was waiting for a call from the sheriff to let me know when this meeting with Charlotte was to take place.

Excited? Very! Dread? Yes.

"I'm so hopeful that Charlotte will do the right thing and tell me what I so need to know," this I keep telling myself.

Waiting! Waiting for Charlotte and the sheriff's department to contact me was not an easy task. I would jump and run every time the house phone rang, and my cell phone was never far from my reach.

*****

The call finally did come from the sheriff's office four months and a few days after Christmas. Charlotte had said after Christmas. To me, this was way after Christmas. I was in the kitchen making dinner. I had given Ruth the day off work because I needed to keep myself busy and keep my mind off this upcoming event. I tried not to be too hopeful for fear that Charlotte was playing games, and her intentions were never to meet with me at all. She had said we would have this meeting after Christmas, and here it was more than four months later.

I was to meet with Charlotte in three days at three o'clock. "Be there on time," I was told, "and don't be late. She will give you only ten minutes. Remember only ten minutes." Not one minute more was the message she sent me through the sheriff.

"She will only give me ten minutes," just repeating these words make me so livid.

The sheriff once again impressed upon me not to take this meeting too seriously, elaborating on the subject by saying, "I have witnessed these kinds of meetings many times, and they usually go nowhere. Just another way to play with or to hurt the victims."

So the sheriff warned me once again before he hung up the phone. "Not to take this meeting with Charlotte seriously, and take this thought with you when you enter the cell where she is housed."

When I told George this news, he let me know he would make the drive with me. He would not have me go alone. I was so glad he was scheduled to be off work and would not be on call for a few days, which made the timing perfect for this trip. When I told Mother the news, she cried. She cried most of the day.

When I asked her if she was okay, she just said, "Lexi, this meeting scares me so much." She avoided the subject the rest of the day.

The next day when Mother didn't come downstairs for breakfast, I became worried about her. I waited another hour, then I headed upstairs. I knocked softly on her bedroom door, wondering what could be keeping her. No answer, so the second time I knocked harder. She opened the door, and I could see she had been crying.

"Mother, are you sick? Why have you been crying? I asked her in a very gentle and concerned tone."

Then I pressed her, "Mother, we need to talk, and you need to tell me what is bothering you."

"Lexi my dear, I am just worried for you," she said as she crossed the room to get a tissue.

While wiping away her tears, she said, "Lexi, it could be really bad news that Charlotte has for you. I don't want to see you hurt any more than you have been already. I couldn't bear it."

"Mother, I have to be strong. Whatever is, is and it cannot be changed. Mother we have to keep a positive attitude about all this," I said this as I was torn apart inside and fearful myself. "Let's try to keep our minds on the good times we will all have together once we finally find Joseph. We will bring Joseph home." And with this said, we bypassed the kitchen and walked out into the cool crisp morning.

Julia would stay with David for a few days, so the matter of school would be taken care of, and since George was going on this trip with me, he would also be driving. I was so very grateful to Julia and to George, which would make my trip a little more pleasant and less worrisome.

The next few days just seemed to drag by so slowly while I waited and tried to be patient. The day I was to meet with Charlotte was an exciting and terrifying day all in one. George and I were up early and had arrived by twelve o'clock. We had plenty of time, so we stopped at Clair's Restaurant for lunch. I was too anxious to eat, I couldn't even drink my cup of coffee. I spilled it twice. Nervous I guess. So I just sat there looking out the oversized window, which overlooked the lake. The wind was blowing strong upon the water. The water was braking savagely upon the edge of the bank. In the distance, it looked like storm clouds were coming our way, and the lake was so different from all the other times I had been here. With it being the tail of winter and a storm coming our way, I was sure this was normal.

As I was sitting there trying to keep my mind on the lake and away from this upcoming meeting wasn't an easy ordeal. I found myself remembering how the lake looked in early spring and summer—beautiful, calm, inviting, with the water glistened with the reflections from the sun's rays—and to add to the pleasure of the lake, the smell of fresh air mixed with the honeysuckle and wild roses was quickly brought to my mind.

However this didn't last long. My mind kept going back to the thought that Charlotte would indeed tell me today where I could find Joseph. Or would she?

George was unusually quiet as he ate his lunch, looking out at the lake with his own thoughts, probably thinking how this day would play out. We talked a little, not much which was unusual for us both. Even with his lack of words, it felt so comforting having him here with me, and knowing no matter what the outcome, he would be here by my side to help me deal with whatever Charlotte might do or say.

George interrupted my thoughts by patting me gently on my shoulder and saying, "It's time to go, Carol, we don't want to be late."

I found myself not wanting to leave. My eyes and thoughts were drawn to the lake, and even with the storm coming in from the north, somehow I knew if I left, the storm would only get worse, and with this said, I began to think this meeting with Charlotte was the real storm that was brewing my way.

My legs didn't want to move; my mind didn't want to go there; and fear gripped my heart at the sudden thought of what Charlotte might tell me. She could tell me almost anything. I felt suddenly sick;

however, I knew I had to do this for Joseph. So George and I left the restaurant in the pouring-down rain.

*****

Three days later, I was still lying in my bed crying—couldn't sleep and couldn't eat just crying. This unfeeling woman named Charlotte had only said about fifteen words to me in the whole ten minutes she allowed me to speak with her. The entire meeting was to a certain degree very bizarre. She sat there facing me, looking all self-satisfied as if she had all the answers, as if the answers I was seeking were tucked away as treasures for only her to enjoy.

I was the first one to speak, "Charlotte, please tell me where Joseph is. I am begging you please."

Her words finally came, "Joseph is no more." I thought my heart would fail me at hearing these words. It was only Charlotte and I in the room. She would not allow George to be part of this meeting.

I was at a loss, I didn't know what to do. I wanted to grab her by the hair and make her talk, and after thinking twice about taking this very action, I knew it would only have me removed from the room. Instead, I blurted out, "Where is Charlie? Charlotte, do you know where Charlie is? Can you please tell me where he is? Charlie the little boy you loved so much?" She sat there stoically and indifferent, looking straight ahead at me but not really seeing me. Her words came slowly without expression. "Charlie is no more." The tears that ran down her face were what unsettled me the most. This horrid feeling of dread that I felt was overpowering.

What did those tears say? Are they telling me more than her words? "Charlotte, you are saying Joseph is gone. Where did he go? Where did Charlie go?" No response, just more tears.

My time was up, I was told by the officer standing outside the door. I didn't care if my time was up; I wanted more I wanted answers. The officer said, "For the second time, ma'am, your time is up." I stood up to leave. As I was about to walk through the door, Charlotte said once again, "Joseph is no more." Then her voice came with what seemed like an anxious tone, "But David is not."

"David! What do you know about David? What, what are you talking about?" I said turning back to face her.

"Don't lose David," were her last words to me just before the officer closed the door behind me.

I don't remember much after that. Everything was fuzzy. Shock, I guess. A fear of the unknown, or was it a fear of knowing?

I was again at a loss. After this meeting with Charlotte, I couldn't seem to shake the feeling that Joseph was gone, forever gone. George was by my side as much as his job would allow. He would hold me in his arms when I cried until I would fall asleep. George had talked to my doctor, and he had ordered a sedative, something that would calm me down for a few days so I could rest; however, there was nothing there to ease the burden of a broken heart.

It wasn't only the words Charlotte spoke that had upset me so. It was the tears that just seemed to keep coming. Those tears were like a signature saying it is all over. I couldn't seem to get the thought of those tears streaming down Charlotte's face out of my mind, along with the tears and the words I felt like I was slipping into a pool never to return.

This stupor that I had fallen into continued for, I don't know, a while, possibly weeks maybe longer, I was just not sure. Time had somehow been lost to me during this period of my life. I couldn't eat, couldn't sleep, and my mind became foggy.

Early one morning, a young lady called to talk with me, saying my doctor had given her my name. She wanted me to join a class of hers, a class for grieving parents who had lost children in difficult circumstances. I paid attention to what she was saying for a while, then I hung up. I was just not interested in what she was saying. I walked over to the window and opened the shade to let the sunlight in. I stood there for a while looking out at the blue sky, then I whispered out loud, "Joseph, I will never stop looking for you. Never!"

The next day, I had to make myself get out of bed; I had to go on. I had to get over this sad state of mind. This terrible stupor I found myself in was overwhelming, and I knew I couldn't go on like this. I suddenly had an urgent determination to join the rest of my family. I have David and a wonderful husband, and of course, my newfound family who needed me. I was determined to be there for them, and that means all of me, so I quickly dressed and, with lots of effort, made my way downstairs.

After making my way downstairs, I realized the house was empty. Everyone was gone. I got to thinking to myself I didn't even know what day it was, and I was at a loss to know how long I had been in this sad state of mind. However, I will not dwell there, and I had some packing to do. First I will take a walk to the lake.

Upon leaving the house and making my way slowly and with some substantial determination, I headed to the direction of the lake. I spotted Blondie, the old faithful neighbors' dog. He was by my side in no time. Blondie always made the walk to the lake more exciting with his sudden movements when he spotted wildlife, a bird or rabbit and occasionally a fleeting deer. I always scolded him for chasing deer, and he was learning. However, his favorite animals to chase were the squirrels. He liked chasing them up the trees. I was always glad it was not a skunk he was chasing; however, I had spotted them on occasion.

Some snow still lay on the ground, but the temperature was mild for this time of year, and the lake was calm with just a few ripples on the water. The sun felt so good, a warm comforting feeling I thought as I removed the scarf from my head.

I sat at the edge of the pier for quite a while just relaxing, watching the geese floating and bobbing their heads from time to time in the cool water, looking for food I would think. When they would come near the edge of the water Blondie would go investigating, and they would swim or fly off to the middle of the lake. However, the biggest part of the morning, that sweet loveable dog was right by my side. I think he must have realized I was sad and not quite myself.

It was nearly lunchtime when I made my way back toward the house. I saw David making his way down the path to the lake, and Blondie ran to meet him. I could hear David calling, "Mom, Mom!"

Then I realized it must be Sunday. David wasn't dressed in jeans; instead, he was dressed in dress pants and a sports coat. Church— that was where everyone had gone.

Upon entering the house, I could smell the fresh aroma of coffee. Mother met me at the door with what was very nearly a shout, "My prayers were answered," then she gave me a big hug and took my hand in hers and said, "Lexi, come warm yourself by the fire and have some hot coffee. I just made a fresh pot."

After giving her a kiss on the cheek, I said, "Mother, I have decided to take a trip, yes, a weeklong trip."

After taking a few minutes to process this, she said, "Lexi, are you sure you are up to a trip?"

"Mother, I have decided we are taking a trip to Keokee."

"Keokee!" Mother was so excited that she started crying. These tears were happy tears. After a good cry, she started talking about all the arrangements we would have to make.

"Lexi dear, I'll have to contact the caretaker so he can get Grandmother's house ready for our arrival. Removing sheets and drop cloths from the furniture. Opening up all the windows and letting in fresh air." He would bring in fresh flowers and a fruit basket for our delight.

The next couple days, we spent packing and making arrangements for David to be absent from school. His grades were great, and he never missed school, so with all his assignments in place for what's left of the week, he should be fine. The week after that was spring break, which made it perfect timing. In the end, he would only be missing two days.

After making these arrangements with the school, I felt much better about the trip. I also felt this was the right time to go. George was going also. He said he wouldn't let me go alone. I was so happy he had taken off work to make this trip with me. I knew that I so wanted him to be there with me.

The trip would consist of the six of us. This was my grandmother's and mother's small town that they loved so. They would definitely accompany me on this trip, and of course, Grandfather, George, and David would be by my side.

David was excited about going to the mountains. "The mountains of Keokee, that is where we are going, right, Mom?" David would ask this question more than once on our trip, along with,

"Mom, are we almost there? How many more miles, Mom?" I would wink, nod my head, and smile at him.

"Yes, David, with every mile, we are getting closer." He was excited and a little impatient to say the least.

*****

The air smelled so fresh and clean. A storm had just passed over, with lots of rain as we made our way to a place in the mountains, where I had planned on visiting for some time now. My hope was that here I would find what I was looking for—the piece of evidence that would bring you back to me. An answer to this mystery that should have been long ago resolved.

Mother had told David about Keokee as we made our way further and further into the mountains. She told him Keokee was located in the Blue Ridge Mountains of Virginia called the Trail of the Lonesome Pine.

My mother and grandmother had been encouraging me for some time to make this trip. Now that I was actually making my way through the mountains, this journey was becoming more exciting with every mile we leave behind.

Mother said, "Lexi, Keokee is your home. You grew up there. Being there may help you to remember." I was hoping with each passing mile and the closer we came to Keokee, my mind would begin to remember this place that I once called home. This place where I grew up, where I went to school and where I started my business career.

Grandmother reminded me once again she had seen many miracles take place in Keokee. "Lexi dear, I am praying all that you are looking for, you will find in the mountains of Keokee."

I thought to myself, *Grandmother, that would be wonderful if only it were that simple.*

David was so thrilled by the winding roads that lay before us, and so was I; this was all new to me too.

I asked myself, "How could I not remember these winding roads?" As I watched each curve and twist as we went higher into the mountains, I was amazed that I could not recall the road that lay before me. My mother told me this was the road I had learned to drive on when I was only a teenager in high school.

Wow, I thought, *I learned to drive on this road, and now this road is not even a distant memory to me, and yet traveling in these mountains had been a big part of my past.*

Finally late into the evening, we arrived at my grandmother's house. A white house with gray shutters and tall trees lined the backyard and spread their branches high above the house. The yard sloped into small hills, and the driveway was uphill from the road. The front porch was rather large, and a big swing hung from the overhang that covered the porch. Ivy had made its way up the far end of the wall and stopped before encroaching on the window. It was early spring here in Keokee, but it seemed more like late winter on the day we arrived. With snow still lingering on the ground and a heavy wind coming in from the north, the house was smaller than I had expected but very charming indeed, with a welcoming appeal. Just beyond the house, you could see the ripples of the water flowing on the lake, as dusk made its way to the mountains.

Just as Mother had said, the caretaker made sure everything was ready for our arrival complete with food in the pantry, fresh flowers in the bedrooms, and a fruit basket on the kitchen table.

Keokee was indeed beautiful. I loved the mountains almost immediately, and they seemed so mysterious. Mr. Carr, my detective whom I had working for me, called me three days after my arrival in Keokee.

He informed me Charlotte had been in contact with him, and she was sending me a present, and along with the present was a message.

"Carol, Charlotte's message to you is, 'Stay where you are. This is the only opportunity you will ever have for the truth about what really happened.'"

I repeated the last part of her statement out loud. "Lexi, this is the only opportunity you will ever have for the truth about what really happened."

Mr. Carr also told me to please stay where I was, and he would come to me. He took about two days to get what Charlotte was sending me released to him. He would have to get permission from the court for it to be released to him.

It would turn out to be a ten-by-ten-inch box. What this box would hold inside or what it would reveal to me was ever present on my mind. It was a terrifying thought not knowing what to expect.

While waiting for Mr. Carr to take care of this urgent matter, I was getting to know some of my extended family. David was having a wonderful time with his newfound cousins—Alex, Dylan, and Jacob whom I had met the night before. Now they were busy playing tag while teasing more newfound cousins Arianne, Kennedy, Danielle, and Gracie whom I had just been introduced to this morning. These girls were now in the middle of a serious hop-scotch game.

I laughed while watching them. They seemed to be having so much fun, which thrilled my heart. George took my hand and said, "Oh, to be a child again."

Food was being prepared and would be served at the pavilion down by Keokee Lake. They were hosting this event as a welcome back for my mother and grandmother. Later, my mother told me it was for me more than for them, for my return.

I found this statement to be very emotional, "For my return."

I was very thankful they would take their time to do this for my mother and grandmother, and especially for me.

The food was wonderful, and every one was so nice. I spent lots of time talking, laughing, and just enjoying myself with my newfound family and friends in Keokee.

Friends that remember me but I don't remember them, which made for odd conversations. Women introducing themselves to me now that were young girls at the time. Girls who I ate lunch with every day at school. Men that were young boys I had dated while in high school also introducing themselves along with their wives and children. Yet for me, there was no memory of them because of this unfortunate event called loss of memory and likely some brain injury. However, they all were very accepting of me and welcomed me into their lives.

Mr. Carr called to let me know he wouldn't be able to make his trip till tomorrow. He apologized for any inconvenience this might have caused me.

I was rather distraught at having to wait another day; nevertheless, there was nothing I could do about the situation but wait.

I asked myself again how long must I wait until this awful nightmare was finally over? The evening seemed to go by so slow, but when the evening was finally over, I was ready for bed. Surprisingly, I slept well through the night.

Early the next morning, I found myself a blanket and poured myself a cup of hot coffee and headed for the front porch where I would lounge for a while only if the weather permitted. Later David and George would join me. There was a mist out on the water probably caused from the storm during the night. As the mist rose from over the water that picked up the rays from the sun made for a beautiful show out on the water, I thought to myself Keokee Lake was indeed a lovely sight this morning. I relaxed as I sat there pondering on the beauty of the mountains that surrounded the lake.

As the day progressed, the lake seemed to come alive. Many activities had been arranged for the afternoon if the weather permits. It looked like it was going to be a nice day, the sun was nice and warming, a lot different than when we arrived.

David, George, and I along with his newfound cousins would compete in seeing who could get the biggest fish a little later in the day. This would be fun, and it would keep Mr. Carr off my mind for a little while any way.

Down by the lake, kids were flying kites; cotton candy was being passed out; and a croquette game was in full swing. Live music with people stepping forward to do solos and duos, which I thought were outstanding performances. It was lively music, music that made you want to dance.

People were waiting good-naturedly to pose for an artist who would turn out their image on paper done with pencil, pastels, and a brush. People just having fun and enjoying themselves. My mother and grandmother knew everyone there, or so it seemed.

The weather was also holding out, sunny but a little chilly. Later in the evening, two bonfires were started, and everyone was gathering around. Marshmallows and hotdogs were being roasted. People were laughing, talking, and just enjoying themselves.

The men and older boys kept the bonfires going on into the night. By night time, the temperature had dropped quite a bit. However, the heat from the bonfires kept the temperature nice enough to endure.

On this lovely night, Keokee Lake seemed to dazzle. Such an amazing sight, with the movements from the rippling water and the light from the moon and a golden glow from the bonfires cast such a glorious sight upon the lake.

We were there when the sun went down. We were there when the moon was high in the sky. In the wee hours of the morning, we made our way back to the house. I told myself I'll sleep in late tomorrow, and in doing so, I won't have to stress myself too much thinking about Mr. Carr's arrival.

However, the sun woke me up early the next morning, as it made its way across the bed, warming my skin as I slept. George was already up and in the kitchen as I tiptoed downstairs hoping not to wake up everyone in the house.

Well, it is early spring, I thought to myself as I made my way outdoors. I could see storm clouds on the horizon. The air was a lot different today than it was yesterday, very cool. To me, it seemed like an icy mist in the air.

"Could more snow be on the way?" I asked myself.

George was in the kitchen as I closed the door behind me, shivering from the cold I had left behind.

"Too cold for me out there this morning," I said this as I took a sip of George's coffee.

"George I have to say I dread today. Do you think I will be able to get through this meeting with Mr. Carr?"

"Carol, you have no choice. I'll be right here with you, and whatever happens, we will have to deal with it together, sorry."

Mother joined us in the kitchen, made her way to the stove, and started preparing breakfast. The bacon smelled so good; however, I knew I wouldn't be able to eat. I was already at the point of being sick just thinking about Mr. Carr's arrival.

The morning seemed to pass rather fast, a lot faster than I had hoped. Mr. Carr had called, and his plane had just landed, George informed me.

I thought, *It won't be long now, and Mr. Carr will be pulling up into the driveway.* I said this as I made my way into the shower, hoping to wash away the tears that just kept coming and this horrible feeling that I can't seem to shake off.

I decided to take my time before I made my way downstairs to where the rest of the family was waiting for me. I made my way downstairs and sat quietly in the sunroom, overlooking the lake while waiting on Mr. Carr's arrival. I was sitting there watching the snow fall when I saw Mr. Carr's vehicle pull into the driveway. It had been snowing now for almost an hour—big beautiful white snowflakes, which were piling up quickly. I had almost hoped the snow would keep him away from my door, away from my living room, away from my mind.

Suddenly the doorbell rang.

George was here with me. He slowly, as if in no hurry, perhaps fearing what was inside that box as I did, made his way to the door. I think he dreaded this meeting almost as much as I did.

"I wanted to run. I wanted to hide. I don't want to be here. I'm scared. I have knots in my stomach, but I know I have to be strong. I have to endure."

The doorbell rang for the second time. I could hear Mr. Carr's deep voice. I closed my eyes hoping this moment would go away, but I heard footsteps approaching as they came closer and closer to where I sat. George and Mr. Carr exchanged a couple of words, which I could not make out, greeting each other I assume.

I closed my eyes and hoped this moment would go away. My hands were shaking. Mr. Carr stood directly in front of me. He didn't say a word to me; he just placed the box on my lap. Panic took hold of me. My throat seemed to be closing. I could barely catch my breath. I thought once again I don't know if I can do this. I finally took the chain that held the key from around my neck. With shaking hands and an aching heart, I put the key into the lock, opened the lid, and quickly began to absorb what lay before me.

Here in this small box were many folded letters stacked on top of one another. The top of the first letter said, "Don't mix these letters up. Read them as I have placed them inside the box."

I opened the first one. All it said was, "I am sorry," signed and dated by Charlotte. Reaching for the second folded letter and my mind still wondering about the first one, I asked myself, "Sorry for what? Kidnapping my son, or sorry for," I stopped there.

The second one I drew from the box. "Joseph is no more. Charlie is no more, but David is."

Reaching for the third letter and quickly opening it, it read, "Six months after taking your baby, I put him up for adoption."

I reached in the box for the fourth letter. "The adoption did take place. He was adopted by a very nice couple. I never met them. I only knew their names." This one was dated and signed by Charlotte. It appeared to be a date about six months after my accident.

Reaching inside the box and carefully bringing out the last letter, "Lexi," the letter read. "You can only imagine how shocked I was when I found out the mother of the family that had adopted Joseph had died of breast cancer. Then years later, Mr. Wainwright married you. This will be a shock to him also. David is your son, and Joseph is no more. They are one."

I was in utter shock at what I had just read. David is Joseph. How could I have not known. However, I did not know. I walked over slowly to where David was sitting. I was at a loss as to what to say or do. George was there by my side, and I leaned on his shoulder and sobbed.

David looked up at me and said, "Mom, are you okay? Mom, did you find Joseph?"

"Yes, David, I found Joseph."

I leaned down and gave David probably the biggest hug I had ever given him while trying at the same time to contain my composure. I did not want to overwhelm David as I was overwhelmed. Saying only to myself, with tears streaming down my face, "Joseph, I finally found you."

Then I guess the reality of it all hit me with full force. Laughter and happiness filled my heart that had been lost to me since the day I realized Joseph was gone. Then looking into David's eyes and saying only to myself this is Joseph, and he is alive, well, and he is happy. Such a burden had been lifted from my heart. Knowing in my heart somehow I must explain all this to David. I must think about this for just a short time. I then turned and walked to the front door that overlooked the lake.

I walked out that door with such a relief knowing Joseph was safe and happy. Carefully closing the door behind me, I walked out into the beautiful snow. It was the most beautiful evening I could remember. The sky was gray, and the snow was coming down fast with big white snowflakes falling. There was a strange peaceful silence about the air, the fir trees white with the weight of the snow that clung to them. Beyond the fir trees were more mountains covered with snow.

I stopped in my tracks; beautiful is all I could say for the sight that lay before me.

Remembering my mother's words, "Stop, listen, and you can hear the snow fall." I stopped, closed my eyes, and just listened; and, yes, all I could hear was the snow falling. It was almost as if I was in a dreamland, as if God had created this moment in time just for me.

About the Author

Lelia Long Collins grew up in the heart of the Blue Ridge Mountains of Virginia not far from Kentucky and Tennessee and was exposed to the colorful storytelling traditions of the mountains at an early age. She is the mother of three grown children and the wife of a twenty-year Navy veteran. She has traveled extensively within the United States and to Germany and the Ukraine. She has a captivating way of weaving a story and pulling her reader into the twists and turns while developing her plot.

JUL 2020

CPSIA information can be obtained
at www.ICGtesting.com
Printed in the USA
FSHW020423190620
71213FS